TYLER WHITESIDES

JANITORS

STRIKE OF THE SWEEPERS

TYLER WHITESIDES

JANITORS

STRIKE OF THE SWEEPERS

ILLUSTRATED BY
BRANDON DORMAN

SHADOW
MOUNTAIN

Library of Congress Cataloging-in-Publication Data
Whitesides, Tyler, author.
  Strike of the sweepers / Tyler Whitesides.
     pages cm. — (Janitors ; book 1)
  Summary: Spencer, Daisy, and their team witness a Sweeper warlock eat Professor DeFleur whole and they must once again launch into a fight against evil.
  ISBN 978-1-60907-907-9 (hardbound : alk. paper)
[1. Monsters—Fiction. 2. School custodians—Fiction. 3. Schools—Fiction. 4. Friendship—Fiction. 5. Magic--Fiction.] I. Title. II. Series: Whitesides, Tyler. Janitors ; bk. 4.
  PZ7.W58793St 2014
  [Fic]—dc23   2014012932

Printed in the United States of America
R. R. Donnelley, Harrisonburg, VA

10 9 8 7 6 5 4 3 2 1

For readers who like to build their imagination—

And for Aubrey and Lance, who helped build mine.

CONTENTS

Contents

Contents

CHAPTER 1

"PINK IS NOT STEALTHY."

I t was raining. And cold. The parking lot of Welcher Elementary School was a giant puddle, with light from the nearby streetlamps glinting white against the slick blacktop.

"April showers bring May flowers," Alan Zumbro whispered, a poor attempt to lighten the mood.

Spencer scanned the empty parking lot, but there was still no sign of Walter's janitorial van. He turned to Daisy, whose teeth were chattering so loudly it sounded like a machine gun.

"We should get somewhere out of the rain," Spencer said. "We'll be soaked and frozen by the time we get inside."

Daisy's shaking hand reached into a pouch on her janitorial belt. "I have this," she said, withdrawing something and handing it to Spencer.

1

"You had an umbrella?" Spencer said. "Why didn't you use it?"

"It's pink," answered Daisy, tugging at her sopping black beanie. "Walter said we should wear dark clothes so we could be stealthy."

"Good point," Spencer said. A hot pink umbrella against the dark wall of the school would be like a lighthouse to anyone watching. He handed the umbrella back. "Pink is not stealthy."

The thought of shelter from the rain vanished as headlights flashed across the wet parking lot. Walter's janitorial van careened into view, stopping a few feet from the school's rear doors.

The old warlock stepped out of the vehicle, his bald head instantly shiny from the rain. Alan led Spencer and Daisy from their hiding place against the wall. The four of them ran the short distance to the school doors, and Walter fumbled with some keys. A moment later, they were inside.

"Where's Penny?" Spencer asked. He found it strange she wasn't there, since the warlock rarely went anywhere without his janitor gymnast niece.

"That's Nicole to you," Walter said with a wink. Spencer would never get used to calling his friends by false names. But it was important now. Two weeks ago, Walter Jamison had been rehired as head janitor at Welcher Elementary School. Of course, he was going under his old alias of John Campbell. And Penny was his new assistant janitor, Nicole Jones.

It was by far the best thing that had happened to

Spencer and Daisy since Walter had been fired earlier that year. The kids had spent the last several months working around Mr. Joe, a simple custodian who didn't even know Toxites existed. Now Walter was back at Welcher full-time, hunting the brainwave-sucking creatures and protecting Spencer and Daisy.

"Penny's not coming tonight," Walter said. "This is a matter for the four of us."

Spencer knew there was only one thing that Walter would keep a secret from Penny. It was something that had happened at the Aurans' hidden landfill after Penny and Bernard Weizmann had left. Walter hadn't been there either, but Alan, Spencer, and Daisy had quietly brought him into the secret.

"This is about the *Manualis Custodem*," Walter said, striding off toward the janitorial closet, the Rebels' secret base.

Spencer felt his breath catch in his chest. If the *Manualis Custodem* was the reason for their late-night gathering, then big things were on the horizon. The book had been a gift from the Dark Auran boys. Its pages held a secret that would change everything in the war against the BEM. The *Manualis Custodem* would tell them how to find the Founding Witches and bring them back. Spencer had given the first edition *Janitor Handbook* to Walter almost two months ago. It was written in a foreign language, so the warlock had set out immediately to find a trusted translator. Then came the long, anxious weeks of waiting.

Now, at last, something was happening.

3

Spencer's wet footsteps left little puddles in the hallway. Walter led them down the stairs and into the cluttered janitorial storage area. Spencer almost slipped on the stairs, but he didn't grab the handrail. There was no telling what kind of germs clung to a public handrail.

Walter grabbed a stack of boxes and slid them aside to reveal a secret door. On the other side, a bare lightbulb flickered on, and the four Rebels moved into the hidden room.

"I received word from our translator last night," Walter said. "Professor DeFleur has finished."

Spencer shared an excited look with his dad. If the translation was complete, then they were one step closer to finding the Founding Witches.

"Such important information cannot be trusted in the mail," Walter said, "so Professor DeFleur arranged to give us the translated manuscript in person."

"He's coming here?" Daisy asked, a residual shiver shaking her voice a bit.

Walter shook his head. "We're going to him."

The old warlock lifted a long-handled squeegee from a rack on the wall. Spencer had seen people use them to clean windows, but he'd never encountered one that was Glopified.

"My latest invention." Walter held the squeegee out for examination. It looked ordinary enough.

"You plan on cleaning some windows?" Daisy asked.

Walter shook his head. "It's for traveling," he said. "Remember the Glopified garbage trucks that the Aurans drive? The backs of their trucks are portals to the dumpsters at the landfill."

Spencer remembered perfectly. They'd escaped from the hidden landfill by jumping into a dumpster. As they had fallen through, they had come out in the back of Rho's garbage truck. The Dark Aurans had destroyed the dumpster behind the Rebels so nobody could follow. Last thing Spencer had heard, Bernard had adopted Rho's garbage truck and was driving it around.

"I was able to figure out a Glop formula that was similar to the garbage truck portal," Walter explained. "I used it on this squeegee."

"We're supposed to jump into a squeegee?" Daisy raised an eyebrow.

"Not exactly," said Walter. "There's a set of two Glopified squeegees. When I run mine across a piece of glass, it creates a magical opening. When the other squeegee is used on a different piece of glass, it creates a portal between the two. We step through our squeegeed glass, and we come out wherever the other squeegee was used."

Alan clapped his hands together, a smile across his bearded face. "Brilliant!" he said. "Why didn't we try something like this sooner?"

"I needed to use the garbage truck as a model to get the right Glop formula," Walter said.

"I could have helped," Spencer said, suddenly feeling left out.

More than two months had passed since he'd discovered his full powers as an Auran. He could Glopify anything with his right hand and de-Glopify with his left. It was as simple as spitting. Literally.

When Spencer became an Auran, Glop was introduced into his bodily systems. Rubbing spit between his hands would activate the Glop and access his powers. It was gross, yes. But Spencer wanted to experiment with it. Walter had forbidden him, talking about a bunch of unknown dangers. Spencer's only experience had been to de-Glopify the Aurans' pump house. And that had left him drained.

"So, who has the second squeegee?" Alan asked.

"Professor Dustin DeFleur," answered Walter.

"A professor dusting the floor?" Daisy said.

Walter looked puzzled. "What? No. Why would he be dusting the floor?"

"That's what you said," Daisy insisted. "Professor dusting the floor."

Walter smiled, finally understanding the confusion. "That's his name. Dustin DeFleur."

"That's got to be a fake name," Spencer said. "Who would name their child Dustin DeFleur?"

"His parents were French," Walter defended. "And don't say anything about his name. He's very sensitive."

"So how is this going to work?" Alan broke in.

Walter stepped over to a rack and retrieved a spray bottle of Glopified window cleaner. In a moment, he had misted the door. It shimmered blue and turned to glass. "The squeegee portal only lasts about fifteen minutes," he said. "One of us should stay here to make sure it doesn't close."

It was quiet for a moment. Then Daisy raised her hand. "Fine, I'll stay."

Walter nodded. "If the portal starts to close, just swipe the squeegee across the glass again."

Spencer checked his janitorial belt. It was loaded with supplies he probably wouldn't need, but it always felt better to be armed when stepping into the unknown. Walter handed the squeegee to Daisy and strapped on his own belt.

"Ready to find out how to bring the Founding Witches back?" Alan said. There were anxious smiles around the room. Then Daisy Gates swiped the Glopified squeegee down the glass door.

CHAPTER 2

"I CALL IT GLOPPISH."

It didn't happen like Spencer expected. A wake of visible magic flowed in the squeegee's path. The glass turned fizzy and bubbly, glowing an eerie green. It stayed like that, a stripe of roiling magic down the door.

"I'm not stepping into that," Spencer muttered.

"Professor DeFleur must be late." Walter checked his watch. "Any minute now."

As the warlock spoke, something happened to the squeegee mark. It changed color, growing darker and then fizzling out. In a flash, everything was different. The squeegee mark was now an open passageway, only a line of magic sizzling around it like a narrow door frame. The view showed a dim library, obviously closed to the public at this time of night.

Spencer jumped with fright when the face of a wizened

old man popped into sudden view. He had some serious mad-scientist hair, all white and frizzy. A pair of round glasses slipped down his nose, and when he smiled, some of his teeth twinkled with gold fillings.

"Quickly!" he whispered hoarsely. "Come in!"

Through the squeegeed opening, Spencer saw Professor DeFleur hobble across the library, a thin wooden cane in hand.

Wordlessly, Walter stepped through the portal, Alan close behind. Daisy caught Spencer's arm as he put a foot through.

"Do you think we can trust that guy?" she whispered. "He looks like he might be . . ." She twirled a finger around her ear, making the universal sign for "crazy."

"He's the leading expert on a made-up language," Spencer said. "He's got to be a little crazy."

"He has nice hair, though," Daisy said. "Same color as yours."

Spencer rolled his eyes and ran his fingers through his own hair, whitened from the shock of using his Auran powers. He followed his dad through the portal.

From the title, everyone assumed that the *Manualis Custodem* was written in Latin. But as soon as Walter had used his bronze nail to open the latch sealing the book, the Rebels realized they were up against something entirely different.

Walter had found a Rebel linguist who specialized in archaic tongues and made-up language variations. Until now, Spencer hadn't learned much about the translator. He knew

Professor DeFleur had worked his entire career for the BEM before they turned evil. Now the old man was a member of a retired janitors' group who called themselves the Silver Swiffers.

Spencer had heard Walter mention the group before. Most were too old to help the Rebels. Many of them didn't even know that there was a problem with the BEM. They were so nonthreatening that the BEM left them alone. Walter had known Professor DeFleur for decades, so when it came time to find a translator for the *Manualis Custodem*, the warlock knew just where to turn.

The retired professor stood before them now, hunched over a table in the dim library, beckoning the Rebels to come closer.

Spencer scanned the area, curious to find out where Professor DeFleur had used the squeegee. One end of the library was made up of side-by-side picture windows. The view through the glass showed a lawn lit by a streetlamp— except for one swatch the width of a squeegee. Spencer could still see into the Rebel janitor closet, Daisy standing only feet away, though they might have traveled several states in a matter of inches.

"Here we are," muttered Professor DeFleur. Spencer hurried over to the table, immediately recognizing the leather-bound *Manualis Custodem*. Beside it was a blue three-ring binder, thick from the pages inside.

"This is the translation?" Alan asked, touching the binder.

Professor DeFleur nodded, his crazy white hair bouncing.

"It was the trickiest of translations," he said. "You see, the original was written in a language that never really existed. A complex, made-up variation on Latin."

"Like Pig Latin?" Daisy shouted through the portal.

Professor DeFleur chuckled. "Something like that. Maybe more like Glop Latin." He leaned his cane against the edge of the table and flipped open the *Manualis Custodem*. "I call it Gloppish. The base language was definitely Latin, but the Witches added these almost hieroglyphic symbols that—"

The terrible sound of shattering glass caused Spencer to double over in fright. He twisted around to see what had happened and realized with a pang of dread that the squeegee portal was gone! The picture window, where Daisy had stood only seconds ago, was broken into a thousand shards.

But far worse than the shattered window was the thing that had broken it. Spencer stared at it for a moment, unable to decide if it was a man or a Toxite. Then the sickening truth struck him.

It was both.

The man standing in the window wreckage wore the standard tan coveralls of a BEM worker. The Bureau seal was embroidered on the chest beside a name tag—Ted. His body was indubitably human, but his hands and face called that into question. His fingers were sharp hooks, like the black talons of a Rubbish. Ted's face was pinched, the skin an unnatural reddish hue around his yellow eyes.

But the worst feature rose from the man's back, where

11

the coveralls were ripped. A massive set of leathery black wings stretched wide and then tucked close.

Spencer stood rooted, mouth agape, as Ted's talon fingers flexed. Next to the deformed man, another large window shattered. A second figure rolled through the wreckage and into view. This was a woman, or, at least, *half* of her was. She had somehow merged with a Filth, so her face was hairy and her eyes were feral slits. Her BEM coveralls were tattered, as countless spiky quills bristled across her back.

Spencer immediately felt a wave of the woman's Filth breath reach him. His eyes fluttered and his legs felt weak. His dad caught him by the arm, and Walter released a spritz of vanilla air freshener to combat the Toxite breath.

Professor DeFleur was scrambling for his cane, sweeping the *Manualis Custodem* and the translated manuscript under his arm.

"The squeegee!" Alan shouted. Spencer saw it lying amidst the rubble from the shattered windows. He didn't know what had happened on Daisy's end, but their only chance of escape was using the squeegee to reopen the portal on the last remaining library window.

Walter drew a pushbroom from his belt. A razorblade glinted in Alan's hand. Spencer felt his dad's breath as he whispered in his ear. "Use the squeegee and get Professor DeFleur out of here."

His instructions were interrupted by the Filth lady. She opened her mouth, exposing jagged animal teeth. When she spoke, her voice was inhumanly deep and raspy. "We are the Sweepers," she said. "Give us the book!"

Walter leapt forward, thrusting his pushbroom at the Rubbish Sweeper. Ted instantly took flight, his leathery wings unfurling and lifting him above the attack. The woman dropped to all fours and charged like a beast, quills raised.

Spencer didn't wait to see what would happen. He grabbed Professor DeFleur by the scrawny elbow and dragged him away from the action. The old man was muttering incoherently as Spencer led him alongside a library bookshelf. They crouched in the shadow, watching Walter and Alan stand against those horrifying Sweepers.

"Wait here," Spencer whispered to the professor. "I'm going to use the squeegee on that far window. Once the portal is open, come as fast as you can."

Without waiting for a response, Spencer sprinted away from the bookshelf, his shoes crunching over shards of glass. He stooped to pick up the squeegee, catching it on the run. He had just lifted the rubber end to the last window when the glass exploded.

Spencer staggered backward as a new figure stepped into view. This man wasn't a Sweeper, but, in so many ways, he was worse.

It was Mr. Clean.

The huge warlock stood before Spencer, white lab coat hanging over his broad shoulders. In that moment, stricken with fear, Spencer realized that he had never stared into Mr. Clean's face. Countless times, he had seen through the man's eyes as Spencer clung to a bronze vision. He'd seen those gloved hands and familiar lab coat, and he would know the warlock's voice if he spoke. But Spencer had never seen his face.

The warlock was nothing like his trademark namesake. Mr. Clean's skin was dark, a detail that didn't really surprise Spencer. He had assumed some kind of ethnicity from Clean's deep, resonant voice. His black hair was trimmed short, though it looked like it might be curly if he allowed it to grow out. There was no earring, no good-natured wink. Just a square jaw and a maleficent smirk on his face.

As Spencer stood, rooted in fear, the BEM warlock reached a gloved hand into his lab coat and withdrew a tiny bottle. His thumb uncapped the vial, the little cork landing at his feet amidst the shattered glass.

"Behold," Mr. Clean said. "I drink to the future." He raised the small vial as though he were offering a toast. Then he lifted the bottle to his lips and threw back his head, draining the mixture in one swallow.

CHAPTER 3

"LIKE A POTION?"

Mr. Clean's body began to tremble. Pale goo began excreting from his skin, shimmering like the sweat on his forehead. His eyes shut and his hands stretched out, the gloves dissolving with an acidic hiss as his fingertips expanded into the bulbous grippers of a Grime.

His white lab coat was smeared in slimy Grime residue, and a serpentine tail flicked behind him. Mr. Clean's eyes were open again, now lidless and bulging, glimmering like the eyes of a wild animal.

The warlock's mouth opened, and Spencer thought the man might scream. But no sound rolled out of Mr. Clean's mouth. Instead, a snakelike tongue flicked out, testing the air.

The deformed Mr. Clean stopped trembling. He took a

step toward Spencer, his movements absolutely silent, like a stealthy Grime.

"What have you done?" Spencer muttered. A horrible transfiguration had just occurred before Spencer's very eyes!

"It has come to this," the big warlock said. His voice sounded deep within his throat, an almost serpentine quality to it. "A Glop formula capable of merging human and Toxite. Nothing can stop my Sweepers." His reptilian eyes shifted their gaze onto something behind Spencer. "Give us the book!"

Spencer whirled to see what had drawn Clean's attention. Professor DeFleur stood in the open, his cane rattling and his thin legs trembling.

What was he doing? Spencer had told him to stay behind the bookshelf until the squeegee portal opened! "Get back!" Spencer jumped, pushing the professor away as Mr. Clean sprang.

The Sweeper warlock landed on the side of a bookshelf, his sticky fingers holding him against the surface like a spider on the wall.

As Professor DeFleur retreated hastily, his cane slipped and the old man went down. The *Manualis Custodem* and the translated binder tumbled to the floor, sliding across shards of shattered glass.

Spencer dove onto the books, using his body to shield them from Mr. Clean. But the Sweeper warlock's attention had fallen on a new victim.

Professor Dustin DeFleur was trying to lift himself up. There was blood on his linen shirt, and his face looked gaunt and pale. Mr. Clean leapt from the bookshelf, landing silently on all fours, his white lab coat spilling around his large, dark frame. Then his Grime tongue lashed out, wrapping around DeFleur's bony ankle.

The retired professor let out a terrified shriek. Spencer reached out for him, but it all happened too quickly. Mr. Clean's tongue withdrew, dragging Professor DeFleur across the floor at an alarming speed. Then, inexplicably, the warlock's jaw seemed to unhinge. His mouth stretched to an unbelievable width as Professor DeFleur was pulled into it. He vanished, a wisp of mad-scientist hair sticking out until the last.

Spencer was too shocked to move. He'd seen a giant Grime eat Slick at New Forest Academy. But this was worse. So much worse.

Mr. Clean rose slowly to his feet. He looked larger than before, as if slightly bloated from his recent meal. His cold eyes turned on Spencer, but before either could move, Alan Zumbro was there.

Alan pulled his son to his feet, Spencer's fingers grasping numbly at the binder and the *Manualis Custodem*. They could have made a retreat if Alan's eyes had not fallen upon Mr. Clean.

Spencer saw his dad go rigid. All color drained from his face, and his hands, ever sure and steady, began to quake. "You . . ." Alan's voice was barely audible. "No . . . not possible . . ."

"Hello, Alan." Mr. Clean's hand darted into the folds of his white lab coat. Spencer saw the nozzle of a spray bottle.

He ducked as a stream of green liquid shot toward them. Alan, rigid with some indescribable fear, took the green solution directly to the face. The result was instantaneous, and Spencer saw his dad collapse into unconsciousness.

"Spencer!" Walter's voice pierced through the danger. The Rebel warlock had overturned a table and misted it with Glopified Windex. The surface was shimmering blue and already turning to glass. During the chaos of Professor DeFleur's death, Walter must have retrieved the squeegee. He held it now, ready to swipe down the glass tabletop.

There was a moment, certainly enough time for Mr. Clean to strike. But he didn't. He seemed to pause in introspection, the green spray bottle still in his outstretched hand.

Spencer wasted no time, tucking the books under his arm and unclipping a Glopified toilet plunger from his janitorial belt. He pulled up his dad's shirt and slammed the rubber cup against Alan's back. The Glopified plunger worked its magic, and Spencer easily hoisted his dad from the floor.

He sprinted across the library, Alan's legs dragging despite Spencer's effort to hold him aloft. He saw Ted, the Sweeper, facedown and motionless at Walter's feet. There was something different about him now. In the urgency of the moment, Spencer managed to realize that the Rubbish wings were gone, leaving only tattered shreds across the back of his tan coveralls.

"Quickly!" Walter shouted. The squeegee portal was complete. Spencer could see Daisy standing only feet away, her eyes the size of dinner plates. Then Spencer leapt through the opening, his unconscious father clipping a shoulder on the edge of the portal as Spencer dragged him through.

"What happened?" Daisy asked. "Did I do something wrong?"

Spencer lowered Alan to the floor. "It wasn't you, Daisy," Spencer answered. "We were ambushed."

Walter stepped through the portal, tossing the squeegee aside and dragging Ted's motionless form.

"What are you doing?" Spencer cried. Bringing the enemy into a Rebel base didn't seem like a good idea. Not only was Ted a BEM worker, he was also a Glopified Sweeper!

"Step back!" Walter shouted once Ted's legs had cleared the portal doorway. In the Rebel janitorial closet, Spencer had a limited view of the library. But what he could see was not comforting.

Mr. Clean was racing forward with unbelievable speed. He was lowering his body, preparing to leap through the portal, when a Glopified razorblade flashed in Walter's hand.

The Rebel warlock thrust his blade into the glass door, shattering the surface and closing the portal.

A heavy silence filled the Rebel closet. Spencer set the *Manualis Custodem* and translated manuscript on the table. Walter gave a deep sigh of relief when he saw them.

Daisy was treating Alan with a light mist of orange healing spray. He gasped and sat up, blinking hard.

"Looks like you got plunged," Daisy said, plucking the toilet plunger from Alan's back.

"Where are we?" Alan asked. "What happened back there?" He shook his head. Green spray had the power to erase a minute or two of recent memory, blocking any knowledge of the person who had used the spray. Spencer knew how disorienting it was to wake up with a gap in his memory. Now it was happening to Alan. And he clearly had no recollection of meeting Mr. Clean.

"Last thing I remember," Alan said, "I was killing that Rubbish guy."

"The Rubbish Sweeper isn't dead," Walter said, nudging Ted with his foot. "We should try to revive him and see what he can tell us."

"Won't it be dangerous?" Spencer said. "The guy was half Rubbish!"

"*Was*," emphasized Walter. "He seems perfectly human now." Walter rolled Ted onto his back. The talons were gone from his hands, and the man's face looked pale but ordinary.

Daisy handed Walter the orange spray, and he misted it over Ted's face. He revived, though not as quickly as Alan.

"Where am I?" Ted scrambled backward until he came against the wall. "What's happening?" His eyes were wide, but the pupils seemed glazed over. He touched his face in panic. "Don't hurt me, please! Who are you people?" Ted's eyes darted around the room but failed to focus on the Rebels standing before him.

"We are members of the Rebel Underground," Walter said. "We want answers about the Sweepers."

Ted's hands continued roving over his own face, an expression of fear growing as he seemed to realize that all his features were plainly human. "You can't send me back, please!"

"What do you mean?" Walter asked.

"Clean shows no mercy to Sweepers who fail him," Ted blabbed.

Alan crouched to look the man in the face. "I drove a razorblade through your chest," he said. "How are you still alive?"

"It's the Glop formula," Ted explained, his unblinking eyes darting nervously around the room. "Mr. Clean developed it."

"How does it work?" Walter asked.

"You have to drink it," he answered.

"Like a potion?" Daisy said.

Ted nodded, but Alan looked skeptical. "You can't drink Glop. Even the smallest amount would kill you."

"Normally, yes," Ted muttered. "But Clean developed a Sweeper Potion. According to the rules of Glopification, anything janitorial can be Glopified. There is nothing more janitorial than the janitor himself."

Alan looked at Walter. The old warlock nodded. "In that context, it may be possible," he confirmed.

"Sweepers take on Toxite characteristics," Ted went on. "We have to be killed twice. The first death only takes the Toxite out of us. And Mr. Clean wanted to make sure we were useless without our Toxite parts." He touched his eyes again.

"You're blind?" Walter asked.

Ted nodded. "When the Toxite half dies, our eyesight goes with it. Some kind of cruel punishment."

Alan stood up. He stepped over to Walter, his voice low. "What now?"

"Don't take me back to the BEM!" Ted cried. "Please!"

"It's all right," Walter said. "We are not your enemy. We'll put you somewhere safe. Somewhere Clean won't find you."

Spencer was surprised by Walter's mercy. But Ted looked frightened and helpless. He was hardly a threat to them now that he'd failed as a Sweeper.

Alan glanced around the closet, seeming suddenly to notice something. "Where's Professor DeFleur?"

It was silent for a moment, and Spencer knew he had to answer. "Clean got him."

Alan reached out a hand to steady himself. "Mr. Clean? He was there?"

Spencer thought back to Alan's petrified reaction when he had seen the Sweeper warlock. Spencer had seen something in his father's eyes. Perhaps a glimmer of recognition? But that wasn't possible. Mr. Clean had never shown himself before tonight.

"Clean hit you with the green spray," Spencer explained. "Sure you don't remember him?"

Alan shook his head. "What did he look like?"

Spencer shrugged. He didn't know how to explain it.

"Big black guy. When he first stepped into the library, he was human. But he drank a Sweeper Potion and turned half Grime right in front of me." He shuddered at the memory of it.

"Did he say anything?" Alan asked.

"He just said your name. Then you were down," Spencer said.

Alan's eyes narrowed. "That coward. He still doesn't have the courage to face me. We will meet again."

"Do not wish that!" Ted said, trembling in the corner. "There is no man more ruthless than Mr. Reginald McClean."

"Who?" Daisy asked. But Ted was done speaking. He lowered his head in shame and defeat.

"Reginald McClean," Walter muttered. "So that's his real name."

"Ever heard it before tonight?" Alan asked.

Walter shook his head.

"Me neither."

Walter glanced at Spencer and Daisy. "You need to take the kids home," he said to Alan. "They've been through enough tonight. I'll stay with Ted, but I want you to come back immediately."

Alan nodded. He stared at the sightless Ted for a moment. Then he took Spencer softly by the shoulder and led him and Daisy up the stairs.

CHAPTER 4

"IT WILL KEEP YOU SAFER."

Mrs. Natcher had come to represent the irony in Spencer's life. Last night, he was fighting evil Sweepers in some far-off library, watching Professor DeFleur get swallowed whole. Now he was taking a spelling test, writing down words like *amphibious*, *hygienic*, and *malevolent*.

Spencer was a good speller, and Mrs. Natcher gave enough time between words that he found his mind wandering all over the place. Spencer hadn't seen his dad or Walter since being dropped off at home last night. He wondered what had become of Ted, the blind Sweeper. Was he still being held in the basement of Welcher Elementary?

But above all, Spencer's mind was swimming with thoughts of what the translated *Manualis Custodem* might say.

He thought of Sach, Aryl, and Olin, the three boys who had been named Dark Aurans. They had saved him from the curse of the Broomstaff—of forever wandering the landfill with a bronze dustpan strapped around his neck. V and the other Auran girls would be angry about the Rebels' escape. Spencer wanted to go back to the landfill and fulfill his promise. He could use his powers to de-Glopify the Pan around the Dark Aurans. He could set them free.

But Sach had said to wait for Rho.

The thought of Rho sent a shiver down Spencer's neck. He had met her at New Forest Academy as Jenna, seemingly helpless and innocent. The truth had come out at the landfill when Rho had admitted to spying on Spencer and leading him to the Broomstaff to be Panned.

Spencer had come frighteningly close to wearing one of those cursed Pans, just like the three Dark Auran boys. The Pan suppressed their magical abilities, only allowing them to Glopify and de-Glopify at the bidding of the Auran girls. They'd been trapped for 198 years in that horrible landfill, and Spencer had almost joined them with a Pan of his own.

But Rho had helped him escape. In the midst of the conflict at the Broomstaff, she'd suddenly changed. Something about Spencer had sparked her to forgive the Dark Auran boys and put the feud behind her. Spencer had expected to hear from Rho by now. But 198 years' worth of bad feelings weren't likely to be resolved in two months.

It was better to focus on the task at hand. The translated pages of the *Manualis Custodem* would tell them how to find the source of all Glop. Alan had given years of his life to find it, and his partner, Rod Grush, had literally given his life. The Dark Aurans explained that the Founding Witches had been trapped in the source, waiting for mortals to rescue them. If the Witches were set free, they could help the Rebels in their fight against the Bureau of Educational Maintenance.

They were nearing the end. Spencer could feel it.

Mrs. Natcher was in the middle of saying the word *deceive* when Mrs. Hamp's voice crackled through the intercom speaker.

"Spencer Zumbro and Daisy Gates, please report immediately to Mr. Campbell in the janitorial office."

For once, Spencer was pleasantly surprised by the secretary's announcement. If Walter wanted to see them, then he would finally get some answers.

Mrs. Natcher looked far less enthusiastic about the announcement. The sixth-grade teacher peered over the rims of her glasses, daring anyone to move during her spelling test.

"Shouldn't we go?" Spencer finally asked.

Mrs. Natcher sighed. "You can make up the test during afternoon recess."

Spencer leapt to his feet, maybe looking a little too excited. Daisy joined him at the door right as Mrs. Natcher called out her usual line.

"Take the hall pass!"

Spencer grabbed the blackened piece of plastic that was once Baybee's leg. The doll had given its life in a Texas high school, exploding like a chalk bomb and buying the

Rebels time to get away from the huge Extension Toxites and the Pluggers who rode them.

The two kids moved silently down the hallway. They were almost to the steps that led into the janitorial storage area when a familiar voice squeaked out.

"And where do you think you're going?"

It was Principal Poach. He was leaning against a drinking fountain, breathing as heavily as though he had just run a marathon. His walrus mustache still had droplets of water clinging to it from a drink he must have just taken.

It was indeed a rare occurrence to see Principal Poach standing, instead of spilling over the arms of his office chair. Rarer still to see him outside his office, wandering the hallway like a responsible administrator.

"The janitor wants to see us," Spencer explained.

"Don't worry," Daisy offered. "We have a hall pass!" She grabbed Spencer's arm and made him display the blackened chunk of doll leg that had belonged to Baybee. It was hardly a hall pass anymore. Now it looked more like a piece of shrapnel.

Principal Poach narrowed his eyes suspiciously. "I'm sure you're up to no good. If I weren't so busy, I'd follow you."

He didn't look busy, leaning for support on the drinking fountain. Principal Poach wiped his brow. "I've been down to the school gym," he said, but Spencer was sure he wasn't exercising. "I got word this morning that the P.E. teacher quit. She moved to Mexico with hardly a moment's notice."

He shook his head. "Now I've got to hire someone new to finish out the year. And good help is hard to find."

"Good luck with that," Spencer said, not seeing what it had to do with Daisy and him.

Principal Poach studied them over. "You didn't scare off the P.E. teacher, did you?"

"What?" Spencer said. "No way!" Whenever anything bad happened in the school, Spencer and Daisy were Poach's prime suspects.

"Maybe she got tired of running laps," Daisy said. "I know I do."

Principal Poach gestured for the kids to move along. Then he bent over the drinking fountain to take another sip, rallying his strength to make it back to the comfort of his office chair.

Spencer and Daisy moved quickly down the steps into the janitorial storage area. The stack of boxes was already slid aside. Chunks of wood were lying on the floor, remnants of last night's shattered portal that were no longer glass after the Windex wore off.

Walter welcomed them into the hidden room, and Spencer immediately noticed the open binder on the table, showing the translation of the *Manualis Custodem*. Other than that, the closet was empty.

"Where's Ted?" Spencer asked. "And my dad?"

Walter walked around to the other side of the table. "Your dad took Ted away. We're turning him over to some other Rebels. We can't afford any distractions right now."

28

"Did you read it?" Spencer asked, his eyes falling to the open binder.

Walter nodded. "Your dad and I pored over every word last night." He touched the open pages of the translation. "It's now clear what we must do."

"I hope it's not a crossword puzzle," Daisy said. "I'm really bad at those."

"I'm afraid it's going to be a bit more dangerous than a crossword puzzle," Walter said. "We have to go back to New Forest Academy."

Spencer shuddered at the name. That place held very bad memories. New Forest Academy was a private school created by the BEM to handpick and educate only certain students while letting the rest of the nation rot out on Toxite breath.

"What does New Forest Academy have to do with finding the source of Glop?" Daisy asked.

"Meet me here at ten o'clock tonight," Walter said. "I want you to be part of the team."

"Who else is coming?" Daisy asked.

"We're keeping it small," Walter said. "Just the three of us, plus Spencer's dad and Penny."

"So you're going to tell Penny about the *Manualis Custodem?*" Spencer asked. They'd kept it a secret since the landfill.

Walter shook his head. "Not yet. Which is why I pulled you from class so I could talk to you two first." He carefully closed the binder. "The BEM will stop at nothing to find out what is written in the *Manualis Custodem*. They have Sweepers now, in addition to the Pluggers, making them more deadly than ever before." He leaned across the table. "Alan and I are the only two people who know what this book says. From translating it, Professor DeFleur had to know also. In a way, I suppose it is for the best that he didn't survive last night. One less person to protect."

Spencer was shocked by Walter's words. The warlock was so serious, he seemed almost uncaring.

"No one else can be given this dangerous knowledge," Walter continued. "I don't want you to know specifics, and I don't want you to mention the *Manualis Custodem* to Penny or anyone else. Understood?"

Daisy nodded promptly, but Spencer took a moment to process it all. Walter was expecting a lot and not giving them specifics.

"You have to trust me on this," Walter said. "It will keep you safer."

Spencer did trust Walter, but he hated being shut out like this. He nodded at last.

"Ten o'clock tonight," Walter repeated. Then he gestured for the two kids to hurry up the stairs. There would still be time to write the word *confidentiality* for the spelling test.

CHAPTER 5

"MAYBE HE'S HOMESICK."

It was five minutes to ten o'clock. The moon let off a hazy glow behind a curtain of leftover storm clouds. Spencer found Daisy in her backyard, leaning against the rickety tool shed in the dark. He had succeeded in sneaking past the Gates family dog, which usually came at him like it had missed a few meals.

"Hey," Spencer whispered. "My dad's in the car just down the street. Walter's waiting for us at the school. We should hurry."

"Spencer." Daisy's voice sounded small in the large, dark yard. "I think something's wrong with Bookworm."

Besides the dog, Daisy had another pet. Bookworm was a Thingamajunk—quite literally a walking heap of trash with a mind of its own. Bookworm had followed Daisy home from the hidden landfill when she had showed it a

31

bit of kindness instead of trash-talking it like everyone else. Bookworm had saved Daisy's life and become resolutely loyal to the girl.

Spencer knew that Daisy kept her Thingamajunk in the toolshed. Her parents probably knew too. Mr. and Mrs. Gates knew all about Glop and Toxites, but their involvement was a secret Daisy had shared only with Spencer.

"What's the matter with Bookworm?" he asked.

Daisy pulled open the door to the toolshed and stepped inside. Spencer knew this might make them late for their rendezvous with Walter at the school, but Bookworm was important to Daisy, so Spencer followed her in.

Daisy reached onto the workbench and flicked on a battery-powered lantern. In the dim light, Spencer saw a formless heap of trash lying in the middle of the shed. This was strange indeed. Usually Bookworm took a humanoid form, with gangly arms and legs. The pile of trash before them looked like someone had upended a dumpster.

"He used to jump around and say hello whenever I'd come out to the shed," Daisy said.

"He says hello now?" Spencer didn't remember the Thingamajunk speaking the slightest bit of English.

"Well," Daisy said, "it sounded more like *gharba-harba-blarba*. But I thought it meant hello."

Spencer stooped to examine the pile of garbage. It didn't smell pretty, and he was reluctant to get any closer. "When did this happen?"

"He's been getting slower for a while," Daisy answered. "But today he hasn't moved at all."

"I don't know, Daisy. Are you sure he's still . . ." Spencer couldn't bring himself to say *alive*.

"Bookworm," Daisy addressed the mound of trash. "I'm going to be very sad if you're dead." She put her hands on her hips.

In response, the pile of garbage began to stir. Spencer stepped back as something lifted out of the mess. It was the Thingamajunk's head, comprised of a dented lunchbox and a moldy textbook dangling down like a sloppy jaw.

Bookworm attempted his trademark smile, textbook covers parting to reveal stubs of broken pencils arranged like teeth in the yellowed pages. Spencer was relieved to see that the pale worms that had inspired the creature's name were finally gone. A pink retainer was wedged among the pencil teeth, a simple gift from Daisy that had changed the Thingamajunk's entire nature.

Bookworm managed his smile for only a second; then his head collapsed out of sight under the trash.

"Maybe he's homesick," Daisy said.

Spencer couldn't imagine that anyone would want to go back to that Glop-saturated landfill. "Or maybe he's tired of being caged up in this tiny shed," Spencer suggested. "Do you take him for walks?" Taking the garbage out for a walk? It sounded ridiculous! Spencer couldn't believe he had just said that.

"We used to run around the yard at night," Daisy said. "But Bookworm kept trying to eat our dog, so we had to stop."

A quick car honk sounded from down the street.

Spencer was surprised that his dad would risk it at this time of night. But Alan was obviously anxious to move forward on the information they'd gathered from the *Manualis Custodem*.

"We'd better go," Spencer said.

Daisy reached out and patted the stinky garbage. "Hang in there, buddy," she said. Then the two kids slipped out of the toolshed and ran across the dark backyard, janitorial belts jangling.

CHAPTER 6

"HOLGA."

Walter looked serious. He stood in the Rebel janitor closet wearing dark blue coveralls and a black cap over his bald head. A Glopified squeegee rested loosely in one hand.

Beside him stood his niece, Penny. She was Walter's weapons specialist and always looked ready for battle, in Spencer's opinion. She had on the same type of navy jumpsuit as her uncle. Her short red hair was tied back in a bandanna, and she wore not one but *two* janitorial belts.

Walter checked his wristwatch. "I have exactly seven minutes to brief you on the mission, so I'm going to ask for your cooperation and trust."

Spencer glanced at Penny. He felt bad that she didn't know anything about the *Manualis Custodem*. It didn't seem fair to keep her in the dark like this. Of course, Spencer and Daisy were shut out now too. Walter and Alan were the only two who knew what the mysterious book said, and they had decided it would be safer to keep it a secret from the kids.

"In five minutes," Walter said, "I'm going to use this squeegee to open a portal to New Forest Academy. We're going to move in and apprehend Director Carlos Garcia."

Spencer's surprised look mirrored Daisy's. Penny looked excited, and Alan simply nodded.

"Tonight we finish what we almost did last November," Alan said. "We're taking the warlock's hammer and nail."

Spencer remembered their wild escape from New Forest Academy, his father barely freed from his dumpster prison. They had managed to swipe Director Garcia's hammer then, but they'd lost it when Dez had betrayed them. . . .

"Holga," said Walter.

"Bless you," Daisy muttered.

"I don't think he sneezed, Daisy," Spencer said.

"We've received new information that has revealed the names of the other two warlock hammers," Walter said. Spencer knew the information had come from the *Manualis Custodem*, and he was again bothered by the secrecy of it. "Holga is the name of Director Garcia's hammer."

"What about the other one?" Penny asked. "The one that Mr. Clean holds?"

"Belzora," Walter said. "Clean's hammer is called Belzora."

Daisy shivered. "That one sounds scary."

Spencer raised an eyebrow at her. "Why does it sound any scarier than Ninfa or Holga?"

She shrugged defensively. "It has a Z in it."

Walter was smiling. "We have no reason to be afraid. Ninfa, Holga, and Belzora are the names of our Founding Witches. They left their power in the bronze hammers so the warlocks could continue to fight Toxites."

Spencer saw Daisy open her mouth to say something. But then she seemed to remember that Penny didn't know about the quest to bring back the Founding Witches. Her mouth dangled open for a silent moment, and then she closed it.

"Here," Walter said, pulling a bulky bundle of clothing from a closet shelf. "Put these on." He tossed the clothes onto the table, and Spencer saw that they were dark blue jumpsuits just like Walter and Penny were wearing.

"What's this?" Spencer asked.

"Your new uniform," Penny said. "Uncle Walter finally succeeded in Glopifying these coveralls."

Spencer lifted one off the table. It was obviously adult sized, so he handed it to his dad. Daisy had found some coveralls just her size, and the remaining outfit looked like it would fit Spencer comfortably.

Spencer held it out for examination. The cloth seemed very plain and, to Spencer's relief, clean. The jumpsuit had long sleeves and pants, with a few pockets sewn into the design. The front zipper started at the seam between the legs and ended at the collar.

"Try them on!" Penny said impatiently. "Make sure they fit!"

"Umm . . ." Daisy hesitated, her jumpsuit tucked under one arm. "Could I get some privacy? I don't feel comfortable changing my clothes in a room full of people."

"You don't have to change, Daisy," Walter explained. "The jumpsuit will fit over your regular clothes."

Alan had already stepped into his uniform, pulling the coveralls over his clothes and zipping up. Spencer removed his janitorial belt and followed his dad's example. He was pleased to discover that the jumpsuit fit comfortably and smelled as though it had been freshly laundered.

"My dad wears something like this when he's fixing cars," Daisy said, stepping into the coveralls. "Except, his jumpsuits are always dirty. And they definitely aren't Glopified." She pulled the zipper partway up and strapped on her weapons belt once more.

"What do the coveralls do?" Spencer asked. It was remarkable to him that he trusted Walter enough to put on a magic jumpsuit without having any idea what would happen.

"Protection," Walter said. "The Glopified coveralls will protect you from any sort of physical impact."

"Like a suit of armor?" Daisy asked.

"Sort of," Penny said. "I've been testing the jumpsuits for the past couple of weeks. They have their limitations."

"Like what?" Spencer asked.

"The jumpsuits won't do anything against Glopified attacks," Penny continued. "Get hit by a pushbroom and you'll still go flying. Get cut by a Glopified razorblade and you'll still bleed. Toxites can also get through the coveralls, so you'll want to duck if a Filth blows its quills."

"If they don't protect us from Glopified weapons," Daisy said, "then what are they good for?"

"The jumpsuits will protect you from any kind of natural physical injury," Penny said. "You can get kicked in the ribs or smashed against a wall and you'll walk away without any pain."

Spencer looked down at his blue coveralls. He felt safer already. "Why didn't we have these before?"

"I just developed the formula last month," Walter said. "Then we had to special-order those child-sized coveralls. Penny brought them to the school this morning so I could Glopify them."

"One more thing," Penny said. "Make sure you zip all the way up." She reached over and tugged Daisy's zipper until it was just below her chin.

"Yeah," Daisy said. "That's embarrassing. One time I went a whole day at school with my zipper down."

Penny shook her head. "It's not that," she said. "The coveralls have to be zipped up completely. If the zipper pulls down even half an inch, your jumpsuit will lose power until you zip up again."

Spencer checked to make sure his zipper was tight.

"Do you have these jumpsuits in a different color?" Daisy asked, looking down at herself.

"What's wrong with navy blue?" asked Spencer.

"Nothing." She shrugged. "I just like variety."

"I don't think the coveralls are going for fashion, Daisy," said Spencer. "I have a feeling that color won't matter so much in the middle of a battle."

"Speaking of battle," Penny said, turning to Walter, "what's our plan tonight? Director Garcia won't give up Holga without a fight."

"We'll need someone to stay here and keep the squeegee portal open," Alan said.

"I'll do it," Spencer volunteered. He wasn't in any hurry to go back into New Forest Academy.

"We'll need you with us," Walter explained. "We'll be counting on your Auran abilities to locate Director Garcia."

Tracking the warlocks was one thing Spencer had grown very good at. But he knew he could do much more. Spencer looked down at his hands, one imbued with power to Glopify, the other with power to de-Glopify. When would he get the chance to try out his full powers?

Daisy raised her hand. "Fine, I'll do it again."

"Again?" Penny asked.

"We practiced with the squeegees yesterday," Alan cut in with a lie. "Wanted to make the kids feel prepared for tonight."

Once more, Daisy opened her mouth to say something. This time it was a soft nudge from Spencer's elbow that got her to close it. They couldn't tell Penny about last night's mission to get the translated *Manualis Custodem*.

Spencer glanced around the janitorial closet for the old book. He didn't see the *Manualis Custodem* anywhere, but he glimpsed the blue binder that held the translation. It was closed, lying on the table with several strips of duct tape sealing the binder shut. More tape secured the binder to the tabletop so no one could even pick it up. It looked as secure as it could be for the time being.

"All right," Walter mumbled, nervously checking his watch. "Any moment now." He took a Glopified spray bottle from the table and misted the Windex across an empty wall on the far side of the Rebel closet. As it turned to glass, Spencer was suddenly struck with an obvious question.

"Who's got the other squeegee?" he asked. In order for the portal to work, someone at New Forest Academy would have to swipe the other squeegee.

"We have an inside man at the Academy," Walter whispered.

"Who is it?" Spencer asked.

Walter took his squeegee and dragged it across the glassy surface of the wall. The portal opened instantly, shimmering green along the border. The narrow view opened into a dim room, one that Spencer didn't recognize from the Academy.

Someone stocky stepped into view, beefy hands gripping the squeegee that had opened the way. His buzzed hair had grown into a short Mohawk, but there was no mistaking that broad face and sneering grin.

"Hey, Doofus! Long time no see!"

It was Dez.

CHAPTER 7

"I DON'T EVEN HAVE A WHISTLE."

Spencer stepped back, his heart thumping. Had the plan gone wrong already? What was Dez Rylie doing with the squeegee?

"Hello, Dez," Walter whispered, handing his squeegee off to Daisy and stepping through the portal.

The realization dawned on Spencer and he didn't like it one bit. "Dez?" he muttered. "Dez is our inside man?"

"Inside *man?*" Daisy said. "That's not even possible. He's only twelve. He'd have to be the inside *boy*."

"More like inside *traitor!*" Spencer said.

"Oh, please," Dez moaned. "That was like, so five months ago. I'm good now." Even his voice made Spencer's skin crawl.

Spencer turned to his dad. "I can't believe we're trusting him."

"We've been in touch with Dez for several weeks now." Alan stepped through the portal. "He's been quite helpful."

"Yeah," Spencer said sarcastically. "If you need help slamming your head against the wall."

Dez scratched his stomach and glanced around the room. "Are you guys coming, or what?"

Penny stepped out of the Rebel closet and into New Forest Academy. Spencer paused beside Daisy in the doorway.

Dez beckoned. "We don't have all night."

"How long do we have?" Spencer asked. "How long until you blow the whistle and Garcia comes running in here with a bunch of Pluggers to capture us?"

"Psh!" Dez rolled his eyes. "I don't even have a whistle."

"Check him for a kazoo," Daisy whispered in Spencer's ear.

"Where are we, anyway?" Spencer pushed his head through the portal and glanced around. Dez had opened the way into a large room with chairs and music stands arranged in tidy rows.

"It's the band room," Dez said. "In the Arts Building."

Spencer hadn't been there before, and the idea of following Dez into a mysterious room didn't sound like a good one.

"How did you get in here in the middle of the night?" Spencer continued to interrogate. "How'd you sneak out of the dorms?"

"Chill," Dez said. "I didn't have to sneak out. Ever since

Garcia caught me making a spit-wad smiley face on the ceiling, he's made me do cleaning duty."

"You mean detention?"

"Whatever." Dez shrugged. "Point is . . . I got these." He jingled a ring of keys in his hand.

"They gave *you* keys to New Forest Academy?" Daisy asked.

Dez made a face. "No way. I swiped them from Slick's old office. It's not like he's going to need them." Dez tucked the ring of keys into his jean shorts. "These should help us get to Director Garcia."

"Not until after we locate his bronze nail," Alan said. They would need the warlock hammer to pull out the nail, but it would help to know exactly where it was so they didn't waste any time after taking Holga from Garcia.

"Duh," said Dez. "Why do you think I brought you here?" He reached into his pocket and pulled out a small flashlight. As soon as the bulb flickered on, Spencer knew it was Glopified. The light was pitifully dull until it shone on a magical item.

Dez turned around and directed his flashlight at the back wall of the band room. Instantly, the white light shot outward like a beacon, glinting between two timpani drums and honing onto a small spot on the wall.

"Come on," Penny said. Dez moved away from the portal, and the Rebels followed him. Spencer raised his eyebrows at Daisy, telegraphing his disbelief that they were trusting Dez. She lifted her squeegee, ready to swipe the portal if it started to close.

Then Spencer stepped out of the janitorial closet at Welcher Elementary School and into the band room of New Forest Academy.

By the time Spencer caught up, the others were hunkered around a tiny glint of metal in the far wall.

"It looks like the real thing," Walter said, running his thumb over it.

Spencer looked at Dez, his eyes narrowed in suspicion. "How did you know the nail was here?"

Dez looked around as if it were obvious. "I spend a lot of time in this room," he said.

"This is the band room," Spencer reminded him. "You always thought musical instruments were dumb."

"That was before I started playing the tuba," Dez said.

"You play the tuba?" Daisy called from the portal.

"Don't make fun," Dez said. "When Mr. Hylton heard how loud I could burp, he told me I should play the tuba."

"Since when do you listen to what the teachers say?" Spencer said.

"I don't," answered Dez. "But the tuba rocks! Every note sounds like a fart!"

"I hate to break up such an educated conversation," Penny said, "but we really need Spencer to tell us where to go."

"If you touch the bronze nail, it should be enough to give you a fix on Director Garcia's location," Walter said.

Spencer took a knee next to the wall. He'd gotten swift and accurate at these bronze visions. It was easy now to pick which warlock to spy on, and he was able to maintain the link for long periods of time without fainting.

Spencer stretched out his index finger and pressed it against the smooth head of the nail. The dim band room fizzed into speckles of white. Then his vision cleared, and he was looking through Director Garcia's eyes.

The Latino man had a hand on a doorknob. He looked over his shoulder, and Spencer gasped to see half a dozen Pluggers mounted on overgrown Extension Toxites. Orange cords connected rider to beast, allowing the humans to control the gigantic, armored Toxites.

It happened so fast. Spencer saw the Pluggers and sensed Garcia's exact location. But before he could pull his finger off the nail, the director threw open the door and charged into the band room. Through Garcia's eyes, Spencer saw the Rebels hunkered behind the timpani, watching Spencer make his connection to the bronze nail.

Spencer willed the vision to end, plucking his finger away from the nail in the wall. The room went white again, and he felt himself falling backward, his head bumping against the kettledrum. By the time he adjusted to seeing through his own eyes, a number of bad things had happened.

Mop strings lassoed Daisy around the middle and pulled her through the portal as the bludgeoning tail of an Extension Filth shattered the glass. In a heartbeat, the portal back to Welcher was gone. Daisy fell among the glass shards, facedown on the band room floor, the squeegee still in her grasp.

The Pluggers were spreading across the room, blocking any chance of escape. Extension Grimes clung to the walls, giant Filths bowled past chairs and music stands, while overgrown Rubbishes rose near the ceiling, the riders held in by the magical rug saddles.

In the center of the chaos stood Director Garcia, adjusting the cufflinks on his pressed shirt. His hair, perfectly styled, whisked away from his olive forehead, and there was a look of excitement on his smooth face.

Dez stood beside him, wearing an aloof expression as Director Garcia put a congratulatory hand on the boy's shoulder.

Spencer felt a rush of anger rise all the way from his toes. He knew it! They never should have trusted Dez!

Director Garcia flashed a white smile and gestured around the band room to the Pluggers awaiting his command to attack. When he spoke, his voice was touched with that familiar Spanish accent.

"Welcome back to New Forest Academy."

CHAPTER 8

"CAN I HAVE IT NOW?"

Spencer took a hasty step backward, his shoulder bumping the band room wall. He saw Daisy push herself up, but a nearby Extension Grime had already overpowered her with its distracting breath.

"I feel like a princess!" Daisy shouted. "I'm lying on a bed of diamonds!" She might have started making snow angels in the shards of glass around her, but the Plugger reached down from the Toxite's saddle and pulled Daisy away from the mess.

Penny released a heavy stream of vanilla air freshener into the band room. Spencer felt the Filth fatigue leave him as Daisy suddenly seemed to realize that she'd been captured. As the freshener wafted outward, Dez's head perked up. The bored and apathetic expression faded from his face, and he turned to look at Director Garcia.

"Can I have it now?" he mumbled.

Garcia looked momentarily annoyed. Spencer knew how he felt; Dez was always annoying. "Later, Dezmond," he said. "I told you I would give it to you later."

"No," Dez said, a stubborn edge to his voice. "You said you'd give it to me once you had them." He pointed at the cornered Rebels.

Garcia sighed, his patience clearly worn thin by Dez's behavior. "Have it your way," he muttered. Then he snapped a finger at a Plugger whose giant Rubbish had just perched across several music stands.

"Nicholson!" Garcia called. "Take Dezmond to get his reward." He paused, then spouted something in Spanish.

The Plugger on the Rubbish's back nodded in understanding, and his beast spread its leathery wings toward the doorway.

"Hey!" Dez grabbed Garcia's sleeve. "What did you say to him?" Garcia pulled away, shrugging. "What was that Spanish?"

"It sounded kind of like Dora," chimed Daisy. "You know, the Explorer."

The Plugger leaned back into the room, his bird hopping impatiently in the hallway. "Do you want the vial or not, kid?"

Without so much as a backward glance at the Rebels, Dez dashed across the band room and out of sight.

"Vial of what?" Alan asked. "What are you giving him?"

Director Garcia looked over his shoulder to make sure

the band room door had clicked shut. "He's not getting what he thinks, I can assure you that much." He smiled.

"You'd better not hurt him," Walter threatened. Spencer's feelings toward Dez were anything but fond. But even Spencer felt a sting of worry for the bully. Dez was mixed up with the wrong people.

"Relax," Garcia said, his voice smooth. "He'll receive little more than a treatment of Rubbish breath. Not that he can be dumbed down much more than he already is . . ." He glanced at his manicured fingernails. "I'm not in the business of harming people. I leave the dirty work to the man who calls the shots." He glanced up from his nails without lifting his chin.

"Mr. Clean," Spencer muttered.

Garcia grinned, but it seemed forced and unnatural this time. Spencer could almost see a thread of nervousness in the director's eyes. "Yes, he goes by that name. And a few others."

"Reginald McClean," Walter said.

Director Garcia nodded. "That's what we call him at the BEM headquarters. On official business, he's Reginald McClean, president of the Bureau of Educational Maintenance. But when he's dealing with Rebel scum, he is the ruthless Mr. Clean."

"I call him a coward," Alan said.

"A bold statement," Director Garcia said. "One you might not be so quick to make when he arrives."

"Mr. Clean is coming here?" Daisy asked.

Director Garcia nodded. "After I dispose of Alan

Zumbro." Spencer shuddered when Garcia's dark eyes locked onto his dad. "Mr. Clean will deal with the rest of you."

"You don't know how dangerous he is," Spencer blurted. "There's something wrong with Mr. Clean—he's transformed."

"Yes," Garcia said. "He's a Sweeper now." The director reached inside his suit coat. "And I must become one too."

Spencer squinted at the small object in Director Garcia's hand. It was a tiny glass bottle, just like the one Mr. Clean had used in the library. The contents of the vial let off a dull grayish glow.

A Sweeper potion.

Garcia's hand was trembling ever so slightly. Spencer knew what he was going to do. He'd seen Mr. Clean swallow a similar Glop formula, transforming himself into a terrible human-Toxite hybrid. A Sweeper.

The idea was horrifying, and Director Garcia didn't seem keen on it either. "You don't have to do this," Spencer said, noticing the man's hesitation.

Garcia paused, his left hand gripping the tiny cork. "I have little choice." He took a deep breath. "Clean will be here any moment."

Spencer remembered what a pawn Garcia was. Mr. Clean was always the one calling the shots from the sidelines. It didn't matter that Carlos Garcia was a warlock. It didn't matter that he was director of New Forest Academy. Clean was the man in charge. Spencer wondered what threats and lies had turned Garcia into such a loyal puppet.

Spencer had just opened his mouth to say something more when the band room door flew open. Garcia whirled around, and Spencer stepped around the kettledrums to see who had arrived.

Dez stood in the doorway, a broken-handled pushbroom in his grasp. His face was twisted with anger and darkened by the shadows of the hallway.

"You liar!" he shouted, pointing the pushbroom directly at Garcia.

Director Garcia relaxed when he realized it was only the boy in the doorway. "Dezmond, what are you doing here? Nicholson was taking you to get the—"

"Shut up!" Dez yelled. "It's in your hand! Give it to me!"

Garcia looked at the small vial of Glop formula in his hand. "I simply cannot do that. This Sweeper potion is meant for me."

"I don't care if it's meant for your old granny!" Dez took an intimidating step forward. "You said I could have it if I brought you the Rebels!"

Garcia shook his head. "I don't have time for this. Where is Nicholson?"

"The chump you sent to lock me up?" Dez said. "I unplugged his Rubbish when he started acting like a jerk. Then I busted my pushbroom over his back. He might wake up in an hour or two." Dez was trudging forward, his broad face red.

Garcia held out a hand. "Not another step, Dezmond,"

he warned. "Think about which side you want to be on when Mr. Clean gets here."

"That's a no-brainer," Dez said. "I'm on my own side." Then he hurled the broken pushbroom like a javelin.

CHAPTER 9

"I'M NOT EVEN IN THE BAND!"

The bristles of Dez's pushbroom caught Director Garcia full across the chest. His polished wingtip shoes left the carpeted floor, and the small vial of Glop formula fell from his hand.

The band room quickly erupted into chaos. Director Garcia soared over the Rebels' heads and crashed high upon the wall, gasping for air from the solid impact. Penny's twin mops streamed out and entangled the nearest Filth Plugger. Alan and Walter both sprang toward the Grime Plugger that held Daisy hostage.

Spencer threw himself down, his hand closing over the little vial of Sweeper potion. Dez was on him in a flash, wrestling Spencer sideways and toppling into the nearest music stands.

"Give it to me, Doofus!" Dez grabbed Spencer's wrist.

Unless something serious had changed in Dez's personal hygiene, Spencer knew the big kid never washed his hands. That alone was almost enough to make him give up the vial of Glop formula.

But there was too much at stake. If Dez got his filthy fingers on that potion, he would definitely try to use it. Ordinary Dez was bad enough—Sweeper Dez would be far worse. If he could even survive the transformation . . .

"It's mine!" Dez grunted. "My potion!" He sounded like such a big baby! Dez swung a fist into Spencer's stomach. Spencer braced for the pain, but it never came. His Glopified jumpsuit had magically reduced the impact, rendering Dez's fists useless. Spencer rolled hard to the side, smashing one of Dez's hands against a chair.

There was a deep-throated croaking sound somewhere overhead. Spencer barely shut his eyes as an Extension Rubbish swooped down, a cloud of black soot issuing from its long beak. Spencer coughed on the grit. In his momentary blindness, he felt Dez suddenly lift away from him.

Spencer dragged himself along the carpet between two rows of chairs, the Sweeper potion clutched in his sweaty hand. Peering between chair legs, he checked on his friends.

One of the Extension Grimes had been destroyed. Its scaly armor was in a formless heap over a puddle of pale goo on the carpet. The dismounted Plugger was lying motionless beside his fallen Toxite.

Penny had just knocked another Plugger from his Filth saddle. Her razorblade flashed downward and severed the extension cord in a burst of magical sparks. The beast reared up, sensing its sudden freedom. With that realization came the animal instinct to hide. But a creature so large was not going to find a hiding spot easily.

The loose Filth charged, its armored head smashing into chairs. The thick horn on its mask impaled a music stand, and it thrashed wildly to lose the awkward accessory.

Spencer saw an opening and stumbled to his feet. Reaching behind his back, he dropped the vial of Sweeper potion safely into his janitorial belt pouch. He'd need both hands for this fight.

Spencer's dad, Walter, and Penny were teaming up on the last Grime Plugger, but a woman on a Filth was trying to rout them. Spencer couldn't see Dez anywhere, but he could hear his annoying voice, so he knew he wasn't far.

It was Daisy who needed help. She stood alone near the back of the room, surrounded by a bunch of percussion instruments. The Extension Filth was hunkered nearby, its wet nostrils flaring like a nervous animal. And the Plugger who had been separated from his ride was moving on foot toward Daisy, a pushbroom in his hands.

As soon as Spencer moved to help her, the stray Filth charged in panic. Spencer saw it coming with just enough time to leap around the large bass drum and come shoulder to shoulder with his friend.

"Hi, Spencer," Daisy said, releasing a shot of vanilla air freshener. There was a rending *boom*, and the bass drum split open. The Filth's huge armored face ripped through the drumheads, desperate for a place to hide. Spencer fell back, the creature's galvanized horn passing inches from his chest.

The Filth began to bellow and buck like a rodeo bull. The frame of the big drum was wrapped around its neck, and somehow one of its front legs had become entangled in the mess.

The dismounted Plugger backed away from the rabid beast. In the confusion, Spencer saw Director Garcia cutting across the room toward Alan. Spencer acted quickly, his mop strings flicking out and catching Garcia around the middle. The man went down, and a flip of the handle caused the mop strings to retract, dragging the director toward Spencer.

Before Garcia could recover, Spencer pounced. His knee came down hard on Director Garcia's chest, knocking the wind out of him. Spencer jerked at the director's suit coat. He and his dad had found Holga there once before, just before they threw Garcia into the dumpster prison. It would be different this time. If Spencer found the bronze hammer, he intended to keep it.

Daisy squared off against the other man, trying to buy time for the search. Spencer couldn't keep Garcia down for long. The director gasped for breath and heaved the boy aside.

On hands and knees, Director Garcia began to scurry away, always avoiding a fight. He might have escaped if Daisy hadn't bumped into the crash cymbals. The round pieces of metal toppled to the floor with a deafening sound. The sharp edge of one cymbal caught Garcia across the side of the head and he collapsed, hair matting with blood.

Daisy gasped when she saw what she'd done.

"Perfect timing on the crash cymbals, Daisy!" Spencer said.

"I'm not even in the band!" Daisy answered. "I didn't crash them on purpose!"

"That's okay," said Spencer, "the kids in the band never do either."

Spencer rolled Director Garcia onto his side. The man was breathing but seemed completely dazed. Before Spencer could complete his search, Dez's voice rasped out from overhead.

"Up here, you chumps! Help me out!"

Spencer's eyes turned toward the high ceiling of the band room. Dez dangled from the armored talons of a giant Rubbish. The Plugger leaned in the saddle, keeping his creature balanced in midair.

Spencer grunted in frustration. Then he turned to Daisy. "Find Holga before Garcia wakes up!"

She plastered the dismounted Plugger with a dose of vacuum dust and dropped down to finish the search for Director Garcia's bronze hammer.

Spencer backed up, his hand reaching into his janitorial belt. Dez was weaponless, but Spencer knew just the tool that would do the trick. As the Plugger winged around, setting a course to smash Dez against the wall, Spencer shouted the bully's name and tossed the weapon into the air.

It was the small handle of a razorblade. Spencer didn't have to explain how to use it. Dez must have seen one before. The bully caught the handle and pushed the button with his thumb. A long, double-edged blade extended, ten times the length of the little handle. The sharp tip pierced past plates of armor and stabbed into the hairy belly of the Rubbish. The wound gushed black dust.

The Rubbish made a horrendous shrieking sound and the talons released Dez. Leaving the razorblade embedded in the Rubbish's gut, the big kid dropped heavily. He smashed through the drumhead of the nearest timpani and came to rest lying cradled in the big kettledrum.

The injured Rubbish made a final desperate swoop for Spencer. At the last moment, he ducked under the xylophone. The reinforced claws clinked along the bars, scraping out an ugly scale. Spencer felt flakes of disintegrating Toxite filter down on him through the gaps in the xylophone bars. He could see the handle of the razorblade wedged between two plates of armor, piercing the creature's belly.

Spencer quickly reached between the broken xylophone bars, and, seizing the handle of the razorblade, he twisted sharply. The damage was too much for the huge Rubbish. Its leathery wings flailed, scraping an eerie glissando across the instrument. Its body spasmed, and it leapt into the air.

The Plugger felt his bird breaking apart and tried to bail from the saddle. But the Toxite's final burst of energy was too strong, and the rider hit the wall with bone-breaking force.

Daisy leapt to her feet, a triumphant grin on her face. "I found Holga!" she shouted, holding the bronze hammer aloft.

Spencer glanced around the room nervously, but no one seemed to be able to devote any attention to Daisy's announcement. The riderless Filth that had tangled itself in the bass drum was gone. The Rebels had killed the other Grime, and its rider was incapacitated. Alan and Walter were flanking the final Filth Plugger while Penny went hand to hand with a BEM woman.

"This way, Daisy!" Spencer grabbed her by the arm. In a second, the two kids were kneeling at the back wall, Dez climbing out of the timpani.

"Let me do it," he said, elbowing between them.

"No way!" Spencer shoved him away. "Go ahead, Daisy."

Spencer was relieved to have his friend pull the nail. It would have been complicated for him to try resisting the bronze visions while holding Holga. The removal process was simple. Nothing would happen to Daisy. She wouldn't even have to exert herself since the magic of the hammer would draw the nail out of the wall. Spencer had done it a few times before. But he had taken it one step further when he had pounded Ninfa's bronze nail into the School Board. That had brought a serious side effect, introducing Glop into his bloodstream and turning him into an Auran.

Daisy pressed the hammer against the flat head of the bronze nail. Immediately, a burst of golden light formed between the two objects. Daisy pulled back, magically plucking the ancient nail from its place in the wall.

The small object fell to the ground, and Dez snatched it. "This is what you guys came for, right?" He rolled the nail between his stout fingers. "Now, how do we get out of here?"

Daisy had clipped the squeegee into her janitorial belt.

But it was useless now anyway, since both squeegees were in the same room and no one was back at Welcher to complete the portal.

Spencer held out his hand, acting as if Dez would fork over the nail without an argument. "You can't be trusted with it," he said.

"You chumps still think I'm a bad guy?" Dez did his best to look shocked. "The whole reason I left you guys was so I could get some cool stuff from the BEM and then betray them."

"Wait a minute," Daisy said. "You betrayed us so you could betray them?"

"Duh," Dez said. "It's called a double cross."

"I can do those with a jump rope," Daisy said.

Alan suddenly ducked over to the kids, his eyes quickly finding the bronze nail in Dez's hand and the hammer in Daisy's. He nodded in approval, taking both items before Dez could protest.

"This way," Alan said. Walter and Penny had succeeded in clearing a path to the doorway of the band room.

Spencer took one final glance at Director Garcia. The man was finally stirring, a hand pressed to the injured side of his head. He was still a warlock, but without the hammer and nail, Garcia was useless.

"It is over!" Director Garcia managed, his hand outstretched. "You will not escape." There was a current of panic in his voice that caused Spencer to stop. "He is here."

Spencer didn't have to ask who Garcia was referring to.

It was Mr. Clean. It was always Mr. Clean, standing on the sidelines and controlling everything.

"He will kill you," Director Garcia said. "And he will kill me for my failures."

Daisy tugged on Spencer's arm, reminding him of the urgency of their escape. Spencer didn't look back at Garcia. He was a villain, and whatever fate awaited him would be the result of his own dark choices.

Spencer and Daisy ducked out the doorway and into the dim hallway, leaving Director Carlos Garcia broken and powerless on the band room floor.

CHAPTER 10

"NO WHIFF FROM ME."

The Rebels burst out of the Arts Building and into the cool night. They paused in the lamplight, scanning the area for enemies as Walter searched for something on his janitorial belt.

"How are we getting out of here?" Spencer whispered to his dad. With both Glopified squeegees in once place, there was no way to make a portal back to Welcher. Spencer knew from his time at New Forest Academy that the private school was sequestered several miles up a canyon road. Going on foot could take them all night.

"Walter had a backup plan in position," Alan whispered. "In case things didn't work out with . . ." He didn't say Dez's name, but Spencer saw his dad's eyes flick over to the kid. It had been risky to use Dez in the first place. Spencer still hadn't decided if the risk was worth it. Dez had double-crossed the BEM and helped the Rebels find Holga and the nail, but what was he really up to?

The old warlock unclipped a walkie-talkie radio from his belt. A slight trace of magic shimmered around the device as he whispered into it; the radio was clearly Glopified. Spencer wondered who Walter was contacting, until a familiar voice crackled through the speaker in response.

"Dr. Bernard Weizmann, at your service."

Daisy shot Spencer an excited glance. They hadn't seen the garbologist since their adventure into the Auran landfill two months ago. He was an odd man, with a tweed jacket, duct-tape necktie, and rubber boots. But, most important, he was a trusted Rebel, which was hard to come by these days.

"I'm in the parking lot," Bernard's voice came through the walkie-talkie. "But you might want to hurry. I think I've been detected." There was a loud sound that caused the radio speaker to pop. "Scratch that," Bernard said. "I *know* I've been detected!"

Walter clipped the walkie-talkie back onto his belt and took off at a run. The group didn't pause again until they stood at the base of the Academy's outer wall. Then, one by one, they unclipped their brooms and drifted to the top of the wall.

Balancing there, staring down into the parking lot with Daisy by his side, Spencer was suddenly reminded of his week at New Forest Academy. They had spied on Slick from this same vantage point. So much had happened since then, and Slick seemed weak compared to their more recent enemies.

Idling in the center of the parking lot was Bernard's garbage truck. Technically, the truck was Rho's, but Bernard had commandeered it when they left the landfill. Since then, he had been driving it around the country, doing whatever garbologists did. It was a sturdy vehicle, and the Aurans had reinforced it with many Glopified enhancements: puncture-proof tires, unbreakable glass, and an engine that could run forever without gasoline.

But even these extra security features didn't stop Bernard's garbage truck from getting surrounded. From high upon the brick wall, Spencer counted eight figures stationed around the vehicle. Several were hammering on the cab's glass, and Spencer knew by the eerie, inhuman way that they moved—these were Sweepers.

"It's Mr. Clean," Spencer whispered. He couldn't tell which of the Sweepers below was the warlock, but he knew. Garcia had said that Clean would be there any moment. But even more than that, Spencer's Auran sense seemed to tell him that the BEM warlock was nearby.

"Yeah," Dez said, squinting. "I think that's him by the front of the truck. Hard to tell from up here."

"You know Clean?" Spencer asked.

Dez shrugged. "He stops into the Academy sometimes. I've seen him around. He likes to yell at Garcia."

"We'll have to find another way out," Walter muttered.

Spencer didn't like what he was hearing, and Daisy voiced his concern. "What about Bernard?"

"He knew the risks," said Walter. "The BEM will hold him alive for questioning. Let's make for the trees."

"Wait," Dez said. "Why aren't we going down there to fight those guys?"

Penny shook her head. "Eight Sweepers, one of them Mr. Clean. They'd tear us apart."

"Not if I go down first," Dez said.

Spencer couldn't hold back a laugh. "Oh, please," he said. "We're supposed to believe that you're some kind of amazing fighter now?"

"I'm not going to fight them," Dez said. "I'm going to tell them that Garcia has you all captured inside."

"But that's not true," Daisy pointed out.

"Duh," said Dez. "It's called deception."

"That's a pretty big word for you," Spencer said.

Dez grinned, taking it as a compliment. "I learned it at the Academy."

To Spencer's horror, Walter began to nod. "It might actually work," the warlock muttered.

"No way!" Spencer said. "He just admitted that he learned deception at the Academy! Remember, this is the same kid that double-crossed us. What if he does it again?"

"Would that make it a triple cross or a quadruple cross?" Daisy asked.

"Let me do this," Dez said. "I'll prove that I'm really on your side."

"I don't know," Penny finally said. "I don't like the idea of having him down there without any way of knowing what he's telling Mr. Clean."

Alan drew Garcia's bronze hammer from a pouch on his janitorial belt. His eyes turned to Spencer. "Could you use Holga?" He offered the hammer to his son. "If Mr. Clean is down there, then you'll be able to see through him, right?" Alan asked.

Spencer nodded, realizing what his dad was suggesting. "I'll be watching you, Dez," Spencer said. "If I even catch a whiff of betrayal, I'm breaking off the vision and we're leaving you behind."

"No whiff from me," Dez answered. "I didn't eat the refried beans at lunch." Then he launched himself from the top of the wall, using a broom to drift down toward the Sweepers and the garbage truck.

When one of the Sweepers raised a cry of alarm, Spencer reached out and grabbed the handle of Holga, pulling the hammer from his dad's grasp.

The night bleached, and when his vision returned, Spencer was seeing through Mr. Clean's eyes. The large warlock turned away from the garbage truck, his gaze instantly finding Dez's silhouette in the moonlight.

Dez touched down on the blacktop and released a hiss of vanilla air freshener to combat any Sweeper breath. Dez was really only susceptible to Rubbish breath, so Mr. Clean's Grime-human mix wouldn't be a problem. Still, Spencer was surprised by Dez's precautions as Mr. Clean moved to greet him.

"What are you doing here, boy?" The warlock's voice was rich and deep as the words rolled off his snakelike tongue.

Dez's eyes were downcast and he didn't look up when he spoke. "Garcia sent me to find you. Wants to know why you're late."

"He's in a hurry to see me?" Mr. Clean asked.

Dez shrugged. "He's got the Rebels cornered in the band room. He's just waiting for you to tell him what to do."

Mr. Clean began to pace slowly around Dez while the boy fidgeted under his gaze. "Fool, Garcia," Clean said. "He has the Rebels in his clutches and he sends a child to find me." He finished his circle and stopped in front of Dez. His voice was low and his words slow. "Are you *sure* the Rebels have been captured?"

As a silent observer, Spencer felt his heartbeat quicken. There was a lot of pressure on Dez, and his "deception" didn't appear to be going smoothly.

"Well, yeah." Dez was trying to sound nonchalant, but Spencer could hear the tension in his voice. "That's why Garcia sent me out here."

Mr. Clean paused for a moment. "Work with me honestly, and I can give you anything you like," he said. "Lie to me, and I shall be very upset." He bent down until his face was close to Dez's. Even through the warlock's eyes, Spencer could see the thick tongue curling out. "Does Garcia really have the Rebels?"

Dez stood petrified in the BEM warlock's gaze. High upon the brick wall, Spencer held his breath, preparing to sever his connection with Holga and tell the Rebels to retreat.

Dez nodded, his mouth tight. Then, finally, he squeaked out a few words. "Yeah. I'm sure."

Mr. Clean straightened and took a deep breath. Dez relaxed a bit, the tension releasing from his shoulders. Then, without warning, Mr. Clean's hand shot out, his sticky, Grimelike fingertips catching Dez by the chest and lifting his feet off the blacktop. "Then who's on top of the Academy wall, boy?"

Spencer felt a pit open in his stomach.

"Chill, dude!" Dez said, his feet kicking the air. "I don't know what you're talking about!"

"I know when someone's lying to me!" Mr. Clean said. "Every time I mentioned the Rebels, your eyes went straight to the Academy wall!"

Mr. Clean dropped Dez roughly to the ground. He turned to the nearest Sweeper, a half-Rubbish woman. "Make sure he doesn't go anywhere. The rest of you come with me!"

The remaining Sweepers moved away from the garbage truck as Mr. Clean turned his gaze to the brick wall. Through his enhanced Sweeper eyesight, Spencer could see five indiscreet bumps across the top of the wall, silhouettes of the hiding Rebels. Then the tall warlock dropped to his hands and scuttled like a Grime across the blacktop.

CHAPTER 11

"ALL ABOARD!"

Spencer finally severed his link, dropping Holga into his dad's waiting hands.

"We've got to move!" he said.

"We didn't need your vision to tell us that," Penny said, pointing. Spencer saw the Sweepers moving toward them at terrible speeds.

"What do we do?" Spencer asked.

"While you were watching Mr. Clean, Walter was talking to Bernard," Alan said. "I think our garbologist has one more trick up his sleeve."

Spencer looked to Walter, who was lowering the walkie-talkie, his face ashen.

"He said to wait here," Walter muttered. "Said he's going to drive by and pick us up."

"Um," Spencer said, "does he know we're on top of the wall?"

Headlights flashed as Bernard spun the garbage truck around and accelerated directly toward the brick wall. Mr. Clean and the Sweepers hesitated as the diesel engine roared toward them.

"Is he going to ram the wall?" Daisy asked, bracing her hands against the edge of the brick. Spencer didn't know what the garbologist was planning. The Auran truck seemed durable, but hitting a brick wall at forty-five miles per hour didn't sound like a good idea.

At the last moment, the truck veered hard, Bernard cranking the steering wheel frantically. But the cumbersome, top-heavy vehicle was moving too fast. Spencer watched in absolute horror as the garbage truck tipped, rolled once, and came to rest on its side, with the wheels slammed up against the brick wall.

"Oh, garbage," Penny muttered. "There goes our escape."

Leaning over the edge of the wall, Spencer saw the Sweepers jeer at Bernard's failed attempt. But before the enemy could resume their pursuit, the garbage truck's engine revved.

Spencer couldn't believe what he was seeing. He turned to Daisy; her wide eyes confirmed that he wasn't going crazy.

Bernard was driving the garbage truck *up* the brick wall!

It shouldn't have been possible, but somehow the Glopified tires were gripping the vertical face and the truck was chugging steadily upward. In a moment, Bernard had reached the top. Turning the truck sideways, he pulled up just below the Rebels. The passenger window rolled down, which seemed a tedious task in the face of the quickly approaching Sweepers.

Staring straight down through the window, Spencer saw Bernard Weizmann, wearing his goofy leather aviator cap and a huge grin. He was sitting in the driver's seat, looking as comfortable as though he were on flat ground.

"All aboard!" the garbologist shouted.

One by one, the Rebels slipped over the edge of the wall and dropped through the open side window. When Spencer's feet passed into the cab, he was surprised to feel a sudden shift in gravity. He dropped comfortably into the truck seat, and although he was sitting parallel to the earth, he felt perfectly upright.

"Welcome back to Big Bertha," Bernard said. He reached out and ruffled Spencer's white hair. "You don't look a day older than the last time I saw you."

Only Bernard could get away with a joke like that. But it was true. Spencer's Auran powers prevented him from aging.

"I can't tell if I'm up or down in here," Daisy said.

"Down is always down inside Big Bertha," answered Bernard.

Penny was the last Rebel to slip through the window. She let out a quick "whoa" as gravity rearranged itself. Then she rolled up the truck's window and turned to the driver.

"Let's roll, Bernie!"

Out of the dark night, a Rubbish Sweeper dove. He hit

the reinforced windshield and clung there, the impact of his attack causing everyone in the cab to jump. Bernard stepped on the gas, and the huge truck lurched forward, the heavy tires passing over a Grime Sweeper clinging to the wall.

The Rubbish Sweeper was digging his talon fingernails against the glass, an angry sneer on his beaked face.

"The bugs here are terrible," Bernard said. "I just can't keep my windshield clean." The garbologist pulled a lever, releasing a stream of windshield wiper fluid right into the Sweeper's face. The hybrid man reeled back, and Bernard engaged the wipers. The wiper arms flicked across the glass, throwing the Sweeper aside.

"Much better," Bernard said. "Now I can see where we're going."

But Spencer wasn't sure if it was better. They were driving on the wall! It was incredibly disorienting.

"How do we get this thing back on the road?" Alan yelled.

Bernard shook his head. "I'm not really sure. This is my first experience with wall driving."

"Wait a second," Penny said. "You mean to say that you rolled this thing against the wall and you weren't even sure it would work?"

"I had my suspicions," Bernard answered, "but it wasn't exactly written in the operator's manual."

"Never mind that!" Walter interrupted. "We've got to come off this wall and get out of here!"

"What happens if you stop the truck?" Alan asked.

"Besides letting the bad guys catch up?" Bernard said. "I don't know."

"I think you should try it," Walter said.

Bernard spun the wheel, veering the truck downward until it was racing along the wall, just feet from the ground. Spencer again felt disoriented, and he had to remind himself that they were actually sideways.

"Everybody hang onto something," Bernard said. Spencer grabbed the dashboard. Daisy grabbed his arm. Then Bernard slammed on the brakes, and the garbage truck came to a squealing halt on the wall.

The huge vehicle clung there for a moment. Then the wheels came off the wall and the truck dropped with a crunch to the ground. Instantly, gravity rushed through the cab, toppling everybody to one side, with Bernard at the bottom of the dog pile. He reached out and rubbed the steering wheel apologetically. "Sorry about that, Big Bertha."

Spencer was still trying to sort up from down when Penny rolled down the passenger window and climbed out. She unclipped a toilet plunger from her belt and clamped the rubber suction cup onto the front of the garbage truck, lifting the vehicle effortlessly.

The Rebels were tossed around inside the cab before Big Bertha was upright again, this time with her wheels on the parking lot asphalt where they belonged. Bernard revved the engine.

"Is it broken?" Daisy asked.

"Of course not," answered the garbologist. "Big Bertha's

magically enhanced. She can drive out of a head-on collision without a scratch."

Penny leapt back into the cab just as the first Sweeper reached them. It was a Filth man, his teeth jagged and his back bristling with deadly quills. He hunched over, quivering for just a moment before blasting his arrowlike projectiles at the Rebels.

Most of the quills pinged harmlessly off Big Bertha's shell as Bernard peeled across the parking lot. But one of the quills shot through the open window and buried itself in the seat between Walter and Daisy.

"Let's roll that up," Penny said, quickly making sure the window was tight again.

"We've got to find Dez!" Spencer said, squinting through the windshield.

The big kid was sitting slouched in the middle of the parking lot with a Sweeper woman standing over him.

"What's he doing?" Alan asked.

Spencer shook his head. It wasn't like Dez to sit patiently as a prisoner. Unless . . .

"It's that Rubbish Sweeper," Spencer said. "Her breath is affecting him."

Dez looked as apathetic as could be. As the headlights flashed across his face, Spencer saw an expression of utter boredom, as though he didn't care that the Sweepers had captured him.

Bernard honked the truck horn, but even the obnoxious noise couldn't rattle the kid from his deep laziness.

"Come on, Dez!" Penny shouted. Still no response.

Spencer glanced in the rearview mirror. Mr. Clean was circling around behind them, rallying the other Sweepers into a deadly charge. There wasn't enough time to get out and shake Dez to his senses.

"Remember that joystick in my old truck?" Bernard asked. "The one that controlled the mechanical arm to pick up trash cans on the roadside?"

Spencer nodded as Bernard pushed a button on the dashboard. A panel slid aside and a silver joystick rose out of the console. "Well, this one is about seven hundred times better."

The garbologist wrapped his hand around the joystick and pressed a red trigger button. Instantly, a mechanical arm stretched out from the side of the Auran garbage truck. The metal arm telescoped out, reaching much farther across the parking lot than Spencer thought possible.

The Rubbish Sweeper who was guarding Dez moved to intercept, but Bernard yanked on the joystick and the arm pummeled into the winged woman, tossing her aside. Bernard pressed another button and the claw grippers opened. Then, double-checking the distance in his side mirrors, Bernard dropped the mechanical arm over Dez.

"Ugh!" Dez grunted, still under the effects of the Rubbish breath. The grippers closed around his middle and scooped him into the air. "This is so boring! Why won't somebody do something fun?"

"This ought to be fun enough," Bernard said, directing the joystick. The mechanical arm retracted, lifting Dez over the open back of the garbage truck. Then Bernard let go of a button, the grippers released, and Dez plummeted into the trash.

"Right where he belongs," Spencer muttered.

Big Bertha roared across the parking lot, New Forest Academy fading in the rearview mirror as they drove down the mountain road.

CHAPTER 12

"WHAT'S NEXT?"

No one spoke until Big Bertha ambled out of the canyon and into some residential back roads. Then Daisy raised her hand.

"Um," she said. "Shouldn't someone check on Dez?"

"Nah," Bernard said. "I'm sure he's fine back there. Probably lounging in the trash like a pig in a mud hole."

Penny rolled her eyes. "I think you're the only one who enjoys lounging in trash."

"That's a shame," he said. "It's quite cleansing."

"Where are we even going?" Spencer asked, watching darkened houses whisk by.

"Back to Welcher," Walter answered. "If everything had gone according to plan, we would have stepped right back into my janitorial closet after stealing Holga. This puts us behind schedule."

"Why?" Penny said. "What's next?"

Alan and Walter glanced at each other. Without the translation of the *Manualis Custodem,* Spencer wondered if they knew what to do. But Walter delivered the answer without hesitation.

"We have to steal Belzora."

"Bel-*who*-za?" Bernard asked.

"The final warlock hammer," Walter said. "The one that belongs to Mr. Clean."

"I thought we just got away from Mr. Clean," Daisy said. "Now we have to go back and fight him?"

Alan shook his head. "Not at New Forest Academy. In order for this to work, we have to take Belzora *and* the bronze nail. That means going straight to the heart of the BEM."

Spencer thought back to a handful of visions he'd had in Mr. Clean's office. "The BEM headquarters are in Washington, D.C.," he said.

"Right," answered Alan. "But that's not where Mr. Clean is hiding his nail. He has a secret BEM laboratory. We know that's where he experiments with Glop, so the nail has to be there."

"And where is Dr. Frankenstein's secret lab?" Bernard asked.

"What?" Daisy cried. "Frankenstein's working for the BEM?"

"Massachusetts," answered Walter. "Outside of Salem. We'll give you more details when we get back to Welcher."

"Why are we going all the way back to Welcher?" Penny

asked. "That's at least an eight-hour drive from here. Won't it be easier to invade the BEM labs if Mr. Clean isn't there? If we strike now, we can get in, find the nail, and be waiting for him when he gets back from the Academy."

"That's a decent plan," said Walter. "But we need a base of operations. Somewhere we can work from."

"Aren't there a couple of Monitor schools nearby?" Daisy asked Spencer. "Maybe they can help us out."

The Organization of Janitor Monitors was a network of students spread across the nation. They spied on their janitors and emailed Spencer the reports. The president of the Monitors was a genius thirteen-year-old named Min Lee.

"Can I borrow a phone?" Spencer asked.

Penny slipped hers from the pocket of her Glopified coveralls and handed it to Spencer. He punched in the memorized number and waited for an answer.

"He's probably sleeping," Daisy said. "My dad says we shouldn't call people after nine o'clock."

Spencer glanced at the clock on the dash. It was well after midnight. He was just about to give up when Min answered, his diction perfect despite the grogginess in his voice.

"Hey, Min."

"Greetings."

"We need your help again," Spencer said. "We're looking for a Monitor school in the Denver area."

"One moment," answered Min. Spencer could hear him typing rapidly on a computer keyboard. "I've pulled up the spreadsheet. There are two Monitor schools relatively close, both reported to have Rebel janitors. The Monitors are Anna Ferguson and Jeremy Hatch."

Daisy was listening in, her ear pressed close to the phone in Spencer's hand.

"Ooh, pick Anna's school," Daisy said. "I remember her. She had cute shoes."

"Uh, how about Anna?" Spencer said. He couldn't believe that he had just picked a Rebel location based upon a girl's shoes!

"The school is Viewmont Elementary," Min said. "The janitor's name is Earl Dodge."

"I need you to get ahold of Earl," Spencer said. "Tell him to meet us at Viewmont as soon as possible. Can you do it?"

"Of course I can," Min said.

"Thanks," Spencer replied, but the phone was already dead in his hand. He passed it back to Penny, who instantly started navigating to Viewmont Elementary School.

"I'm not sure how I feel about rushing in like this," Walter muttered. "There are things back at Welcher that we need."

"It's fine," Alan quietly assured. "We'll swipe Belzora and then get back to Welcher to double-check the instructions."

Spencer was sure they were talking about the *Manualis Custodem*, but no one dared mention it in front of Penny and Bernard. Luckily, those two were arguing loudly about which way was right and which way was left.

"Are you worried about its security?" Alan whispered.

The warlock shook his bald head. "I duct-taped the translated binder to the table in the closet. Only my fin-gerprints can peel it up. The pages would be destroyed if anyone else tried to get them."

"What's the problem, then?" Alan asked.

"I didn't dare secure the actual *Manualis*," Walter said. "It's a very old book. I didn't want to damage it. The best I could do was hide it in a drawer in my janitorial office. It isn't safe. Anyone could get their hands on it."

"Even if someone got to it," Alan said, "the book is latched and locked. It would take a warlock nail to open it. We have Holga and the nail with us here. Your nail is set in the walls of Welcher Elementary, but as long as you have Ninfa, no one can pull it out. That leaves Mr. Clean. So it makes even more sense to move on him as fast as we can."

Walter nodded. "What if Clean doesn't go back to the BEM laboratory? That would leave us sitting in the enemy base."

"I can check," Spencer chimed in. "I can spy on Mr. Clean and try to figure out his plans."

"Excellent," Walter said.

Spencer held out his hand, and his dad slid the cool, hard handle of Holga into his palm.

CHAPTER 13

"WHAT MORE CAN YOU LOSE?"

The visions didn't bother Spencer at all anymore. When his eyesight returned, Spencer got an immediate fix on Mr. Clean's location. The tall warlock had just entered the Arts Building at New Forest Academy. He moved with silent, serpentine grace as his half-human Sweepers scuttled down the dark hallway behind him.

Clean's slime-covered hand pushed open the band room door. In a flash, he was staring into the face of Director Carlos Garcia. The Latino man was pressing a red hand against the bloody gash on the side of his head. His face was pale and his fingers trembling.

Despite all the evil that Garcia had done, Spencer hated seeing him so helpless and terrified. Spencer instantly shifted his perspective, his vision fading to white for just a moment before returning through the eyes of Garcia. It was more frightening from this angle, looking up at Mr. Clean's Sweeper face. But at least Spencer didn't have to see the panic in Garcia's eyes. Now he was seeing through them.

"You have failed me again," Mr. Clean said.

"But I thought . . ." Garcia began.

"Why have you not taken the Sweeper potion?" Clean bellowed. "Were my instructions unclear?"

"They were very clear, sir." Garcia's eyes dropped to the floor. "The potion . . ." he stammered. "I may have lost the Sweeper potion."

"Lost the potion, lost the Rebels, lost your warlock hammer," Mr. Clean said. "What more can you lose?"

"Please, no," Garcia said, his hands raised in pleading. "You still need me. What about the Academy?"

"You think the Academy needs you?" said Mr. Clean. "You think *I* need you?" He laughed, a deep gurgling sound in his slime-choked throat. "Soon the Academy will have a new director."

Garcia took a staggering step backward as Mr. Clean reached into his white lab coat. When his strong hand withdrew, he was holding a dirty rag by one corner.

"As a child, I enjoyed vexing my younger sister," Mr. Clean said. "Of all my methods, she hated this the most." As he spoke, he slowly wound the rag, twisting it from end to end. "A simple dishrag, when flicked just so, would leave a terrible mark—a bright welt that would have her whimpering for hours."

Director Garcia tried frantically to back up, but Clean's

Sweepers had ringed him in, hissing and crowing with unnatural sounds.

"And so I thought," Mr. Clean said, striding a step closer, "if a simple rag would leave a welt, what would a Glopified rag do?"

"You cannot do this!" Garcia shouted. "You cannot do this to me! I've been your companion! Your friend from the beginning!"

"You were never my friend, Carlos," said Mr. Clean. "Only my puppet." He lifted the twisted rag. "And now I must deal with you. But I can assure you, your death will be clean. Because if there's one thing I hate—it's a mess."

The Glopified rag whipped outward, glistening and rippling with magic. A scream escaped Director Garcia's lips, and then the tip of the rag cracked against his chest with a sound like a gunshot.

Then nothing.

No fading vision into pinpricks of white. No change in perspective. Spencer was suddenly sitting in the garbage truck, seeing through his own eyes, with Holga still resting in his palm.

"What happened?" Daisy asked.

Spencer shook his head. He couldn't form words. He tried to jump back into Director Garcia's vision, but there was nothing there. So he did the next best thing, and when he focused on Mr. Clean, Spencer made the link, seeing through the Grimelike eyes of the tall warlock.

Mr. Clean was still standing in the band room, just tucking his terrible Glopified rag back into his lab coat. Before him, in the space where Garcia had stood only seconds ago, was nothing but a wisp of vapor, clinging in the air like mist after a summer storm.

Mr. Clean waved his hand dismissively, sending a current of air rippling through the immaterial remains of Director Carlos Garcia.

"What now, sir?" rasped a Filth Sweeper at Clean's side.

"We must return to the laboratory," Mr. Clean said. "The Rebels have taken Garcia's hammer. We must assume they will be coming for mine. But first . . ."

The warlock's gaze searched across the room until he found two of Garcia's Pluggers huddled against the back wall, their Extension Toxites lost after the fight with the Rebels.

Mr. Clean turned to his gang of Sweepers. "No one must know what happened here," he said. "Feast yourselves on those Pluggers. They are not worthy of the beasts they ride."

The Sweepers shrieked and croaked, their sounds of delight causing Spencer's stomach to turn. He dropped Holga into his lap and returned to the cab of the garbage truck.

"Well?" Alan asked. "Did you catch his plans?"

But Spencer couldn't talk about it yet. Director Garcia was dead. Spencer pressed his hands against his face and tried to forget what he had just seen.

CHAPTER 14

"SPEAKING OF GARBAGE . . ."

Spencer didn't like waiting in the parking lot of View-mont Elementary School. Even though it was late and Big Bertha's headlights were turned off, he still felt rather conspicuous.

They were still waiting for the Rebel janitor whom Min had promised to contact. But if he didn't arrive soon, they'd have to continue on. It wasn't smart to linger out in the open for too long. Not with Mr. Clean and his group of Sweepers on the loose.

Alan and Penny had slipped down the street to a gas station that they'd seen on the drive in. It was only a few blocks away, and if they were successful, they would return shortly with a bag full of corn dogs and chips.

The moment they'd parked, Dez had crawled out of the trash in the back of the garbage truck. He'd grumbled a few angry words at Bernard before seating himself on Big Bertha's front bumper to mope.

Spencer and Daisy were leaning against the side of the big truck as Walter and Bernard made a few routine checks over the vehicle.

"Whoa," Daisy said, looking suddenly over at Spencer. "For a second I thought your head was the moon."

"Huh?" He raised an eyebrow. Daisy said a lot of strange things.

"It's your hair," she explained, as though it made perfect sense. "Looked like a full moon for a second."

Spencer put a hand on his head. He would never get used to his new Auran look. Activating the Glop in his bloodstream to destroy the landfill pumphouse had given his body such a shock that his hair had turned stark white. He had tried dying it, like Rho had when she was at New Forest Academy, but it wasn't worth the effort. The dye never seemed to take—it would wash out in a day, leaving his head shimmering like the moon.

Bernard came around the side of the garbage truck. "She's in good shape," he said, patting Big Bertha's side. "No harm done from a bit of wall-driving."

"Did Rho say you could keep her truck?" Spencer asked.

The garbologist shrugged. "She didn't say I couldn't. Besides, she's got more important things to worry about. I'm taking good care of Big Bertha."

"Good care?" Spencer said. "It's full of garbage."

"*You're* full of garbage," replied Bernard. "Big Bertha's full of treasures!"

"Don't tell me you're actually going to sort through all that junk," Spencer said, pointing to the truck.

Bernard grinned. "I've got to rebuild my collections. Some of us see the true value in garbage. Isn't that right, Daisy?" He clapped his hands together with a sudden thought. "Speaking of garbage . . . how's the old Thingama-junk doing?"

"Bookworm?" Daisy shook her head. "Not good."

"What's wrong?"

"I think he's sick," Daisy said. "I used to take him for walks, but he doesn't even stand up anymore."

"What're you feeding him?" Bernard asked.

Daisy went wide-eyed and shrugged. "I didn't think he needed food. He's made of garbage."

"Just because he's made of garbage doesn't mean you should treat him like trash," said Bernard. "He's probably starving, poor thing."

Daisy's bottom lip began to quiver. Spencer thought she might cry. "I'm a bad, bad owner. I can't even be trusted to keep the garbage alive!" She buried her face in her hands.

"It'll be all right," Spencer said. "I'm sure we can find something that Bookworm likes to eat. Remember the other Thingamajunks at the landfill? They loved eating nasty stuff. Like that stink bomb that Aryl threw at us."

"I don't know," Bernard said. "At this point, he might be hard to resuscitate. Bookworm may need a massive trash-fusion."

"What's a trashfusion?" Daisy asked.

"You know," Bernard said. "Like a transfusion, but with trash."

"Will we have to take him to the hospital?"

"Nah," Bernard said. "I've got a home remedy that might work for a trashfusion."

"What do you mean?" Daisy asked.

"Rotting garbage," answered Bernard, pointing a thumb at Big Bertha. "Come with me. I'll show you what I've got in mind."

Daisy followed the garbologist around the back of the garbage truck, but Spencer stayed where he was, taking a moment to breathe in the cool springtime air and digest everything that had happened in the last two nights. He'd seen some pretty frightening images that clung to his brain.

"You look troubled." Walter Jamison's voice startled Spencer. He hadn't seen the old warlock approach. "What's on your mind?"

"It's nothing," Spencer said.

"You want to talk about it?"

Spencer didn't realize his emotions were so transparent. Since it was obvious that Walter wasn't going to drop the matter, Spencer decided to let it out. "I was just thinking about Garcia. Mr. Clean just . . . *vaporized* him with that Glopified rag." Spencer shook his head. "And they were supposed to be on the same side. Then, last night in the library. Professor DeFleur . . ." This time he didn't finish the sentence.

Walter leaned against Big Bertha and put a comforting hand on Spencer's shoulder. The boy took a deep breath and went on. "I mean, the BEM is just getting stronger and stronger. And now they have Sweepers." He looked at Walter's face, wrinkled and weary. "Do you really think we can win?"

Walter's hand slipped from Spencer's shoulder and the old warlock blinked slowly a few times. When he answered, it was with a question. "What do you think it means to win?"

It seemed like an easy answer, and Spencer gave it right away. "It means that we beat the BEM. We get what we want, and we all go home safe."

"If that's your definition of winning," Walter said, "then I'm afraid my answer is no. We won't win."

Spencer felt his heart sink, as though Walter's pronouncement would seal the Rebels' defeat. He looked down at the ground. "Don't you have hope?" Spencer muttered to his old mentor.

"I'm full of hope, Spencer," said Walter. "If what we're doing is right, then I believe we will win."

"But you just said . . ." Spencer began.

"Winning doesn't mean we all go home safe," Walter cut him off. "That is a thing of fairy tales and bedtime stories. Real life will demand much more of us, and we have to stand ready to pay whatever price is needed to gain the victory." Walter sighed heavily, as though trying to exhale some of the weight on his mind. "Because victory *will* come to those who fight for what is right. It won't come without its fair share of pain and suffering. No victory comes without sacrifice. But it *will* come. We just have to stay the course."

Spencer nodded. "I just don't want anyone else to get hurt." He was thinking of Professor DeFleur, swallowed whole. That could have happened to any of them in the library.

"I wish the same thing," Walter said. "This isn't a game. We're fighting for the future of humanity. When our final goal is this important, the stakes go up. You're young, Spencer. And I wish there were some way to shield you from the consequences of this conflict. But the truth is, we'll all have to put our lives on the line to stop the BEM. That's what it's going to take if we really want to *win*."

Now it was Spencer's turn to sigh. "I know," he whispered. Then he looked back at Walter's face. "But soon we'll have the Witches on our side. They've got to count for something."

Walter smiled. "Indeed."

Headlights flashed as a pickup rambled into the elementary school parking lot. Walter clapped his hands together. "Looks like help has finally arrived."

CHAPTER 15

"DID YOU SAY PORT-A-POTTY?"

There was nothing special about Viewmont Elementary School. Except maybe the Rebel janitor, Earl Dodge.

It was just after one o'clock in the morning when the Rebel team got settled inside the school. Earl was wearing blue plaid pajamas, black cowboy boots, and a ten-gallon hat. He flicked a toothpick back and forth under his bristly handlebar mustache.

"Now, let me get this straight," Earl drawled. They were all sitting, rather cramped, in the janitorial office. "You're just gonna stroll on into a high-security laboratory and take down the most powerful man in the BEM?"

Walter nodded. "Will you help us?"

"Sheesh!" Earl said. "You fellers are daft. If I'da known we'd be raiding the Bureau, I wouldn't have worn my pj's."

"We don't need you to come with us," Alan said. "We

need you to stay here and keep the portal open so we can get back."

"Phew," Daisy said. "Glad it's not me again. I didn't do so good last time."

"You did fine," Spencer said to her. "It wasn't your fault we were working with a traitor." He shot a venomous glance over his shoulder at Dez, who stood slouched against the door frame.

"Not cool, Doofus!" Dez answered. "I'm not a traitor anymore. The BEM's dumb. I hate those guys."

"You really expect us to believe you?" Spencer asked.

"You know how much stuff they promised to do for me?" Dez said. He stood up straight, his lip curled in a sneer. "They lied and lied, like a million times. The BEM didn't do jack for me! Garcia wanted to lock me up with a bunch of Rubbishes till my brain turned to mush. I'm glad he's dead!"

Walter stood up, his arm outstretched in a reassuring manner. "We understand that you're upset, Dez. But you're with us now, and we'll protect you."

"Yeah, right." Dez slumped against the door frame again. "You guys are no better."

"As you can see," Bernard said to Earl, "our team is very united."

The cowboy janitor chuckled. "All right," he said. "I'll squeegee a portal for you. But don't you gotta have some-body in Massachusetts with a squeegee too?"

"We do," Walter said. He unclipped a squeegee from his belt and handed it to Earl. Dez had lost the squeegee he'd used at New Forest Academy, and Daisy's was useless without it. Spencer figured that this new squeegee Walter gave to Earl must belong to a new pair.

"Agnes Maynard," Walter continued.

"And she's inside the BEM laboratory?" Penny asked.

The warlock shook his head. "No, but she's as close as we can get. Agnes is a part-time janitor at a middle school only a few blocks from the entrance to the lab. She agreed to open a squeegee portal for us, but that's all she'll do. We're on our own when we get there."

"What do we know about the entrance to the lab?" asked Penny.

"All of our information comes from Agnes," Alan answered. "She said it's inside a construction site, fenced around with chain-link."

"That's all they have for defenses?" Bernard said. "I've been climbing chain-link fences since I was knee-high to a Thingamajunk."

"The chain-link fence around the construction site isn't the hard part," Alan said, "although it may be rigged with traps, and there will probably be guards. Once inside the construction site, Agnes said the place is riddled with mines. One misstep can spring a trap loaded with Agitated Toxites. We need to make our way across the site and enter a Port-a-Potty."

Spencer shuddered and Daisy giggled.

"I'm sorry," Bernard said. "Did you say Port-a-Potty?"

Alan nodded, like it was the most serious thing he'd ever said. "A portable outhouse. That's the entrance to the BEM's secret laboratory."

Spencer sighed. "We don't have to flush ourselves down the toilet again, do we?" He'd had his fill of that when they were searching for the map to the Auran landfill.

"Agnes doesn't know what happens inside the Port-a-Potty," his dad said. "BEM workers go in, and they don't come out for days."

"Sounds like bowel trouble to me," Bernard muttered.

"It'll be trouble, all right," Alan said. "Agnes believes that we'll need a Sweeper once we get into the Port-a-Potty. No one gets in or out without one of those hybrid monsters escorting them."

"How are we going to get a Sweeper to help us?" Penny asked.

"We know the Sweepers were invented in the BEM laboratory," Walter said. "So we should expect the place to be swarming with them."

"What's the best way to deal with them?" Bernard asked.

"A fatal blow will knock the Glop out of them," Walter explained. "With it goes their eyesight, leaving them blind and quite harmless."

"You're sure they can't transform again?" Daisy said.

Walter shook his head. "It takes a potion to change them into Sweepers. As long as they don't drink another, they shouldn't be much of a threat. But they also won't be much help to us, since we'll probably need them in Sweeper form to get past the security features inside the Port-a-Potty."

The mention of Sweeper potions reminded Spencer of something. "There might be another way," he said. "I stole the Sweeper potion that Director Garcia was supposed to drink. Maybe we can use it to trick the Port-a-Potty's security and get into the lab without a Sweeper."

"Good thinking, kid!" Bernard said.

Spencer turned around and grabbed his belt from the back of the chair where he'd draped it. "I put it in this back pouch," Spencer said, digging his hand into the pocket. He rooted around, his heartbeat quickening as his fingers failed to find the small vial of Sweeper potion.

"Wait," he muttered. "Where . . ." Spencer swallowed hard. "It's gone."

"Maybe it done fell out?" Earl said.

"Impossible," Spencer said. "These are spill-proof pouches. Stuff can't fall out!" A sinking feeling started in his stomach, and he knew exactly what had happened. Spencer leapt to his feet, eyes darting around the cramped janitorial closet. "Oh, no," he muttered, his gaze falling on the empty door frame. "Where's Dez?"

CHAPTER 16

"I'LL TAKE MY CHANCES."

Spencer was the first one into the hallway. He spotted Dez almost instantly, standing at the end of the hall, the green exit sign lending creepy illumination to the scene.

Spencer took off at a sprint toward him, unclipping a mop from the janitorial belt in his hand. As Spencer's footsteps slapped the hard floor, Dez turned.

"Not a step closer, Doofus!" the bully shouted, thrusting out his hand like a policeman directing traffic.

Spencer wouldn't have stopped if Penny hadn't grabbed his arm. He reeled back, not even aware that the other Rebels had followed him into the hallway. They were all there now, trying to figure out the best way to stop Dez from doing something stupid.

The hallway security light glinted off a tiny glass vial

in Dez's hand. The boy threw the cork to the floor, and a sulphuric odor wafted from the open bottle.

"Take it easy, Dezmond," Walter said calmly, stepping to the front of the group. "Think about what you're doing."

"Back up!" Dez shouted.

"We can work this out," Walter said. "But you have to set down the potion."

"No way!" answered Dez. "If I put this down, then you guys win and I'm back to being treated like a nobody!"

"That's not true," Walter continued. "You're an important member of this team."

"Whatever!" Dez yelled. "You guys didn't even let me ride in the front of the truck on the way here. I had to sit in a big pile of stupid smelly garbage!"

"I object!" Bernard said. "My garbage is not stupid."

"But Dez has a point about the smell," Daisy said.

Bernard shrugged. "So I haven't dumped it in a while. So maybe a few things are rotting back there. Doesn't mean the kid has to insult my trash!"

"I'm going to insult everybody's trash!" Dez yelled, raising his potion like a toast. "And then, when I'm a Sweeper, I'm going to *kick* some trash!"

"You can't use the potion, Dez," Walter cut in. "It won't work on you."

"Don't try to talk me out of this!"

"Think about the rules of Glop," Walter said. "Only janitorial items can be Glopified."

"What about the rest of the Sweepers, then?" Dez said. "How come it worked on them?"

"They were janitors," Walter explained. "They were officially employed to clean, which made them fit the rules." The warlock shook his bald head. "If you drink that Glop potion, it will kill you, Dez. You're just an ordinary student."

"Well, I'm not going to be ordinary anymore," Dez muttered. "And when I'm a Sweeper, you guys will need my help. I'll be the most powerful person on your pathetic Rebel team."

"Actually," Spencer said, "I'm pretty sure Walter just explained that you'll be dead."

Dez sneered. "Well." He shrugged. "I'll take my chances."

Penny sprang forward, but it was too late. The vial of Sweeper potion touched Dez's lips and he threw back his head, draining the formula in one gulp. The Rebels froze in total shock at what was happening.

Dez stood perfectly still for three whole seconds. Then his body jerked violently. The glass bottle flung from his hand and shattered into tiny fragments on the hard floor. A second spasm seared through his body, throwing him up against the wall. His eyes clamped shut and his face was pinched in pain.

"We've got to do something!" Daisy shouted, stepping toward Dez.

But the bully threw out his hand. "Stay back!" His voice caused Spencer to shudder. It was changing, growing suddenly throaty and raw. Then, all at once, Dez's outstretched hand flexed. His fingertips split and black talons emerged, hooked and wicked looking.

The skin on Dez's face flushed a bright red. It grew wrinkly and tough, like old leather. His eyes snapped open, and Spencer jumped back. Dez's gaze looked the same, but there was a pinkish hue to his eyeballs that seemed altogether unnatural.

The bridge of his nose darkened and turned hard, widening across his cheekbones like a broad beak.

Then there was a tearing sound. Spencer couldn't tell if the rending was cloth or skin, and he grimaced as Dez let out a horrible shriek. Leathery, black wings rose from his shoulders, unfurling wide enough to span the hallway.

Then it was over, and Dez Rylie collapsed on the floor.

CHAPTER 17

"I LOOK TOTALLY AWESOME!"

It didn't take long for Dez to revive. When his eerie eyes fluttered open, Spencer was sure he would attack. Instead, Dez rose slowly to his feet, examining his taloned fingers and flexing his huge bat wings.

Then he began to laugh.

"Boo-ya!" he shouted. "I look totally awesome!"

Spencer glanced at Daisy. "That's not the word I would use," he muttered.

Earl was holding onto his cowboy hat, as if he feared a gust of wind from Dez's wings might blow it off. "So that's a Sweeper?" he drawled.

Dez thrust a hooked finger in Walter's direction. "Told you so, old man! I knew the potion would work on me!"

Walter was shaking his head, eyes unblinking. "I don't understand . . . how did you survive?"

"I don't care how," Dez said. His transformation seemed to delight him. "I'm amazing! Next time those chumps at New Forest Academy mess with me, they'll get the hook!" He swiped a sharp finger through the air.

Spencer suddenly had a thought that made everything fall into place. "Weren't you in detention at the Academy?" he asked Dez.

"Does it matter?" he answered. "Nobody's putting me in detention now!"

"It matters," Spencer said. "Wasn't Garcia making you clean the school at night?"

"Yeah," Dez said. "I kept trying to get my name off the list, but Garcia wanted to punish me bad."

"That's why it worked," Penny finished Spencer's train of thought. "The Sweeper potion worked on Dez because, technically, he was a temporary janitor, cleaning New Forest Academy."

"Shouldn't we knock him out already?" Daisy asked. "You know, since he's a bad guy now."

"I'm not a bad guy," said Dez. "I'm the same guy I always was." Then he grinned. "But now I have wings."

"We need to get him back to normal," Walter muttered.

"Didn't you just say that a fatal blow to a Sweeper will knock the Glop out of them?" Bernard said.

Walter nodded. "But it will also leave them blind."

"Maybe I can de-Glopify him," Spencer said, holding out his left hand. "With my Auran powers."

"Nobody's taking away my better half!" Dez yelled. He flapped his large wings, and his feet lifted from the floor for the first time. "Woo-hoo!" Dez touched the ceiling and coasted back to the floor.

Spencer could see that Walter was caught in a dilemma. The warlock rubbed a hand across his face. "We don't know what side effects it will have on Dez if you de-Glopify him. He may still go blind from having the Glop withdrawn."

"I agree that we need to get him back to normal," Penny said. "But didn't Agnes say that we'll need a Sweeper once we get inside that Port-a-Potty?" She pointed at Dez, who was now doing a dance move that looked kind of like the Funky Rubbish. "Let's use him while we've got him," Penny said. "Turn him back after we steal Belzora."

Spencer was shaking his head. That was exactly Dez's plan. He wanted to make himself feel important and indispensable. Giving in to him would just fuel his selfishness.

But Walter nodded in agreement. It was decided.

"I'll give Agnes a call," Alan said, pulling a phone from his pocket. "Let's get those portals open before Mr. Clean gets back to the lab."

Spencer and Daisy followed the other Rebels back toward the janitorial closet.

"This is going to be bad," Spencer whispered. "Dez can fly."

"At least he's a Rubbish, so his breath doesn't affect us," she said.

"I wish it would affect himself," Spencer said. "He used to be vulnerable to big Rubbishes."

"I think he's immune now," said Daisy. "It's hard to smell your own breath."

There was a rush of air overhead, and Dez suddenly landed between them, his big bat wings folding around Spencer and Daisy like an awkward group hug. "Isn't this going to be fun?"

Spencer could think of a dozen words to describe what it would be like working with a Sweeper Dez. *Fun* was not one of them.

CHAPTER 18

"SHE'LL NEVER SEE ME COMING."

The squeegee portal opened, and Earl tipped his cowboy hat to the woman standing on the other side.

Agnes Maynard was a rail of a woman. She was dressed in dark clothes with a big ring of keys on her belt. Her gaunt face was creased in ways that made Spencer think she'd spent most of her fifty-some years worrying.

"Come quickly," she said, gesturing for the group of Rebels to step through the squeegee portal. Penny did so first, scanning the area for any kind of trap or betrayal. When she judged it to be safe, she nodded to the others.

"Best of luck to you," Earl said.

"We won't forget your part in this," Walter said.

Earl winked. "That's assuming y'all survive!"

Spencer didn't find the cowboy janitor's words to be very encouraging. But it was too late to turn back now. He

107

and Daisy stepped up to the doorway, hearing his dad give Earl some last-minute instructions.

"Agnes is going to let her side of the portal close," Alan said. "But we'll be taking her squeegee with us into the laboratory. We need you to keep swiping on your side so we can use our squeegee to get back at any moment."

"How long should I keep her open?" Earl whispered.

Alan shook his head, and Spencer could tell that his dad didn't like the question either. "The only reason you should close that portal is if it opens to a mess of Sweepers on the other side. Then you shatter the glass and dispose of the squeegee."

"Aye, aye, captain," said Earl. He tipped his large cowboy hat one last time; then all the Rebels were through the portal and following Agnes down the darkened hallways of a middle school in Massachusetts.

Dez tried to fly above the group, but he was still clumsy with his newfound wings. He grazed the ceiling and dropped heavily to the floor behind them.

"I can't wait to get outside and stretch my wings," he said. "I feel like a bird in a cage."

"Maybe if we give you a cracker, you'll stop talking." Spencer muttered.

Daisy started digging in her pocket. "I think I have a Ritz in here." Then she shrugged. "Nope. Just crumbs."

Agnes glanced back at Dez. "Where did you find the Sweeper?" Spencer heard her whisper to his dad.

"You said we'd need one when we enter the Port-a-Potty," Alan said.

"I didn't think you'd bring your own," said Agnes. "How do you know we can trust him?"

Spencer still wasn't sure they could, but Walter cut in. "Because he wasn't a Sweeper fifteen minutes ago."

"It's a risk," Agnes said, so matter-of-fact that Spencer couldn't tell how she felt about it.

A moment later, they were outside, but Dez wasn't unfurling his leathery wings. Penny had a solid grip on the boy's shoulder. Spencer was pretty sure his Sweeper strength could lift her off the ground, but Penny's threat stopped him from trying.

"Take off, and I clip your wings."

"Whatever." Dez shrugged away from her grasp. "You guys need me."

Penny nodded. "We need you," she said. "We don't need your wings."

They moved beyond the school property and followed Agnes down a street lined with massive trees. After a while, the road turned to hard dirt, ribbed with washboards. They stepped out of the trees and back into the moonlight, where Spencer saw the dirt road bend down a slope to the right.

Agnes quickly dropped to her knee on the edge of the road, and the other Rebels followed her example.

At the base of the gentle slope was a construction site. It was large, treeless, and ringed entirely by a chain-link fence. The fence looked ordinary enough and stood no higher than about twelve feet. Floodlights filled the site with harsh, artificial brightness, and Spencer could see warning signs hanging every few feet along the fence.

DANGER
CONSTRUCTION AREA—KEEP OUT

The dirt road ended in a dusty parking area outside the fence, where Spencer noticed only a half dozen cars. He didn't know why he had expected to see more, since the BEM workers who knew about the lab were likely to be Sweepers or Pluggers. Neither of those groups needed vehicles when they could move with the speed and agility of Toxites.

The only break in the chain-link was an open gate wide enough to admit even the largest Extension Filth. Standing before the gate were two Sweepers. Spencer couldn't see the details of their faces, but even at this distance he could tell that one was a Filth and the other a Grime.

Beyond the guards, the construction site looked plain. A crane loomed over a stack of large pipes and rusty re-bar. There were several perilous-looking dugout holes, with backhoes parked on the piles of excavated dirt and broken chunks of concrete. Splintery wooden pallets were tossed next to a heap of loose bricks.

But at the center of the construction area, clearly visible in the floodlights, stood a single Port-a-Potty.

There was nothing extraordinary about the way it looked. It was a Port-a-Potty, and Spencer had seen plenty of them in his lifetime. The plastic sides were fire-engine red, with a domed top and a small ventilation pipe rising from one corner. Spencer's instincts had always been to stay away from germ-infested Port-a-Pottys. It seemed strange now to risk his life to get inside one.

"There is something else I should tell you," Agnes whispered. "It has come to my attention that Mr. Clean has found a way to Glopify the chain-link fence. You won't be able to climb it."

"We have brooms," Penny said. "Why would we climb it when we can just fly over?"

"That's the problem, you see," said Agnes. "Imagine a force field lying flat across the top of the fence, covering the entire construction site like a blanket. Anything that touches the force field from above or below will be destroyed."

"What about the crane?" Alan asked. It was clearly rising high above the twelve-foot fence.

"The crane has been reinforced," said Agnes. "The force field is sealed around it. The only opening is that gate."

She took a deep breath through her nose. "This is where I leave you," Agnes whispered. She handed her Glopified squeegee to Alan, who clipped it into his janitorial belt.

"Sure you don't want to join us?" Bernard asked. "I bet there's plenty of room in the john."

Agnes didn't even crack a smile. She clasped Walter firmly on the shoulder, gave him a businesslike nod, and retreated into the darkness.

"What now?" Daisy asked. Spencer could tell she was a

bit shaken by the fact that Agnes had revealed the dangers of the Glopified fence and then left.

"Looks like those two Sweeper guards have Glopified walkie-talkies," Penny said. "We'll need to take them out fast, before they can radio in for help."

"You guys handle those two," Dez said, pointing down to the gate. "I'll take out the third one."

Spencer looked at him, annoyed by the fact that he wasn't even crouching down. "Third one?"

"Yeah." Dez pointed. "There's a Rubbish Sweeper perched on top of the crane."

The tip of the crane was high above the construction site and well out of the glow of the floodlights. Spencer squinted, but he couldn't make out a figure anywhere.

"You're lying," Spencer said. "You're just looking for an excuse to test your wings."

"I don't see anything either," Daisy said.

"Duh," said Dez. "That's 'cause I have eagle eyes. I can see pretty good in the dark now. When I turned into a Sweeper, my eyesight got entranced."

"*Enhanced*," Spencer corrected.

"Whatever," said Dez. "There's a Sweeper lady up there." He squinted. "I think she's got a walkie-talkie too."

"If Dez's Rubbish eyes can see her," Walter said, "then her Rubbish eyes will spot us long before we make it to the fence."

"Let me take her out!" Dez insisted.

Spencer rolled his eyes. "Oh, please. You've been a Sweeper for *maybe* twenty minutes. She'll eat you alive."

"She'll never see me coming."

"Dez has a point," Walter said. Spencer threw his hands up in the air. Why did they continue to side with Dez? He always got them into trouble!

"That crane is too high for even the strongest broom to carry someone up," Walter continued. "That Rubbish Sweeper probably feels quite secure up there."

"An aerial attack would give us the benefit of surprise," Penny said. "But I don't think Dez should handle this alone."

"What are you saying?" Dez asked.

"I'm saying that you're going to fly me up there and drop me right down on top of that Sweeper lady," answered Penny. "I'll hit her with the green spray and she won't remember a thing about it when she wakes up."

"Why not take her out completely?" Bernard asked.

"Mr. Clean can't be far behind us," she said. "If he shows up and all of his guards are blind and de-Glopified, he'll know we beat him here."

"Green spray erases only recent memories," Walter said. "That means you'll have only a minute or two from the time she spots you. Anything beyond that might not get erased and she'll wake up with a memory of the fight."

"I'll be faster alone," Dez said.

"Absolutely not," replied Walter. "You're flying Penny up there."

Dez was shaking his head. "No can do. Penny's too big. I don't think I can carry her that high."

"Are you calling me fat?" Penny glared, hands on hips.

"Use a plunger," said Bernard. "She'll be weightless."

Dez shrugged. "I don't have one."

"Here," Daisy said. She unclipped a Glopified toilet plunger and tossed it to him. Dez's taloned hand closed around the handle, but it slipped through his grasp and landed on the dirt road. He bent over, his awkward hands making several attempts to grasp the wooden handle. At last he got it, but when he turned to face the Rebels, the plunger slipped through his fingers again.

Penny raised an eyebrow. "I'm not flying anywhere with Butterfingers."

"It's not my fault you weigh so much," Dez said. He didn't bother trying to pick up the plunger again. "I'll just have to go alone."

"How's that going to work if you can't hold the green spray?" Bernard pointed out.

Alan shook his head. "We'll find another way."

"What about me?" Spencer said. "I'm probably the smallest in the group." Technically, Daisy was, but Spencer wasn't about to suggest that Dez take flight with her. He looked at Dez. "Can you carry me?" He said it like a challenge, knowing that would push the bully into agreeing faster.

Dez scoffed. "Easy!" Before anyone could react, Dez threw his arms around Spencer and leapt into the air.

CHAPTER 19

"LET'S JUST SEE WHAT HAPPENS."

Dez's Rubbish wings unfurled, bearing Spencer through the thinnest branches of the nearest tree and straight into the starry sky.

When they were well above the treetops, Dez began attempting some aerial acrobatics. He started with a tight barrel roll, causing Spencer's stomach to heave uncomfortably. Then he cut a wide loop-de-loop, soaring out over the construction site.

"I'm the baddest person who ever lived!" Dez called.

Spencer's mouth was clamped shut in fear, but he managed to work out a sentence. "Shouldn't we be more sneaky?"

"Relax, dude." Dez had leveled out now, and Spencer saw that they were high above the tip of the crane. "I had my eyes on that Rubbish lady the whole time. She was looking the other way."

Spencer hated knowing that, in this very moment, Dez Rylie was solely in charge of his fate. All the Sweeper kid had to do was open his arms and Spencer would plummet to his certain death. The thought of it caused Spencer's hand to stray to his janitorial belt. He didn't know what would save him in a fall, but it felt a little better just to touch a broom handle.

Dez was gliding now, making a big circle above the crane like a vulture over carrion. Spencer could finally see the Rubbish Sweeper. She was a fat woman squatting at the very tip of the long, angled crane arm. She looked odd, balancing there with her wings tucked back. Spencer half expected her to topple at any moment.

"How close can you get me before she spots us?" Spencer whispered. He wasn't sure if his voice had carried in the wind until Dez responded.

"You worry too much about the details." Dez looked down at Spencer, a horrible look of mischief in his bloodshot eyes. "Let's just see what happens."

Dez's wings folded back and he went into a steep dive. The rushing air stole Spencer's breath as they zoomed down behind the unsuspecting Sweeper.

When they were still some distance away, Dez pulled up hard, his wings snapping out and catching the wind like sails. "I'll handle this one," Dez said. Then his arms opened, and Spencer fell hard onto the angled arm of the crane.

It should have knocked the wind out of him, but

Spencer's Glopified jumpsuit absorbed the impact and he felt no pain. Still, he let out a cry of fear and surprise. There was really no way to hold it in at such a terrifying height. Spencer clung to the metal crane arm as he tipped his head to see the Sweeper above him. She leapt to her feet with surprising agility for a woman of her size. Her wings curled outward to steady her as pink eyes honed on Spencer, who was clinging helplessly a few feet down.

The Sweeper's taloned hand reached for the walkie-talkie at her side. No sooner had she unclipped it from her belt than Dez Rylie struck like a diving falcon. His force knocked her from the tip of the crane, and she reeled in the air for a moment before her own wings caught her fall.

Her walkie-talkie clattered down the crane arm. Spencer reached out, but it bounced over the edge, spiraling toward the construction site below. Spencer watched the little black device fall, illuminated by the floodlights.

When the walkie-talkie was about twelve feet from the ground, it struck the invisible force field that spanned the top of the chain-link fence. Magic rippled like water disturbed by a thrown stone. It sent an audible hum across the entire construction site, lighting up the whole force field for one brief second. Then the walkie-talkie exploded into unrecognizable fragments.

Spencer's eyes were wide. Agnes wasn't joking about the Glopified fence. His grip around the crane arm tightened as he realized that a fall would completely obliterate him.

The exploding walkie-talkie would have surely alerted the two Sweeper guards at the gate. But Spencer couldn't worry about them at the moment. The Sweeper was flapping her wings. She didn't look very graceful or experienced, but that didn't stop her from rising toward Spencer's precarious position on the crane.

Spencer cast his eyes around frantically. "Dez!" he yelled. Stealth was no longer a thought in his mind. "Where are you?"

From somewhere below, Spencer heard the kid's voice. "Just let go, Doofus! I'll probably catch you!"

"*Probably?*" Spencer yelled. There was no way he was letting go. The plan was shot and time was ticking away. If they didn't spray the Sweeper soon, the green solution would be unable to erase the whole skirmish from her mind.

The fat Rubbish woman shrieked below him. Her wings painstakingly bore her plump body up toward Spencer and the crane.

With sweaty hands, Spencer drew his green spray bottle. He figured he'd have one good shot before the Sweeper reached him. If he hit her, she would plummet down and explode in the force field. He didn't like the idea, but did he have a choice?

Dez suddenly flapped up beside him, feet finding purchase on the tilted crane arm.

"Give me that green spray," he said. "She's so slow, I think I can blast her in midflight."

"I thought your clumsy hands couldn't hold on to anything," Spencer said.

Dez shrugged. "That was before." He reached down and

easily plucked the spray bottle from Spencer's grasp. "I just didn't feel like carrying Penny."

Spencer didn't have time to yell at Dez for lying. In the next moment, the fat Sweeper rose into view, her sharp fingers reaching out for Spencer.

Dez aimed the spray bottle and shot a stream of green solution into the woman's face. Her pink eyes rolled back as consciousness slipped away from her. Then her leathery wings spasmed, one of them catching Spencer across the shoulder and knocking him back. He slipped from the crane arm and found himself in a gut-wrenching free fall.

The unconscious Sweeper flopped through the air beside him, the two of them falling so close together that Spencer could have reached out and touched her. He scrambled for a broom at his belt, but the fall was petrifying as he rushed toward the force field.

Spencer was bracing himself to be blown to bits when a dark shadow passed overhead. He was jerked around, slamming into the round body of the unconscious Sweeper. Then Spencer was lifted away, dangling upside down by his right foot and pressed uncomfortably close to the large Sweeper woman.

Dez was carrying them both! Spencer could see the bully's face in the floodlights, and he didn't even look strained by the effort of bearing two people into the sky.

In a moment, they were back at the top of the crane, where Dez dumped the large Sweeper woman in a heap. Spencer thought she would roll right off, but her wings kept her draped there like a dirty rag on a faucet. He hoped they'd

been fast enough for the green spray to work. Assuming it had, the Sweeper would wake up with no memory of the fight, wondering where her walkie-talkie had gone.

"What was that all about?" Spencer yelled. Dez was now holding both of his ankles as they soared back toward the Rebels at the gate.

"Oh, you mean that part where I saved your life?" Dez said.

"No," said Spencer. "I mean that part where you weren't strong enough to pick up Penny, but you had no problem holding me and that fat lady!"

Dez made a face. "I told you, I really didn't want to carry Penny. She wouldn't have let me try out my flight skills. But I knew you couldn't stop me."

Spencer raged silently, upside down, until Dez deposited him at the gate where the other Rebels were waiting. Penny was standing over the Filth Sweeper and the Grime Sweeper. Both of them were unconscious, with droplets of green spray on their faces.

"They shouldn't remember a thing when they wake up," Penny said.

Daisy turned to Spencer and Dez. "What happened up there?"

"We got our Sweeper," Dez reported.

He made it sound so simple. Spencer was about to elaborate when the Filth Sweeper's walkie-talkie sounded.

"Edwards," said an unfamiliar crackly voice. "You got action in the construction site?"

The Rebels all stared at one another for a stunned moment.

"Edwards? If you don't answer, I'm sending someone to your location."

Spencer didn't know where the person was calling from. He didn't know how long it would take to send reinforcements. All he knew was that the Sweeper called Edwards would not be answering the call.

CHAPTER 20

"A CLASSIC AMERICAN CHOCOLATE."

E dwards!" The voice on the other end of the walkie-talkie sounded irritated.

Bernard dropped to his knees and unclipped the Sweeper's radio. Lifting it to his mouth, the garbologist pressed the button and spoke. "Hello. Yes! Edwards here. We are all right now. We are A-OK. Fine and dandy." He paused, then added, "Thank you for asking."

It was silent on the walkie-talkie for a moment. Then the voice said, "Our sensors showed a shock wave at your location. Looks like something hit the force field."

Bernard swallowed hard and continued. "Umm. Yes. Something *did* hit the force field, now that you mention it."

"Well?" the voice on the other end was growing impatient. "What was it?"

Bernard's eyes flicked around the surrounding area, and

Spencer could see he was scrambling for any kind of help that could get them out of this. Then the garbologist smiled and gave an answer.

"It was a toasted marshmallow."

Penny smacked Bernard softly on the back of the head. He looked at her with an innocent expression. Taking his finger away from the button, he whispered to her. "Maybe I'm hungry, okay?"

"A toasted marshmallow?" asked the voice.

"Yes indeed," Bernard answered into the radio. "And I've got graham crackers and Hershey's chocolate to go with it."

"The boss would clean you up if he knew you were messing around with the force field again," said the voice. "He'll be back any minute, and I've got half a mind to tell him that you've been making s'mores!"

"Sorry," Bernard said. "I promise it won't happen again."

"Better not," said the voice. Then, "Over and out." The walkie-talkie went silent, and Bernard clipped it back onto the Sweeper's belt.

"S'mores?" Penny yelled. "What the heck was that?"

Bernard bent down, lifting a brown paper from the dirt. It was an empty Hershey's wrapper, and, by the look of it, someone had tried to grind it into the dirt with the heel of a shoe.

"Hershey's bar," Bernard said. "A classic American chocolate."

He dropped the wrapper and carefully plucked

something small out of the dirt beside it. Spencer squinted to see it clearly. It looked like the broken corner of a cookie.

"Graham crackers and milk make a wonderful snack," Bernard said. "But the presence of the chocolate could mean only one thing: s'mores."

"What about the marshmallows?" Daisy asked.

Bernard grinned, picking up a thin stick with a bit of sticky white residue on the tip. To Spencer's horror, he licked the gooey marshmallow remnants. "Jet Puffed, if I had to guess. This is recent, and I don't smell a campfire. The only other heat source is that Glopified fence." Bernard shrugged and dropped the stick. "It seemed logical that the Sweeper had tried it before. Guard duty can be mighty boring, and sometimes you need a midnight snack."

"Wow," Daisy said, clearly amazed by the garbologist's ability to read what others took for trash. Penny just rolled her eyes.

"We should get moving," said Alan. "How long before the Sweepers wake up?"

"Fifteen minutes," Walter said. "Twenty at the most."

"That doesn't give us much time to maneuver through the construction site and get inside that Port-a-Potty," Alan remarked. "Agnes said the place is probably riddled with mines. One false step could send a load of Agitated Toxites at us."

"We can't afford a fight in there," Walter said. "If even a single mop string hits that force field, it'll blow up in our hands."

Penny tightened her janitorial belt. "We'll just have to watch our step."

"What about a flashlight?" Spencer asked. "We could use a Glopified flashlight to scan for traps."

Spencer was pleased that his idea was met with nods of agreement. Alan dug a small flashlight from his belt pouch. But when he flicked the switch, nothing happened. The light was designed to be dim unless illuminating another magical object. But even when Alan pointed it directly at the Glopified fence, which they knew was charged, they couldn't see the beam clearly.

"Is it on?" Daisy asked.

Bernard leaned around and peered directly into the flashlight. He drew back squinting. "Definitely on and working," said the garbologist.

"Then why can't we see the beam?" Alan asked.

Bernard glanced around the perimeter of the construction site. "It must be the floodlights. They're so bright they're masking the flashlight."

"I'll fly up there and punch my fist through the big lights," Dez said, flexing his talons.

"Why are you so destructive?" Daisy asked. "Why can't you just turn them off like a regular person?"

"Where's the fun in that?" Dez said.

"Looks like there are five banks of floodlights positioned around the outside of the fence," Walter said. "If you can shut them down, that should do the trick."

But Spencer didn't like this. He didn't want Dez to feel any more powerful than he already did. Spencer judged the distance up to the first floodlight. It was easily within broom range.

While Dez went on boasting about how fast he would be able to shut off the lights, Spencer unclipped a broom, sprinted two steps, and rocketed up to the first floodlight.

After his experience on the crane, the height didn't seem nearly as frightening. He reached out and grabbed the light post, reigning himself in. He felt the intense heat from the row of lights and was grateful to be perched on the post behind them.

Now that he was up there, Spencer wasn't sure how to shut them off. As his broom regained gravity and he settled uncomfortably in his perch, Dez's idea of smashing the lights suddenly seemed half-decent.

Then he saw a little fuse box mounted behind the right side of the light. There was a small metal cover on it, but Spencer knew immediately what it was. His siblings had tripped the breakers at Aunt Avril's house enough times that Spencer was well acquainted with the fuse box there.

He had to lean an uncomfortable distance to reach the little door. From this angle, he could see that there was a slot in the metal covering just large enough to reach a finger through and trip the switch. It was stiff, but he managed to flip it off with an audible *click*.

Immediately, the lights on his pole went dark. Pleased with his success, Spencer pulled his hand away from the fuse box. The moment he released the switch, it clicked back and the floodlight kicked on again, startling Spencer so much that he nearly fell from his perch.

"What's going on up there?" Bernard called.

"There's a switch," Spencer answered. "But it won't stay off!"

"Can you tape it down?" asked Walter.

It was a good idea, but the slot in the metal covering was barely big enough for his finger. He'd never be able to get a strip of duct tape in place. "There's a covering."

"See?" Dez shouted. "You need me to smash it!"

"What about Windex?" his dad said. "If you turn the cover to glass and break it, could you get some tape in there?"

Spencer looked down. Leaning as he was, the force-field fence was directly below him. A single shard of glass could cause another explosion, and Spencer didn't think the Sweepers in the lab would believe another s'more story from Bernard.

"It's not going to work," he said. "The only way this light is staying off is if I hang out up here and hold the switch."

Penny had moved off during the conversation, drawing a broom from her belt and floating up to the next light pole. As she reached out, her set of floodlights darkened momentarily. But it didn't last.

"Same problem over here!" she called.

Spencer saw his dad and Walter exchange brief words. Then Alan called out. "Stay up there, Spence. We're sending Dez, Bernard, and Daisy up the other light poles. Once they're in position, you'll have to keep the lights off while

Walter and I use the Glopified flashlight to mark a path through the construction site."

Spencer didn't like the idea of splitting up, but there wasn't much he could say about it from his spot on the light pole.

"We'll mark every footstep with a piece of duct tape," Walter explained. "Once we reach the Port-a-Potty, you can let the lights turn back on and make your way across."

Spencer glanced at the unconscious Sweepers by the gate. This was a pretty elaborate plan to be executing under such a tight deadline.

CHAPTER 21

"KEEP YOUR HEAD DOWN!"

Daisy, Bernard, and Dez moved into position on the light posts with surprising ease. One by one, the floodlights around the construction site went dark. After the hot brightness, everything seemed extra dark. Spencer blinked hard, waiting for his eyes to adjust.

He saw a dim glow from the gate. That would be his dad's Glopified flashlight. As Alan brought it around, the little beam flared, darting to illuminate the Sweepers' bodies and the force-field fence.

Alan and Walter stepped through the gate, and Spencer watched the flashlight beam change directions. The two men moved at a rather slow pace. At least, it seemed that way to Spencer, whose arm quickly grew stiff from his leaning out to reach the fuse box and hold the little switch.

From time to time, one of the floodlights would flare

as someone's grip slipped on the switch. Spencer did it twice, and Daisy more times than Spencer could count. Dez was the only one not to falter. When his arm grew tired, Spencer saw him unfurl his wings and flap in the air beside his light pole.

The call finally came from Alan. Spencer could barely make out the Port-a-Potty in the dark center of the construction site. He couldn't see his dad or Walter standing beside it, but the flashlight was turned off, and Alan's words carried well enough.

"All right!" he shouted. "Come on!"

Grateful that the tedious task was over, Spencer released the switch, and his set of floodlights poured brightness into the construction area. One at a time, the big lights turned on as the Rebels abandoned their posts and met up at the gate.

Penny nudged the Grime Sweeper with her foot. "Can't have more than about five minutes left," she muttered.

"Can't you give him another shot?" Daisy asked.

Penny shook her head. "Once he's out, he's out. A second spray doesn't make it last any longer."

Bernard was down on one knee, just inside the fence.

"Looks like Hansel and Gretel left us a trail of bread crumbs," said the garbologist.

Daisy peered over his shoulder. "I don't know. It looks like duct tape to me." In the brightness of the floodlights, Spencer could clearly see little strips of tape stuck to the ground, each a footfall apart.

Bernard rose and extended his right foot. He set it down

right on top of the strip of tape and shifted his weight. "We'll have to go single file," he said. "Don't step anywhere except on the tape."

Dez made a face. "This is a waste of my time. I can just fly over there."

Penny pointed up. "Be my guest. But don't blame me when your wings hit that force field and you blow up."

"Fine." Dez folded his arms. "But I'm going first."

"Too late, kid," said Bernard, who was hopping to the third piece of tape. "I'm already on the trail. Get in line."

Dez cut in front of Spencer and Daisy, while Penny seemed satisfied to take the rear. They moved at a steady pace, trusting the markings on the trail with every step. The footfalls were mostly regular, although every so often a leap was required. Spencer didn't see a single sign of any mines. He believed they were there. From what he'd seen up on the pole, his dad's flashlight had been dancing between Glopified objects all the way across the site.

The duct-tape markings didn't follow a straight line, but wove gradually toward the Port-a-Potty. Dez's wings kept flicking out, and Spencer was afraid that he might take flight at any moment.

"This reminds me of a place we went camping last summer," Daisy said. Spencer didn't know why she wanted to make conversation at such a crucial time. "We had to hop from rock to rock to get across a little stream. And if you slipped off, you got wet."

"Good idea," Spencer said. "Think of it like that." Anything to put her at ease.

"Except this is different," Dez said. "Slip off now and you're dead."

Daisy was silent for a moment, hopping from tape to tape. "Yeah," she said. "This isn't as fun."

Spencer tried to center each step over the strip of duct tape, but it became tricky as the trail led them over a mound of broken concrete. He leapt from chunk to chunk, sometimes sliding a bit on the sloped surface.

"Keep your head down!" Bernard shouted as they neared the top of the pile. Spencer instinctively ducked, having not even realized that he was dangerously close to the top of the force field. It was an added challenge to follow the markings while hunched over, and Spencer could hear the soft, magical hum of the invisible net overhead.

They were still some distance from the Port-a-Potty when Penny made the announcement that everyone was dreading.

"They're waking up!" Her voice was an urgent whisper, and Spencer didn't need to check over his shoulder to know that she was right. They had taken too long.

Spencer remembered the disorienting feeling of reviving from green spray. That might buy them another few seconds, but then the Sweepers would surely spot them and raise the alarm.

"Run!" Penny hissed.

Bernard took off, his clumsy rubber boots touching down only for a brief second on each piece of tape. Dez was moving fast too, and Spencer was determined to keep up.

It was awkward to run when the marked footfalls had

been set by a person walking. Spencer thought he must have looked ridiculous, like someone hopping over hot coals. He was barely looking where to put his feet down, following so closely behind Dez.

Had Spencer been thinking more clearly, he wouldn't have trusted his path to the Sweeper kid in front of him. He'd learned not to trust Dez with anything, and in the next second, Spencer remembered why.

Dez was leaping along, only yards from the Port-a-Potty, and skipping every other marking. Dez jumped, his legs tucking up under him as his black wings stretched out. The boy had misjudged the trail's direction and veered too far to the left. And Spencer, following too closely, went right after him.

As Dez's Rubbish wings glided him safely back to the pathway, Spencer's foot came down hard on an unmarked spot of ground.

He froze, fully expecting a burst of little Toxites to erupt from the ground at his feet. When nothing happened, he exhaled slowly and looked down.

"Don't move," Penny said. Bernard and Dez had reached the Port-a-Potty, and Daisy was almost there.

"What am I stepping on?" Spencer asked. He could see a line running under the sole of his right shoe.

Penny, still safely on the marked trail, stooped to examine it. "Looks like a rubber band," she said. "It's long. Stretched tight. The ends are buried in the dirt."

Spencer felt a trickle of sweat drip down his side. His eyes flicked back to the gate where the Grime Sweeper was hunched over the Filth guy. The guards were still coming around. At least the Rebels hadn't been spotted . . . yet.

"What's the holdup?" Alan called.

"I think I'm standing on a trigger," Spencer answered.

Daisy's eyes went wide. "You're standing on Tigger?"

Penny reached out a hand and touched Spencer's shoulder. "You're just going to have to make a run for it." Then she turned back to the group of Rebels at the Port-a-Potty. "Let's open that door and get inside."

Walter grabbed the handle, and the door of the Port-a-Potty swung open without a fuss. The floodlights shone inside, and Spencer could see that it looked no different from every portable toilet he'd spent his life avoiding.

Seven people. It was going to be a very tight fit.

The Rebels were still squeezing in when Penny turned to Spencer. She released a preemptive spray of vanilla air freshener around the boy. "You ready?"

He nodded. Spencer tensed his body, mentally preparing for whatever might happen when he took his foot off that Glopified rubber band.

"Go!" Penny said, and Spencer darted forward at full speed.

Spencer heard the twang of the stretched rubber band as the two buried ends ripped from the ground. Attached to each end was an Agitation Bucket brimming with little angry Toxites.

The contracting rubber band pulled the two buckets out of the dirt and into the air with tremendous force. Spencer barely ducked as the buckets collided above his head. Plastic cracked and the Toxites came spewing out like water from a broken pipe.

There was no time to fight. In a hailstorm of monsters, Penny had Spencer's arm, pulling him along, heedless of the duct-tape trail markers. Spencer knew his foot triggered at least one more Toxite mine, and he felt the sting of sharp quills on the back of his legs.

His hand dropped to his janitorial belt, unclipping a dustpan and twisting the handle. The metal pieces fanned into an impressive shield, and he held it over his head as he sprinted. Dive-bombing Rubbishes pelted off his defenses, and Penny used a razorblade sword to swipe blindly at the Toxites over her shoulder.

When Spencer reached the Port-a-Potty, the other Rebels were packed inside. He threw himself through the small doorway, slamming up against his dad. Penny was right behind him. She seized the flimsy plastic door, hurled a chalkboard eraser back at the oncoming Toxites, and pulled the door closed.

CHAPTER 22

"IT'S A BIT CRAMPED."

It was much darker inside the Port-a-Potty. Only the tiniest bit of light from the floodlights crept in around the doorway. The Port-a-Potty seemed to be under attack from every angle. Angry little Toxites slammed repeatedly into the plastic walls, some scratching and pecking to find a way in.

Then, gradually, the activity slowed as Penny's chalk bomb paralyzed the monsters. It grew still and eerily quiet.

"So," Bernard said, "this is the secret BEM laboratory?" He shouldered up against Spencer and Alan. "It's a bit cramped."

"This is only the entrance to the lab," Walter said. "Though I don't quite see where to go."

"We better figure it out quick," said Penny. "Those

Sweeper guards have probably radioed in for backup by now. The chalk cloud outside won't hold them off for long."

"Agnes said we'd need a Sweeper once we got inside the Port-a-Potty," said Alan.

"Need me to do something awesome?" Dez said. He was taking up a lot of real estate, with his wings curling around the walls of the small booth.

A flashlight clicked on. It was dim at first, illuminating under Alan's chin, as if he were about to tell a ghost story. Then the bright beam shot out and honed in on Dez.

"Hey!" he said. "Don't shine that thing in my eyes!"

Alan struggled to point the flashlight away from Dez. When he managed, the bulb dimmed once more. "We're looking for something Glopified in here," he explained. Since there was no way to maneuver in the close quarters, Alan passed the flashlight so the Rebels could take turns shining it at things.

"I swear," Dez said, "if somebody shines me in the face again . . ."

"It's not our fault you're so big and Glopified," Spencer said.

"I think I found it!" Daisy's voice squeaked from the corner of the Port-a-Potty. Spencer craned his neck around, trying to glimpse what the girl had illuminated with the magical flashlight. "I was sitting on it!"

It was the toilet seat.

Glancing under Walter's arm, with his face pressed to his dad's chest, Spencer could see that the flashlight was beaming brightly on the plastic seat of the Port-a-Potty toilet.

Walter reached out and lifted the seat. He examined it briefly, then let it fall back into the downward position. "The light is only catching the seat ring," said the warlock.

Spencer was relieved. As long as there was nothing magical about the hole, he could deal with the seat.

"What should we do with it?" Daisy asked.

"Don't you mean, what should I do with it?" Dez said. "That Agnes lady said it would take a Sweeper to get into the lab. Maybe I'm supposed to bust off the lid," said Dez. "Throw it against the wall like a Frisbee."

"Let him open and close it," Bernard said. "Maybe that'll be the ticket."

It was the general consensus of the group that Dez needed to be in contact with the Glopified toilet seat. There was a considerable amount of shuffling and grumbling in the Port-a-Potty as Dez made his way over to the seat.

"Watch it!"

"That was my foot!"

"Ouch!"

"What's that smell?"

Then Dez was finally in position. He reached out a taloned hand and lifted the seat. In true Dez fashion, he slammed it down a little harder than necessary.

"Well, that didn't work," Dez grumbled. "Maybe I should crack it in half."

"What is it with you and breaking things?" Spencer said.

"Just be glad it's not your nose, Doofus," Dez retorted.

"You're just jealous because I actually have a nose instead of a beak," said Spencer.

"Beaks are cooler than noses," said Dez. "I can peck stuff."

"Excuse me," Bernard cut in, "but I don't give a Sweeper's behind what your beak can do. We've got to find the way into the lab."

"Sweeper's behind," Penny repeated, much too serious to take it for the joke it was meant to be. "Sweeper's behind . . . Glopified toilet seat . . ." She snapped her fingers. "That has to be it! Sit down, Dez."

"Wait," Daisy said. "I was sitting on the seat earlier, and nothing happened."

Bernard scratched his head. "You think Dez's bum is the key to get into the BEM's secret lab?"

"He *is* a Sweeper," Alan pointed out.

"No way," said the kid. "Sitting down is boring. I've got better skills than that."

"Just sit down on the seat," Walter demanded.

"Fine." Dez shoved his legs into the group, tucked his wings in tightly, and sat down on the plastic toilet seat.

The Port-a-Potty responded instantly. It lurched and shot straight into the air like a rocket. Spencer could feel the pressure of gravity almost strong enough to buckle his knees.

"What's happening?" Daisy cried.

"Whatever you do, Dez," said Penny, "don't stand up!"

The Port-a-Potty jerked hard, and everyone inside thumped against the back wall. The flimsy plastic door flapped open on its hinges, and Spencer caught sight of the earth far below. His head reeled with the motion and he thought he might be sick.

Dez was clinging to the toilet seat with both hands, holding his backside tight against the plastic ring while shouting gleefully as though he were on a roller coaster.

The flying Port-a-Potty was making a gentle turn through the sky. Out the dangerously open door, Spencer saw that they were now over a vast expanse of utter darkness. He couldn't tell what it was until he saw moonlight reflected on the waves.

They were flying over the Atlantic Ocean!

The Port-a-Potty lurched again and began a quick descent toward the water.

"I think we better get that door shut!" Alan yelled above the rushing wind.

Penny, holding tight to the door frame with one hand, leaned out and grasped the loose door. She grunted hard, jerking it against the wind and slamming it shut. She found a locking latch and switched it from *vacant* to *occupied*, barring the door closed just as the Port-a-Potty plunged into the Atlantic.

Spencer could sense the change in outside pressure. It was quieter but seemed heavier. A tiny rivulet of water ran along the seam of the door, but other than that, Spencer was surprised to find the portable booth completely dry.

"Incredible," whispered Walter. "The BEM laboratory is under the ocean. No wonder we've never come close to finding it."

"They must have more funding than the Rebels," said Bernard.

Daisy shuddered. "Yeah, but at least we don't have to worry about sharks. I don't think sharks eat Port-a-Pottys." She giggled nervously. "Do they?"

They continued downward for some time. The deep sounds of the ocean seemed to press in on them. In the utter darkness, the walls were not visible, and Spencer couldn't figure out how the Port-a-Potty wasn't collapsing under the pressure of the sea.

"Umm." Dez broke the silence. "I kind of have to use the toilet. But for real. Sitting here isn't helping. Can I get up now?"

"No," Walter said. "You must stay seated. There's no telling what will happen if you stand up."

"If it makes you feel any better," Spencer said, his face pressed into his dad's armpit, "it's not like the rest of us are really that comfy either."

The Port-a-Potty lurched and came to an obvious halt. The Rebels stood cramped and silent for a whole minute, unsure how to proceed. Then Penny unlatched the door and tested it slowly.

There was no resistance—the plastic door swung on its hinges. A bit of water dripped from the top of the doorway, as though they'd just weathered a minor thunderstorm instead of diving deep into the Atlantic Ocean.

They had docked at the very entrance to the BEM's secret laboratory.

CHAPTER 23

"WHO'S IT GOING TO BE?"

An empty hallway opened before them, with a row of lights built into panels along the wall. Penny was the first to spring into the hallway, drawing her twin mops from her janitorial belt. Then, one by one, the inhabitants of the Port-a-Potty spilled out, like clowns from a circus car. Dez was the last one to leave. He stood up and stretched his legs, moaning as though he'd been forced to sit for hours.

Leaving the door to the Port-a-Potty open, the team moved slowly down the hallway. Spencer drew his dustpan shield and kept a razorblade closed in his other hand.

They stepped out of the hallway and into a large, sterile room. Stainless-steel tables were set at perfect right angles, with beakers and test tubes carefully arranged across their surfaces. There was an acrid smell in the air, with a familiar sulphuric undertone of Glop. A Bunsen burner flamed in the corner, as though an experiment had been abandoned halfway through.

And the awful silence seemed to weigh as much as all the ocean water above them.

"Where is everybody?" Daisy finally whispered.

"Not very hospitable," said Bernard. "I expected a welcome party."

"It doesn't matter," Walter said. Spencer could tell that the old warlock was equally disturbed by the empty lab but didn't want to show it. "We're looking for the bronze nail," said Walter. "We'll be waiting for Mr. Clean. Once he arrives, we take Belzora, extract the nail, and squeegee back to Earl."

Spencer let out a breath he didn't notice he'd been holding. If only their plans were ever that simple! If only their plans ever played out the way they were supposed to! Spencer had a feeling in his gut that nothing about this was right.

They took a moment scouring the large room for the bronze nail. Spencer knew it wouldn't be there, so near the entrance to the lab and out in the open. He knew his companions sensed it too, and their searching seemed half-hearted.

Soon the Rebels were gathered at the far side of the room near a set of elevator doors. No one said anything as Alan pressed the button and the elevator opened. They moved silently in. After the cramped confines of the Port-a-Potty, the elevator seemed almost spacious for the seven Rebels.

There appeared to be six floors to the lab. But this building was different from city skyscrapers. The Rebels had entered on the top floor, and the other five levels seemed to descend deeper into the ocean floor.

Walter pushed the button for the bottommost level. "We'll start there and work our way up," he said softly. The doors to the elevator closed, and Spencer felt a little hiccup in his stomach as the elevator moved downward.

For a moment, Spencer felt as though he were in a fancy hotel. He wished they were somewhere ordinary. The depths of the lab made him feel claustrophobic. He watched the numbers change as they passed each floor.

3 . . .

4 . . .

5 . . .

The elevator jolted to a halt. Alan pressed the button to open the doors, but nothing happened. Quickly growing desperate, he pressed a few more buttons at random.

"We must be stuck between floors," he said. "We'll have to—"

But Alan was cut off by a voice. It spoke slowly through the speaker in the side of the elevator.

"Welcome to the experimental laboratory of the Bureau of Educational Maintenance."

Spencer recognized the voice immediately, so slimy and rich, even through the intercom. But how was it possible? Mr. Clean was supposed to be behind them. How could he have beaten them to the lab when the Rebels had been occupying the Port-a-Potty?

"It is indeed a rare visit," Mr. Clean said, "to have Rebels come so deep. You are the first. And you will also be the last."

Walter had drawn a plunger from his belt and clamped it onto the elevator door. He pulled, hoping to wrench open their escape, no matter where it led. The Glopified plunger made good suction, but the door held fast.

"There has to be another way out," Alan whispered to his Rebel companions.

"The elevator is quite secure," said Mr. Clean over the intercom. "The time for daring escapes is past."

Penny reached up toward the top of the elevator. Spencer saw what she was reaching for; it looked like a small hatch. Once, Spencer and Daisy had squeezed into the air vents at Welcher Elementary School to escape Garth Hadley. But here, the opening above looked too small even for them.

"The hatch is locked," said Mr. Clean. "I would advise you to leave it alone."

Penny lowered her arms. Spencer could tell that she wasn't giving up. She just needed to think it through and weigh Mr. Clean's subtle threat.

"Don't listen to him," said Dez. "He's the bad guy, remember? I can handle this." He leapt up, wings fanning to give him an extra boost as he knocked the other Rebels back. His taloned fingers punctured into the hatch covering, and he tore it away.

Something dropped when Dez pulled the hatch open. The small object fell past the bully and struck the floor in the center of the elevator.

It was a chalkboard eraser. And it was already venting paralytic dust by the time anyone realized what had just happened.

"Look what you did!" Spencer yelled as Dez touched back down.

"Oh, man," Dez said. "I hate this stuff!" He bent down, trying to use his large wing to cover the chalk bomb, but the white cloud billowed out too quickly.

"Tisk, tisk," Mr. Clean said. "You should not have opened the hatch. Luckily, we have security measures in place in case an emergency like this should arise."

The Rebels were all covering their faces, breathing shallowly, trying to postpone the inevitable paralyzing effects of the chalk dust.

"There is a small cubby below the elevator buttons," Mr. Clean continued. "You will find something inside that will provide pure air in any situation. It will protect you from the chalk cloud."

Spencer's eyes darted to the spot that Mr. Clean had mentioned. Sure enough, there was a small slide-away door just below the buttons. He wondered why no one was moving to open it. His dad and Walter shared a glance full of distrust at Mr. Clean's suggestion. Spencer saw the stubbornness in his dad's eyes, and he knew that Alan would rather fall paralyzed than play into Mr. Clean's game.

It was Walter who caved, after seeing Daisy gasp and

choke. The old warlock reached out and slid the small door away. Through the haziness of the elevator, Spencer saw Walter retrieve a construction worker's dust mask. It was of simple design, made to cover the nose and mouth with a single elastic to hold it on behind the head. But there was a major problem.

"Oh," Mr. Clean said. "Something I failed to mention . . . there is only *one* dust mask."

Walter held it out, his face reddening from anger and lack of pure air. He ran his other hand through the cubby, but this time, Mr. Clean had not lied.

"Who's it going to be?" asked the BEM warlock.

Walter held it out, too noble to take it for himself. "One of the kids," he gasped.

Spencer, Daisy, and Dez looked at each other.

"I'm taking it!" Dez said. He lunged for the mask that dangled from Walter's hand.

"I don't think so!" Spencer said, reaching into his janitorial belt. If one of them was walking out of this, it wasn't going to be Dez. Spencer tossed a Funnel Throw of vacuum dust, catching Dez in the small of the back and suctioning him to the floor.

Spencer crawled over to Walter and pulled the mask from his hand. But he didn't put it on. If one of them deserved to escape, it should be Daisy. She was here because of him, and Spencer wasn't going to let her suffer for it.

"Here," he managed, holding the mask out to Daisy. She was curled on the floor and didn't look up. White chalk dust had gathered on her head, and, for the moment, her thick hair was as white as Spencer's.

"Take it, Daisy!" He nudged her, but she still didn't stir. He felt the panic begin inside him. He was too late. Daisy had already faded.

He sat beside her, his back pressed to the cold metal wall of the elevator. There was nothing he could do about it. Hating himself for being the one, Spencer lifted the mask until it covered his nose and mouth. He pulled the elastic band around the back of his head and took deep breaths of pure, refreshing air.

Spencer's eyes welled as his friends collapsed around him. They drifted off, one by one, growing helpless and paralyzed, until only he remained.

CHAPTER 24

"WHAT DO YOU WANT FROM ME?"

The elevator lurched. The number above the door changed to six, and a chime announced his destination. The door slid open.

"Spencer," said Mr. Clean, his voice cutting through the thick fog of the elevator. "I knew they'd pick you." Spencer was angry about the statement. It was supposed to be Daisy!

"Now," instructed Clean, "take off your janitorial belt and step outside."

Spencer rose slowly to his feet. His fingers felt numb as he unbuckled the belt and dropped it heavily to the floor. Obeying Mr. Clean seemed like the worst idea, but he didn't know what else to do.

He checked the pockets of his coveralls, but he didn't have even a single pinch of vac dust hidden. Haltingly, like a sailor walking a plank, Spencer shuffled out of the elevator. The door closed behind him, trapping most of the chalk cloud so that only a ghostly wisp filtered out into the hallway.

Two Filth Sweepers were waiting for him, standing side by side and blocking any chance Spencer might have had to run. One held a Glopified mop; the other clutched a garden rake in his clawed hands.

"Go ahead," rasped the Sweeper with the rake. "Try to run."

Spencer took a step back, bumping into the closed elevator doors. He eyed the new tool, wondering what a Glopified rake would be capable of. Spencer tried to keep his face steady and brave. There was obviously no point in running.

"Aww," moaned the Sweeper, disappointed by Spencer's submission. "It's more fun when they try to run."

"Hurry up and cage him," the Sweeper with the mop said to his companion. "The boss is not a patient man."

Before Spencer could react, the Filth man swung the rake around like a fighting staff and slammed the handle against the floor at Spencer's feet. In the blink of an eye, the metal tines at the top of the rake flowered outward with a whir. The Sweeper stepped back, withdrawing his hand just in time as dozens of metal prongs closed around Spencer.

The rake didn't hold him tight, like the strings of a Glopified mop would have. When the effect was finished, Spencer found himself perfectly enclosed in a cage. At the center of the cage, the rake's handle stood upright beside him. From the top, the metal tines curved downward above his head, like a domed birdcage. In the speed of the magic, Spencer barely noticed that the rake's prongs had also slid beneath his feet, securing into the base of the wooden handle and closing him completely inside.

Wordlessly, the two Filth Sweepers grabbed opposite sides of the cage and hoisted Spencer into the air. They lumbered down the hallway, leaving Spencer to cling to the center handle as his rake cage rocked back and forth with the gait of their spiky bodies.

They'd carried him several yards before Spencer realized that their breath wasn't affecting him. He'd been so worried about the new Glopified rake that he hadn't thought twice about the nature of his enemies. Two Filth Sweepers at close range should have had him fast asleep, but the dust mask he was wearing seemed to be blocking their exhalations.

They moved swiftly along. There were many Sweepers on this level, and they all broke from their various tasks to stare at the Rebel boy with the white hair, borne helplessly along in a giant cage. Then they arrived, the Filth Sweepers setting Spencer down as they came to a halt before a set of double black doors.

One of the Filth Sweepers stepped forward and knocked on the door. Mr. Clean's deep voice resounded from within. "Bring in the boy!"

The Sweepers flung open the doors and hoisted Spencer's cage once more. When they set him down again, Spencer was clinging to the metal tines of the rake cage, taunted by the fact that he could reach through the bars

but wouldn't be able to squeeze out. With a nod, the two Sweepers that had carried Spencer moved back to secure the doors.

The office was plain. There were no paintings or fixtures of any kind, just a lamp in each corner that cast the room in long shadows. At the center of the room was a desk, adorned only with the simple intercom system that Mr. Clean had been using.

The Sweeper warlock sat reclined in an office chair. His sticky, Grime fingers were steepled below his chin, and his serpentine tongue kept flicking out to taste the air. Behind Mr. Clean's head was a large, circular window. Spencer couldn't imagine how thick the glass must have been to hold against the pressure of the water. An exterior light illuminated the deep sea around the window, and Spencer thought that Mr. Clean must have the world's largest fish tank in his office.

But it wasn't the round sea window that caught Spencer's attention. It was the glittering bronze nailhead sticking out of the wall above it. Spencer took a deep breath. It was all within reach—Belzora tucked into Mr. Clean's lab coat, and the nail just above his head. If only Spencer weren't caged . . .

Spencer decided to begin the conversation, not wanting to leave that advantage to Mr. Clean. "How did you beat us down here?" he asked, his voice muffled through the dust mask he still wore.

"Oh, the simplicity of youth," said Mr. Clean. "Do you really think the Port-a-Potty is the only entrance to this facility? Ever since your warlock created a Glop formula for the squeegee, coming and going has been quite simple. As you should know."

"You stole the squeegee formula?" Spencer asked. He hated the thought of Mr. Clean being able to step out of any glass surface.

"What I stole, and what I didn't, is no concern of yours," said Mr. Clean. "Let us begin by talking about what *you* stole." He leaned forward. "Where is the *Manualis Custodem?*" Mr. Clean asked.

The question took Spencer by surprise. How did the BEM know about the original *Janitor Handbook*? He let go of the cage bars and found himself leaning against the rake's handle. "I don't know what you're talking about."

Mr. Clean chuckled softly. "Don't lie to me, boy. I saw you with your father and Walter Jamison, retrieving the translation from that old man."

Spencer remembered the horror of seeing Mr. Clean swallow Professor DeFleur in one single gulp. He thought of the old, leather-bound book. The *Manualis Custodem* was lying vulnerable in Walter's desk drawer in the janitor's closet of Welcher Elementary. He had to keep it a secret.

"Walter wouldn't tell me where he hid the book," Spencer said. "And he destroyed the translation when he thought we were trapped at New Forest Academy."

Spencer was pleased by the way his lie came out. In truth, the translated binder was also at Welcher. But Walter had duct-taped it down, so only the old warlock's fingerprints could remove it.

Mr. Clean made a soft gurgling sound deep in the back of his throat. "I will find the book."

"Even if you do," Spencer said, "you won't like what it says." The *Manualis Custodem* was the key to bringing back the three Founding Witches. Only they would be powerful enough to set the BEM back on its proper course in fighting Toxites.

"I do not like to leave a task unfinished," said Mr. Clean. "My search for the Auran landfill began years ago. You have swiped the prize, but I shall reclaim it."

"If you'd done half as much work as my dad, then maybe you'd have found it," Spencer said. He was feeling defiant. If Mr. Clean had planned to hurt him, he reasoned, the warlock would have done it already.

"Yes," Mr. Clean said. "Your father did much of the work in solving the clues to find the Auran landfill. And alongside him was that unfortunate Rod Grush. Did you ever meet him?"

Spencer shook his head. His mom didn't like Rod and wouldn't permit him at the house. She said he was a man obsessed by his work, a phrase she later used to describe her own husband after his disappearance.

"Rod was a thinker," Mr. Clean said. "But he was flawed. Your father grew to know him well as they worked through the clues. But they were both blind followers. They trusted the Bureau and never even thought to ask where the first clue came from."

Mr. Clean reached under the desk and picked something up with one hand. It was an old wooden box. It would ordinarily have been too big for a single hand to hold, but Mr. Clean's Grime fingers gripped it well, and he dropped it on the desk.

"This is the Warlocks Box," said Mr. Clean. "The Witches made it, hundreds of years ago, and knowledge of the Box has been passed down from warlock to warlock."

Spencer stared at it curiously. Walter had never mentioned anything about a Warlocks Box.

"The Founding Witches prophesied of a Hopeless Day," Mr. Clean continued. "They said that a day would come when there would be no good left in the world—only corruption and sin. In that day, the three active warlocks were to use their hammers and nails to open the Box."

Mr. Clean tipped open the lid and angled it so Spencer could see that there was nothing inside.

"The Box is empty now. The prophesied day is upon us."

"You opened the Warlocks Box?" Spencer said.

"A little more than two years ago." Mr. Clean nodded his slimy head. "The world is full of wickedness, Spencer. It rages around us like wildfire. That which was good has been forced into darkness. That which was joyous has been dimmed."

Spencer shook his head. He was thinking of his family and friends. There was plenty of good left in the world! This couldn't be the prophesied Hopeless Day. Mr. Clean had opened the Warlocks Box too soon!

"Carlos Garcia believed as I did," said Mr. Clean. "And the third warlock, who wielded Ninfa, was a man named

Gerald Hunter. We were united in our view of the world. This was the only way to open the Box."

"What was inside?" Spencer had to know.

"The first clue," answered Mr. Clean. "The first clue in a series of thirteen that would lead us to the hideout of the Auran children. If we could reach them, the Aurans would tell us how to proceed."

Spencer bit his tongue. The Aurans had given him the *Manualis Custodem* and told him that he needed to find the source of all Glop and bring back the Witches.

"We decided to send capable civilians to solve the clues," said Mr. Clean. "We settled on Alan Zumbro and Rod Grush. But they worked too quickly, and we were not ready to meet the Aurans at that time. Unforeseeable setbacks were holding us up. Gerald Hunter was questioning the Hopeless Day, regretting the decision to open the Warlocks Box."

"What happened to him?" Spencer asked. He'd never heard of the man before this conversation.

"Walter Jamison learned his identity and attacked," said Mr. Clean. "Your old Rebel stole Ninfa and made himself a warlock. After that, Gerald Hunter was of no further use to us. I took care of him . . . the Clean Way."

Spencer shuddered at a memory from earlier that night. "Just like you did to Director Garcia?" Spencer said.

Mr. Clean smiled. His hand strayed to his belt, and when he lifted it again, there was a dirty rag dangling from his grasp. He laid it on the table, an unspoken threat hanging in Spencer's mind.

"What do you want from me?" Spencer finally asked, taking hold of the cage bars once more.

Mr. Clean shrugged. "I already asked. Where is the *Manualis Custodem?* We had spies around the old professor," he said. "We know that the Aurans gave it to you."

"I don't know where it is," Spencer lied.

Mr. Clean took a deep breath. "Very well," he said, rising abruptly to his feet. "You are free to go."

Spencer's hands slipped from the bars. "What?"

"You may leave," said Mr. Clean. "If you don't know where the book is, then you are no good to me."

The warlock stepped around his desk and approached Spencer's cage. The boy shrank back as Mr. Clean reached his sticky hand through the bars and took hold of the rake handle at the center of the cage.

"The rake can only be opened by an outside hand," Mr. Clean explained. He twisted the wooden handle, and the metal cage instantly reverted back to an ordinary-looking rake. Spencer stumbled, suddenly free of his imprisonment.

Mr. Clean shoved the rake into Spencer's hands. "Go," he said.

"I'm not leaving without my friends," Spencer said.

"Brave words," said Mr. Clean. "You may take the girl and the Sweeper boy. I assume you had an escape plan? A squeegee, perhaps?"

Spencer swallowed hard. Mr. Clean was going to let him walk out of this? "What's the trick?"

"Trick?" The Sweeper warlock shrugged. "No tricks. Just a promise." Spencer waited for him to explain. "I will keep the other Rebels here for questioning," Mr. Clean said. "If you leave and never come back, they will live on. If you, or any of your friends, attempt a rescue . . ." His lips curled in a sneer. "I will kill them all."

Spencer's heart was racing. This didn't feel right. Mr. Clean didn't leave survivors. Now he was *allowing* Spencer to leave? What was his game?

"I don't trust you," Spencer said.

"I don't care," answered the big Sweeper. "I'm offering you a way out. Don't be a hero. Get your friends and go."

Spencer backed up, hefting the rake in his hands. He wanted to cage Mr. Clean, grab Belzora, and rip out the nail. It was futile, of course. The Sweepers would strike him down before he could take two steps.

The Filth Sweepers opened the door, and Spencer moved back into the hallway, retreating silently back to the elevator. The chalk cloud had settled inside, coating everything in a white sheet.

Spencer felt a knot of emotion in his throat. Bernard, Penny, Walter, his dad. Was there nothing he could do for them? He dropped to one knee at his dad's side.

"I'm sorry, Dad," he whispered. Spencer's hand found the squeegee that Agnes had given Alan. The one that would open the portal back to Earl Dodge.

Spencer strapped on his janitorial belt, snapped the rake into a vacant clip, and drew out his bottle of Windex. In a blue flash, the back wall of the elevator had turned to glass. He brought the squeegee around and dragged it down the transparent surface.

The portal shimmered into view. On the other side, Earl jumped to his feet, cowboy hat tipping back in surprise. Spencer grabbed Daisy's legs and dragged her through.

"Boy, howdy!" Earl cried. "She don't look too good!"

But Spencer barely heard him. He reached through the portal, seized Dez by the ankle, and heaved the big kid through to Earl's side.

He stood there, petrified by the sight of his dad and other friends, paralyzed and probably wondering what was happening. Then Mr. Clean's voice came through the intercom once more.

"Remember our agreement, Spencer."

He thought about jumping through and grabbing his dad. Maybe he could get one of the adults through the portal before . . .

The Filth Sweeper stepped forward, lips peeled back into a hideous snarl. His clawed hand swung and the glass shattered, closing the portal to a place that Spencer could never go again.

CHAPTER 25

"I CAN WORK WITH THAT."

It was dawn by the time Daisy and Dez revived from the paralyzing effects of the chalkboard eraser. Spencer had slept only the littlest bit when Earl was standing guard. Spencer had thought up a dozen rescue plans, but none of them ended well in his mind. He wasn't giving up on the others, but right now, something else was of greater importance.

The *Manualis Custodem* had to be protected. Mr. Clean would send people to look for it. And the first spot they'd check would be . . .

"Daisy and I have to go back to Welcher," Spencer announced when everyone was sitting upright.

Dez sighed heavily. "Fine," he said. "I'll do it."

Spencer looked at him curiously. "Do what?"

"I'll fly you chumps back to Welcher," he said, flexing his muscles.

"Welcher's in Idaho," Daisy said. "We're in Colorado."

"You don't think I can do it?" Dez asked, his pride insulted.

"Do you know how many miles that is?" Spencer asked.

"Does it matter?" Dez said. "I've got these babies." He unfurled his big wings with such force that the rush of air caused Earl's cowboy hat to blow back.

"Now, it's fine and dandy if y'all want to go flying," said Earl. "But driving makes a bit more sense to me." He reached in the pocket of his pajamas and pulled out the key to Bernard's garbage truck. Spencer recognized it by the mess of key chains that the garbologist had collected from his dumpster dives: a lucky rabbit's foot, a couple of smashed tourist pennies, a stress ball, a tiny flip-flop sandal, and something that looked like a turtle shell.

"How did you get that?" Spencer asked. Bernard was very protective of his garbage truck.

"That odd fellow handed me the key just before he stepped through the portal," said Earl. "Told me that if things went south, I should drive the truck down to Texas and leave her abandoned."

Spencer grinned. "We're not taking her down to Texas." He held out his hand, beckoning for the key.

Earl laughed, his handlebar mustache curling up. "I ain't letting you drive, kid," he said. "How old are you, anyway?"

"It doesn't matter," Spencer said. "That's a Glopified garbage truck. It was made to be driven by kids."

Technically, the Aurans who created and drove the garbage trucks weren't kids. They were over three hundred years old. But they looked like kids, and so Spencer assumed there were Glopified safeguards that would allow him to drive the truck without trouble.

Earl just tilted his head, an expression of fatherly worry on his face. "I'll see you back to Welcher myself. Least I can do after what you young'uns have been through."

Spencer shook his head. Earl couldn't go to Welcher. They had worked too hard to keep the *Manualis Custodem* a secret, even from Penny and Bernard. It wouldn't be safe to let Earl find out about it.

"Thanks, but we have to go alone," Spencer said to Earl. "There's something in Welcher that we have to take care of. Daisy and I will send word as soon as we get something figured out. Until then, you and Dez should stay here."

Dez reached out and smacked Spencer on the back of the head. It hurt a bit more than usual because of his hardened fingers. "You're not leaving me behind, Doofus. You need me."

"I'm sorry," Spencer said. "There's something in Welcher you shouldn't know about. Something that could put you in a lot of danger."

"I don't care," said Dez. "I don't know why you're being all secretive. But if you leave me behind, I'll go straight to the BEM!"

Why did he always do that? Spencer gritted his teeth in utter frustration. The worst part was that he totally believed

Dez's threat. Spencer's anger built until he couldn't control it anymore.

"Fine, Dez!" he yelled. "Have it your way. But it's not my fault if you end the world!"

Earl was still standing there, the key to Big Bertha dangling in his hand. Spencer took a deep, calming breath, ran a hand through his white hair, and turned to the janitor cowboy.

"You really shouldn't come," Spencer said. "You've probably got a wife and kids, and they need you to come home." He was thinking of his own dad's mysterious two-year disappearance. He wouldn't bring that on another family.

"Actually," Earl said, "I'm single." He tipped his hat to no one in particular.

"Don't you have a dog?" Daisy asked.

"Nope."

"What kind of cowboy doesn't have a dog?" Spencer asked.

"What about a cat?" Daisy asked.

"Nope," Earl said again. "Just a goldfish."

"Okay. I can work with that," Spencer muttered. "Think of your goldfish, Earl. Who's going to give her little flakes of food if you die?"

"Actually," said Earl, "I've been trying to get her to go belly-up for about a month now. Them little flakes are getting expensive."

Spencer was getting frustrated. "I'm not letting you

come with us!" he insisted. There was too much at stake with the *Manualis Custodem*.

"Then I guess you'll have to lock me up," Earl said with a big grin.

Spencer shrugged. "You asked for it." His hand flashed to his janitorial belt, drawing the Glopified rake that had held him prisoner only hours ago. Mimicking the Sweeper's actions, Spencer thrust the rake, handle first, right at Earl's feet.

The swift bars closed around him, causing Earl to jolt in surprise. The key to Big Bertha flung from his grasp, landing with a clink just out of reach.

"Whoa!" Dez said, clapping his hands in approval. "Where'd you get that?"

"Picked it up in the BEM lab," Spencer said as he retrieved Big Bertha's key chain from the floor.

"Hey, partner!" Earl said, a hint of nervousness in his voice. He grabbed the bars and shook them, rattling his cage hopelessly. "Y'all come and let me out, now."

Daisy stepped forward to help him, but Spencer grabbed her elbow. "Come on, Daisy," he said, drawing her toward the door of the janitorial closet. "We've got to get on the road."

"Hey!" Earl shouted. Now there was panic in his voice. "What about me? This is treason!"

"It's for the best," Spencer said, pausing at the doorway. "School will start in a few hours. Somebody will find you. All they have to do is reach through the bars and twist the rake handle."

"I can't let them find me like this!" Earl said. "I'm in my pajamas!"

Spencer nodded. "You look fine."

Then the three kids were moving down the hallway of Viewmont Elementary School. The dawn light hadn't spread enough to illuminate the building, but Spencer could see a glow to the east.

"Why are we going back to Welcher?" Daisy finally asked.

Spencer glanced at Dez. He didn't want to say it, but the Sweeper kid was bound to find out eventually. "Mr. Clean is looking for the *Manualis Custodem*. We've got to protect it."

"You talked to Mr. Clean?" Daisy asked. "How'd you get away?"

Spencer felt uncomfortable talking about it. "He let me go."

"I knew you couldn't fight your way out of there," Dez said.

"He told me that I was free to take you guys with me," Spencer explained. "As long as we don't try to rescue the others, he won't hurt them."

"So what are we going to do?" Daisy asked.

"Rescue the others," answered Spencer. "After we get back to Welcher and hide the *Manualis*."

"You keep saying that fancy word," Dez grumbled. "Are you trying to sound smart? 'Cause you just sound like a nerd."

"The *Manualis Custodem* is a really important book,"

Daisy said. "And it sounds like Mr. Clean will do anything to get it."

"Like letting Spencer go?" Dez said.

Spencer stopped in the middle of the hallway. His heart was pounding, and he knew that Dez could be right for once.

"That's what I would do," Dez went on. "Capture you, tell you what I want, and then let you go. You'll run straight to it."

Spencer pressed his hands to his face, angry and embarrassed that he'd missed the obvious. And worse, that Dez had pointed it out.

"This doesn't change anything," Spencer said. "The *Manualis Custodem* is sitting out in the open. We'll just have to make sure that nobody follows us."

"That might be kind of tricky," Daisy said. She pointed out the window to the parking lot.

Big Bertha, the garbage truck, was parked exactly where Bernard had left it. But surrounding the big vehicle were half a dozen Pluggers.

CHAPTER 26

"PIECE OF CAKE."

There were two of each breed of Extension Toxite, with riders kicked back in the saddles, as though they'd been waiting for quite some time.

"They must have come down from New Forest Academy," Spencer said.

"We really could have used Earl's help about now," Daisy pointed out. "Three of us and six of them?"

"I think I count for at least two people," Dez said. "I'll swoop in there, plunge the truck, fly it back over here, you guys jump in, and I'll drive us out of here."

"You are *not* driving Big Bertha!" Spencer said. To emphasize his point, he jingled the key chain.

"Why do you always get to do the cool stuff?" Dez complained.

"Because," Spencer said, "I'm responsible and you're not."

"And Spencer has white hair," Daisy said.

The boys looked at her. "What does that have to do with anything?" Spencer asked.

Daisy shrugged. "I don't know. I just thought we were talking about your qualities."

Spencer turned back to Dez. "Do you really think you can plunge Big Bertha without getting caught?"

"Piece of cake." Dez reached over and took a plunger from Spencer's belt. Then he sprinted down the hallway.

"How can Dez think about cake at a time like this?" Daisy asked.

She and Spencer moved to the nearest doors and waited for whatever trick Dez might have up his sleeve. It occurred to Spencer that the bully might take off and leave them behind. It was an uncomfortable thought, especially now that Dez knew about the *Manualis Custodem*.

But the next moment proved Spencer wrong. Dez came soaring off the roof of Viewmont Elementary School, a streak of black in the faint dawn light. There was a huge Extension Grime sitting on top of Big Bertha. Dez was upon the rider before he could sit up in the saddle.

The BEM Plugger screamed as Dez jerked him from the slimy monster. The extension cord at his waist went taut and then snapped in a burst of sparks. The Extension Grime perked its head up, pale eyes wide. Severed from the rider, it no longer received the calming flow of electricity. It saw the school, with residual student brainwaves lingering there, and became instantly possessed with the wild drive to get inside.

The huge Toxite leapt from the garbage truck and skittered forward, shaking out of its armor like a snake shedding skin. Spencer and Daisy backed up frantically as the monster compressed its body, squeezing bonelessly through the minuscule gap under the door.

The Toxite breath hit Daisy in a wave of distraction. "Hey, Spencer!" she called. "Which do you like better: hopscotch or jump rope?"

It took Spencer a moment to realize that the huge Grime wasn't attacking. It was happy to be in the school and scuttled off down the hallway. Earl would have his work cut out for him when he got out of his cage.

Daisy's wits returned to her, and she suddenly looked confused. "Did I just say something about hopscotch?" she asked.

There wasn't time to answer. Dez had dropped the Plugger and was winging around. The Rubbish riders took flight. Although Spencer would never admit it aloud, Dez was clearly the superior flier. The Pluggers were riding Rubbishes, but Dez *was* one.

He weaved between the two Pluggers, slammed the plunger against the top of Big Bertha, and flapped his way back toward the school.

Dez was anything but graceful, as evidenced by the way he set the garbage truck down. He swung Big Bertha around, sending the front bumper through the nearest school window and causing Spencer and Daisy to hit the floor as glass showered around them.

Dez twisted the plunger handle, detaching the vehicle with so much momentum that Big Bertha skidded backward and crushed the school doors, blocking the planned exit for Spencer and Daisy.

The Pluggers were swarming on Dez, but he took to the sky like a rocket. Spencer unclipped a broom and drifted through the shattered window. Daisy was right behind him as they landed just beside Big Bertha's door.

Spencer fumbled with the key and shoved it into the little lock, muttering under his breath. "This garbage truck can drive on walls, but it doesn't even have one of those remote unlock buttons?"

A Filth Plugger appeared around the cab of the truck. The beast roared, and Daisy flicked a mop in its direction. The strings tangled around the creature's face, but she didn't wait to see how the rider reacted. Spencer had the cab door open, and Daisy dropped the mop handle to follow him inside.

Spencer and Daisy were both wedged into the driver's seat as she pulled the door shut.

"Okay," Spencer muttered. It took a second to locate the ignition. He thrust in the key and turned it. The engine cranked over and over, but Big Bertha didn't want to start. The Plugger had guided his Extension Filth to the truck door. The huge creature was slobbering on the driver's side window, its heavy claws raking against the glass.

Spencer slapped the steering wheel in frustration and tried turning the key again. "Come on!" he yelled.

"Give it a little gas," said Daisy.

Spencer looked down at the pedals beneath his feet. He felt a trickle of sweat on his forehead. "The gas is the one on the right, isn't it?"

"Haven't you ever driven a car before?" Daisy asked.

Spencer stared at her. "I'm twelve," he pointed out. "Have you?"

Daisy nudged Spencer into the middle seat. She dropped her right foot down, pumping the gas pedal while she cranked the key in the ignition. Big Bertha responded perfectly, the Glopified engine coming to life with a diesel purr. Daisy grabbed a lever and put the truck into gear. Spinning the wheel, she guided the garbage truck across the school parking lot.

Spencer's eyes were huge, his mouth dangling half open. "Since when do you know how to drive?" he finally managed.

Daisy shrugged. "My dad's a car mechanic and I grew up in Idaho." She swallowed hard. "But I'm not very good. And my dad said I should never drive unless he's in the car with me."

"Just pretend I'm your dad," Spencer said.

Daisy shook her head. "No. That's just weird."

Dez was suddenly flapping alongside the garbage truck. "Roll down the window!" he yelled. "Let me in!"

"Keep driving!" Spencer said to Daisy. "We've got to find the freeway and get back to Welcher." He slid across the cab and rolled down the side window. Dez reached out and pulled himself in. He didn't look comfortable, bent in half, with his wings flapping behind him like flags in the wind.

Once Dez was inside the truck, Spencer shoved him into the middle seat and rolled up the window just as a wet Grime tongue splatted against the glass.

"Hey," Dez commented, "I didn't know Daisy was driving! From the outside you look like an old man."

"Don't bother her, Dez," Spencer defended. "She's trying to concentrate."

"I was being serious," answered the bully. "There's something different about the glass. It makes the driver look like an old dude. Must be an octopus illusion."

"*Optical* illusion," Spencer corrected.

Dez shot him a glare. "That's what I said."

"At least I won't get arrested," Daisy said. "No wonder the Aurans never get caught. They've been driving these trucks for decades, and everyone thinks it's an old man behind the wheel."

Daisy blew past a stop sign without even yielding. "Did we lose the Pluggers?" Spencer asked.

"I took out a Grime and a Rubbish," Dez bragged. "The others are probably too scared to come after us."

Just then a Plugger on Filthback pounced into the road. A dustpan shield was in his hand, and a pushbroom was leveled to launch the garbage truck into the air.

CHAPTER 27

"WE'RE DOOMED."

Daisy screamed and threw her hands up. Dez reached over and jerked on the wheel. Big Bertha missed the Plugger by mere inches, hopping over a curb and smashing a fire hydrant. A geyser of water erupted, dousing the windshield and causing the Filth to rear back.

Daisy was back in control, with both hands white-knuckled on the steering wheel. "I can't see a thing!" she screamed. Water was streaming down the flat windshield, making everything look distorted as they barreled blindly down the street.

"Use the wipers!" Spencer said.

Daisy flicked a little stick beside the wheel, but instead of the windshield wipers, she activated the right-turn signal.

"That's not it," Dez said. He leaned across her and

twisted something. The headlights turned off, leaving them driving with what little light the dawn was providing.

"Just stop for a second!" Spencer shouted. Daisy slammed on the brakes. The Pluggers would surely catch up, but it was better than driving blind.

Spencer yanked open the glove compartment and drew back in disgust. Besides the gag-worthy smell, there were several fuzzy lumps that appeared to have once been muffins. Spencer didn't know if Bernard had forgotten about them, or if the garbologist was performing some weird experiment.

In addition to the moldy muffins and a crinkly road map, Spencer saw Holga and the bronze nail they had stolen from Garcia. But what he was looking for was buried under some tissues in the very back of the glove compartment. It was an operator's manual.

Spencer gathered his courage, held his breath in case of deadly spores, and reached into the glove compartment. He pulled the operator's manual free and slammed the compartment door, shutting away the nasty muffins.

"We're doomed," Daisy muttered. "We'll never make it back to Welcher. We can't even figure out how to use the windshield wipers!"

Spencer found what they needed in the index. He flipped to the page, looked at the diagram, and then leaned across the cab and turned on the windshield wipers.

Spencer held up the operator's manual in victory. There was a thump on top of the cab that caused all three kids to look up instinctively. In the next second, the huge face of an Extension Grime was creeping down Daisy's side window, tongue probing for a way in.

Daisy stepped on the gas pedal, and the truck lurched forward. But the Grime's sticky hands held tight.

They made their way out of the neighborhood and onto a larger street. Spencer saw the Grime's throat begin to pulse outside Daisy's window. He saw the skin stretch like a bullfrog as the mouth began to fill with acidic slime.

"Faster, Daisy!" Spencer yelled. "You've got to throw this guy!"

"I'm just following the speed limit," she said. "The sign said 25 mph! I don't want to get a ticket!"

"And I don't want to get dead!" shouted Dez. He leaned over and pushed on Daisy's leg, causing her foot to bear down on the gas pedal.

The Grime spewed its venomous load onto Daisy's window. Spencer smelled the burning acid as the slime oozed down the glass. Then the Grime's tongue was back at it, working to find a way into the cab.

Daisy suddenly giggled. "Sometimes," she said, "if the mood is just right, I think those red lights look like eyeballs."

Spencer didn't know what red lights she was talking about until he looked out the windshield again. Just yards ahead, a stoplight had turned red. Cross traffic was moving through the intersection, cars full of tired people with early-morning jobs.

"Let go of her leg, Dez," Spencer said. "We have to stop."

"I'm not pushing her anymore," Dez answered. He held up his hands to prove his innocence.

Daisy seemed deep in thought. "Why are street signs always so negative? I mean, that one says, 'no right turn.' It would be a lot nicer if it said, 'you may go straight or turn left.'"

"It's the Grime breath," Spencer realized. The venom must have weakened the glass enough for a brainwave-numbing draft to get through. "She's a distracted driver!"

He clipped out his vanilla air freshener and released a long spray in Daisy's direction. She blinked hard, and then Spencer saw the danger register on her face.

"RED LIGHT!" she screamed, and she slammed hard on the brake.

Big Bertha skidded to a halt, the nose of the garbage truck jutting into the intersection, barely missing the cross traffic. There was a chorus of honking, and the Extension Grime flew off the roof. The Plugger hit the stoplight and launched from the saddle. His extension cord became entangled on the overhead traffic light, and he dangled there, unconscious. The impact unplugged the Grime, and it moved fluidly through the intersection and out of sight.

Spencer glanced in his side mirror. "Two Pluggers on Filths closing fast."

"There's still one Rubbish out there too," Dez added. Spencer didn't question him. It took one to know one.

The traffic light turned green and Daisy drove through, leaving the intersection in a chaotic mess of fender benders, with a random guy dangling by an extension cord from the traffic light.

"Phew," Daisy said. "That was a close one."

The sound of a police siren wailed out from behind the garbage truck. Spencer checked his mirror again, noticing a patrol car pulling up tight to Big Bertha's rear bumper.

"I hate it when this happens," Dez muttered. Spencer didn't want to know what previous experiences Dez had had with the police. Daisy had tears in her eyes as she began to slow down.

"What are you doing?" Spencer asked her. They couldn't stop now, no matter who was trying to pull them over.

Daisy glanced at Spencer. "Will you visit me in jail?" she asked.

"You're not going to jail," Spencer said. "The Aurans must have had a way of dealing with this."

He turned back to the operator's manual, thumbing through pages until he found a section titled, "Frequently Asked Questions." He had to find an answer before Daisy's resolve wore out and she surrendered.

"Here!" he said, his finger tracing a line in the manual. He read aloud. "What do I do if the police try to pull me over?" He cleared his throat and read the answer. "The Glopified Garbage Truck 2.0 has a special feature that should prevent anyone from following you unwanted. Simply tap the brake three times quickly. The truck's Glopified brake lights will confuse the driver of the vehicle behind you, making them unable to remember why they were following you in the first place. The pursuer should depart quickly."

Spencer looked up from the operator's manual. "Tap the brakes!" he said.

"Already did," answered Daisy. Behind them, the police car turned off its siren and lights and veered away onto a side street.

"I got to get me one of these," Dez said, patting the dashboard.

"Too bad it won't shake the Pluggers," Spencer said. "They're gaining on us."

"Hey," Dez said, "that's the freeway! Take a right." Dez pulled on the steering wheel again. They squealed around a corner going way too fast. Narrowly missing a guardrail, they merged onto a northbound freeway.

"Faster, Daisy!" Dez demanded. "Let's see if those Pluggers can keep up with us now!"

But even at 65 miles per hour, the Pluggers were catching up. Spencer watched the creatures come, leaping and bounding past slower cars on the freeway, beast and rider invisible to everyone but the kids in the garbage truck.

"I should just fly out there and take them down," Dez said.

"We're going too fast," Spencer said. "If you jump out of this truck, it'll probably rip your wings off."

"You got a better idea?" Dez said. One of the Extension Filths had caught up to them. The Plugger on its back urged the beast forward, and the kids heard the quills scrape into Big Bertha.

"There's got to be something . . ." Spencer muttered as he thumbed through the table of contents. "Chapter 8," he said. "Offensive and Defensive Capabilities of the Glopified Garbage Truck 2.0."

Spencer turned to the page, annoyed that Dez kept coaching him to read faster. Spencer skimmed down the page, mumbling and skipping portions as he looked for something that might help them in their current predicament.

"The Glopified Garbage Truck 2.0 is equipped with various defensive capabilities that should prevent you from crashing. The entire shell of the vehicle is heavily reinforced and armored, with shatterproof glass and punctureproof tires. The front and rear bumpers are Glopified to minimize damage. In the unlikely event that the truck should become totaled and can no longer function, a self-destruct button is located under the driver's seat. Detonate the truck and leave no evidence behind."

Dez tried to reach under Daisy's seat.

"What are you doing?" she yelled. "Do you know what self-destruct means?"

"Chill," Dez said, withdrawing his hand quickly. "I just wanted to check if it was really there."

"Here we go!" Spencer said, reading again. "The Glopified Garbage Truck 2.0 is equipped with four trashcannons, two on each side of the vehicle."

"Whoa!" Dez said. "Trashcannons?"

Spencer read quickly. "To arm the trashcannons, the rear of the truck must be loaded with garbage."

"Got that," Dez said. "I had to ride in it last time."

"Disengage the safety by flipping a small switch below the steering console."

Dez shouldered up against Daisy, rummaging around until he found what he was looking for. As soon as he flipped the switch, Spencer heard the trashcannons prepping for action. He glanced in the side mirror. Two ports had opened on the side of the garbage truck. He could see the rims of two metal trash cans resting in the openings like cannons on a pirate ship.

Spencer turned back to the operator's manual. "The trashcannons are now ready to be fired. Simply press the numbered red buttons to release a slug of high-powered garbage."

Spencer hadn't even finished reading when Dez's hooked finger slammed down on the third button. There was a deafening boom, and Big Bertha shuddered. The rear trashcannon on Spencer's side exploded, releasing a missile of compressed trash with unbelievable force.

The Plugger on the Filth didn't stand a chance. His mount was instantly blown to dust, and he was sent skidding and rolling off the side of the freeway.

"Eat trash!" Dez yelled. The second Filth Plugger pulled back, trying to devise a strategy that wouldn't include getting major road rash.

"Slow down," Dez said to Daisy. "Get us in range."

She let off the gas, and Big Bertha quickly slowed. The Filth rider tried to adjust his belt, scrambling with the dial on his battery pack, but the beast was too eager for a fight.

"Almost there," Dez said, watching out the window. "Turn to the left a bit."

Daisy changed lanes rather sharply, and while the truck was angled, Dez fired the front trashcannon on Daisy's side.

It was a distance shot, and Spencer wasn't sure if it would hit. The garbage slug flew at the Filth Plugger, bits of high-powered trash breaking apart like buckshot. The Extension Filth went down under the hailstorm, throwing its rider and severing the cord.

"Haha!" Dez shouted. "Just like a video game!" Spencer thought he was having way too much fun with this.

"One more to go," Spencer said.

"I'm guessing that guy on the Rubbish is somewhere above us," said Dez.

"Out of range."

"Yeah," Dez mused. "We need to draw him down to our level." He shoved past Spencer and rolled down the side window. Spencer squinted his face against the sudden strong wind.

"What are you doing?" Spencer shouted.

"We need bait!" Dez reached out and grabbed Spencer by the shoulder, his talon fingers digging painfully. With one swift motion, he hefted Spencer up and shoved him out the window.

Spencer thought he was dead. He waited to hit the road and tumble to a painful end. But instead, he dangled there beside the window, Dez holding him easily at arm's length.

"Are you out of your mind!" Spencer yelled. He couldn't look down; the road rushing past below him made him feel sick. Daisy screamed and let off the gas when she realized what Dez was doing.

The Sweeper kid turned back to her. "Keep driving, Gullible Gates!" he threatened. "Hit the gas, or I drop him."

Big Bertha lurched forward again as Daisy began to accelerate. Dez shouted out to Spencer, "You should probably kick and squirm a little more. You're the bait! You have to look alive!"

Spencer had been trying desperately not to squirm, since wriggling out of Dez's grip would likely cost him his life. "Pull me in, Dez! This is crazy! Pull me in right now!"

"Take it easy," Dez said. He turned his beaky nose to the air and drew in a long sniff. "That Rubbish is close; I can smell it."

"He's close, all right," Spencer said. He could see the Rubbish directly overhead, keeping pace with the garbage truck. "But he's not going to take the bait. That Plugger just saw two of his friends get blasted. He's not coming down."

Dez grunted and pulled Spencer back into the cab. "Well," he said, "it was worth a try."

"Are you out of your mind?" Spencer said, strapping on his seat belt. He sucked in deep breaths of air to steady himself. "It was *not* worth it! You just dangled me out the window like—"

"Hang on!" Daisy yelled. "I've got an idea."

All of a sudden, they were four-wheeling off the edge of the freeway and up a steep embankment with a high retaining wall. Big Bertha chugged and jolted. Then Daisy turned the wheel so sharply that two tires came off the ground.

Spencer thought for sure they would roll down the embankment and land upside down on the freeway. But then, just as they'd done on the wall of New Forest Academy, Big Bertha's tires adhered to the concrete retaining wall. They were driving sideways, with the two trashcannons on Spencer's side pointed straight into the air.

Dez brought his fists down on both buttons at the same time, rocking Big Bertha with a tremendous *boom!* The garbage projectiles shot straight into the air, taking the overhead Rubbish and its Plugger by complete surprise.

The big bird was coming down, its wings shot to tatters. Just before the creature dissolved, the Plugger leapt from the saddle, tapping a broom and soaring out of sight.

Big Bertha came off the retaining wall, its tires finding new purchase where the steep embankment rose. The truck bumped back to the freeway and merged alongside a few stunned drivers.

Daisy flipped the safety switch under the steering console, and the trashcannons powered down, folding out of sight. The ports closed, and Big Bertha returned to looking as normal as she could.

They drove in silence for a moment before Daisy finally said what all of them were thinking. "Does anybody know how to get back to Welcher?"

CHAPTER 28

"GOOD TIMES, GOOD TIMES."

Spencer woke up in the parking lot of Welcher Elementary School, appalled to find Dez Rylie behind the steering wheel and Daisy asleep in the seat beside him.

"What happened?" Spencer said, his voice accusatory as he sat up straight. "Did you green-spray Daisy so you could drive?"

"Relax," Dez said. "She was getting drowsy behind the wheel, so she let me take over."

"How long was I asleep?" Spencer didn't like the fact that he couldn't remember drifting off.

Dez shrugged. "Maybe five or six hours." He pointed his hooked fingers out the window. "We're home now."

Five or six hours? "Why didn't *you* get tired?" Spencer asked.

"It must be my Rubbish half," Dez said. "I've been awake for a whole night, and I'm not even feeling it."

Dez's superpowers were really getting on Spencer's nerves. Now he didn't even need to sleep?

The map that they'd found in the glove compartment lay open on the seat next to Dez. Spencer snatched it and shoved it back into the compartment.

"I'm surprised you got us here," Spencer said.

"I can read a map," Dez said. "I know you think I'm an idiot, but I actually learned lots of stuff at New Forest Academy."

Maybe he was being a bit too hard on Dez, Spencer thought. The bully did seem different after his time at the Academy. He was still incredibly annoying, and Spencer wouldn't trust him with anything. But Dez actually seemed a tiny bit smarter.

Daisy woke up suddenly, sitting at the edge of her seat. "We're home already?"

Spencer checked his watch. It was two o'clock in the afternoon. "What day is it?" he asked. Staying up all night had really thrown him.

"Wednesday," said Daisy.

It was crazy to think of all that had happened overnight. They'd gone to Colorado and infiltrated New Forest Academy. They'd stolen Holga, and Director Garcia had been killed. Then they'd gone to Massachusetts, taken a flying Port-a-Potty into the Atlantic Ocean, and been captured by Mr. Clean. Now they were home in Welcher once more. But so much was different. They were alone.

"Okay," Spencer said. "There's a little more than an hour left in the school day. We've got to get down to the janitor's closet and secure the *Manualis Custodem*."

"And we're going to have to do it without a hall pass," Daisy pointed out.

"I don't need a hall pass," Dez said. "I don't even go to school here anymore." He shut off the garbage truck and tucked the bulky key chain into the back pocket of his jeans.

The three kids moved across the parking lot. Spencer knew that most of the school doors were locked during the day, so they'd have to enter through the front.

As Spencer pulled open the door, Daisy grabbed his arm. "Wait," she said. "We can't go in there with him." She pointed at Dez.

"What's that supposed to mean?" the bully asked, sticking out his chest to look more intimidating.

"Look at him," Daisy said.

Spencer hadn't considered how Dez would appear to people who hadn't used magic soap. Would he look normal to them? Or would his features be distorted and inhuman, as they looked to Spencer and Daisy?

"Listen," Dez said, "if that guy doesn't look weird to Mrs. Hamp, then I'm pretty sure I'm good to go." He pointed into the school, where the secretary was conversing with someone at the front office.

The man was definitely a Sweeper, long slimy Grime tail twitching behind him. Mrs. Hamp looked as bored as ever, clearly oblivious to the fact that the visitor was half monster.

Daisy's eyes went wide and Spencer froze. It was as he had feared. Mr. Clean had already dispatched someone to search the school.

"You two can stand there like lame statues," Dez said, "but I'm going in." He stepped through the front door and sniffed the air. "Never thought I'd say this," he muttered, "but it's good to be back."

Spencer didn't let him reminisce. In a flash, he and Daisy were dragging Dez past the front office, where Mrs. Hamp was handing the Sweeper a visitor pass. "The library is down the hall to the left . . ." she was saying. But Spencer knew the man wasn't going to the library. First, he would surely search Walter's janitorial closet.

The three kids moved fast, heedless of Welcher Elementary's strict no-running-in-the-hallways rule. Spencer was determined to beat the Sweeper to the *Manualis Custodem*.

Dez smiled at a few landmarks along the way. "Remember that time I threw a bowl of melted ice cream in Mrs. Natcher's face?" he said as they passed the cafeteria. "Good times, good times."

Then they were there, Spencer leaping down the steps three at a time. The secret closet in the back of the storage area was open. Spencer's heart pumped an extra beat. He didn't know if they'd left it that way, or if someone had already been here.

His heart didn't slow until he reached Walter's desk and

began ripping open the drawers. There, in the third one down, was the leather-bound *Manualis Custodem*. Spencer scooped it up and quickly checked to make sure the latch was still closed.

"That's it?" Dez said. He swiped the old book from Spencer's hand and held it out for examination. "I can't believe we came back for this. It doesn't even have a picture on the cover."

Spencer grabbed the book back. "Careful," he scolded. "It's old."

"And it holds the secrets to saving education," Daisy added.

"Yeah, yeah," muttered Dez. "So does my armpit."

"We've got to go," Spencer said. "As soon as that Sweeper comes down here, this place is going to get ransacked." He glanced around the room. "We should take whatever supplies we think we'll need. I'm not sure when we'll be coming back."

"I don't need any weapons," Dez boasted. "I've got these." He flashed his talons through the air. Spencer rolled his eyes. If Dez didn't want to take any Glopified gear, Spencer wasn't going to force him.

Daisy and Spencer replenished their vacuum dust and filled their clips with fresh supplies. Glopified weapons could max out and become useless if overused.

"Ready?" Spencer said once their preparations were complete.

"What's in the backpack?" Daisy asked as Spencer

pulled the straps over his shoulder. It was Walter's pack, and Spencer knew exactly what was inside.

"We'll need it for later," he said vaguely. "Right now, we've got to worry about getting the *Manualis* out of here."

The three kids left the janitor's closet, sealing the secret room behind the sliding stack of boxes. They moved quietly up the stairs and into the hallway. They wouldn't have to pass by the front office again, since the school doors weren't locked from the inside. It was a straight shot down the hallway and out to Big Bertha waiting in the parking lot. There was only one risk in this more direct route. They would be passing right by Mrs. Natcher's classroom.

"Keep your head down," Spencer whispered to Daisy. There was a window in Mrs. Natcher's door, and Spencer knew they'd be in trouble if the grumpy old teacher happened to be looking out into the hallway.

"I don't know why you guys are scared of Mrs. N.," Dez said. "All she ever did was send me to detention."

Something wet came out of nowhere. It latched onto the *Manualis Custodem* with a splat and yanked the book from Spencer's hand. As it retracted, Spencer realized what it was.

A Grime tongue. And it had snagged the *Manualis* like a frog catching a fly.

Daisy let out a sharp cry of alarm. She fumbled with the air freshener, giving a spritz before the Toxite breath could affect her.

It was the Sweeper they'd seen at the front office. They hadn't seen him above, clinging to the ceiling. Now the

191

Manualis Custodem was clenched between his teeth as he moved to scuttle away.

Dez took two steps and bounded into flight. His wings popped open and he soared up, catching the Sweeper by the tail and ripping him off the ceiling. Dez spun him through the air and hurtled him down toward Spencer.

"Here comes another!" Daisy cried, drawing a mop from her belt.

Spencer gave the Grime Sweeper a Palm Blast of vac dust, leaving him suctioned to the floor of the hall. The second Sweeper, a woman merged with a Filth, was almost upon them when the door to Mrs. Natcher's classroom opened.

"What on earth . . . ?" the teacher cried.

CHAPTER 29

"YOU GUYS ARE GOING TO GET AN F."

Mrs. Natcher's lips pursed and her hands went straight to her hips. A few of the more eager students were gathered around the teacher in the doorway, trying to contain their giggles at the sight of Spencer and Daisy in full janitorial gear, looming over a man lying on the floor with a book in his mouth.

The Filth Sweeper saw she had an audience and drew up short. She tucked her spiky body around a corner to wait. Spencer was suddenly grateful for his classmates and teacher. Mr. Clean wouldn't want so many witnesses.

"Where have you two been?" Mrs. Natcher asked.

"Sorry," Spencer said. "We're just a little tardy."

Mrs. Natcher pointed to her watch without looking at it. "Tardy?" she exclaimed. "There are only thirty minutes left of the day." Her tight, plucked eyebrows suddenly furrowed. "Why are you holding a mop, Daisy Gates?"

Daisy looked at the Glopified weapon in her hands, like she was surprised to see it there. "It's for our book report?" She didn't sound too convincing.

"Book reports are due tomorrow," said Mrs. Natcher.

Daisy shrugged. "Just wanted to be ready."

"Good heavens!" Mrs. Natcher stepped out into the hallway. "What have you done to this poor man?"

"He was stealing our book," Spencer said. "So we stopped him." Technically, it was true.

Then, to Spencer's horror, Mrs. Natcher bent down and pulled the *Manualis Custodem* from the Sweeper's mouth.

"He might have been trying to *eat* our book," Daisy said. "We weren't sure."

Mrs. Natcher pointed a stiff finger back toward the classroom. "In your seats at once!" she ordered.

"You're not the boss of me," Dez said.

It suddenly seemed to dawn on Mrs. Natcher who the third child in the hallway was. "Dezmond Rylie!" she gasped, and Spencer thought he saw a bit of fear in her cold eyes. After all, Dez *was* a teacher's nightmare.

"What are you doing here?" Mrs. Natcher said, once she regained her composure. "I was told that you left our school to study at some," she turned up her nose, "private academy."

"Yeah, well . . ." Dez shrugged. "Turns out the Academy was run by jerks."

"You're back?" Mrs. Natcher looked horrified. "They

don't pay me enough to teach you." She shook her head. "I need a nap."

Spencer hurriedly stepped into the conversation. They had to get away. The Sweeper on the floor was already recovering from the vac dust. "Dez is just here to help us with the book report," Spencer said.

"That's tomorrow," Mrs. Natcher said again.

Spencer nodded. "Okay. We can bring Dez back tomorrow."

Mrs. Natcher looked wide-eyed at the prospect. "That would be such an inconvenience." She studied the *Manualis Custodem*, running her fingers across the tattered edges of the pages. "Since you seem to be prepared, I'll let you present today." She looked at Dez and swallowed hard. "Let's just get this over with."

Then Mrs. Natcher turned back to the classroom and snapped her fingers. "Everyone! Take a seat in the reading corner!" The teacher tucked the *Manualis Custodem* under her arm and reentered the classroom.

"What are we going to do?" Daisy whispered as they stepped through the doorway.

"We're going to lock the door and give a book report," Spencer answered.

"On the *Manualis Custodem*?" Daisy could barely keep her voice down.

Spencer nodded. "I'm hoping they won't remember it when we're done."

Dez shut the door behind him, and Spencer saw him turn the lock. It was strange to have him appear so blatantly

Sweeper to them when everyone else in the room obviously saw him normally.

Spencer and Daisy stood awkwardly in front of their classmates, wearing navy blue coveralls and janitorial belts. Dez stayed at the door, watching the Sweepers through the hallway window.

Mrs. Natcher herded the students to the reading corner. She seated them on the carpet and pulled up a chair for herself. She balanced the *Manualis Custodem* in her lap and shuffled a few papers, surely preparing to deliver a harsh grade to Spencer and Daisy's book report.

"Before we begin," Spencer said, "I need everybody to scoot in close." The students looked puzzled, and some gave a halfhearted shuffle. "Closer," Spencer insisted. He would have only one chance to make this work. His classmates were right up at his feet now, pressed close together, with Mrs. Natcher seated right behind them.

Spencer stepped over to a shelf near the window where Mrs. Natcher kept the classroom fan. The old fan hadn't been turned on since Dez had flipped a spit wad into it last September. Spencer hoped it still worked.

Angling the fan just right, he turned it on maximum setting, sending a wind over his classmates that ruffled their hair and caused Mrs. Natcher to hold onto her grading papers.

"What are you doing?" Daisy whispered.

Spencer shrugged to play innocent. "It was getting kind of warm in here."

A bit of moving air didn't improve Mrs. Natcher's mood.

She cleared her throat. "We're not getting any younger," she said. Spencer interpreted that to mean, "Hurry up." Mrs. Natcher's patience was as thin as he'd ever seen it.

"Okay," Spencer said, stepping in front of the students again. He swallowed hard, fidgeted a bit, and then began. "We chose to do our book report on the first edition *Janitor Handbook*." Daisy looked at him with surprised eyes.

"Author?" Mrs. Natcher droned without looking up from her papers.

"Ninfa, Holga, and Belzora," he said.

"Something unique about the book?" said the teacher.

"The *Janitor Handbook* holds a secret that will save the world," Spencer said. His classmates chuckled.

"Might want to hurry up!" Dez called from the door-way. "Looks like the Sweepers are thinking about busting in here!"

Mrs. Natcher was examining the *Manualis Custodem* a little too closely now. She turned it over in her wrinkly hands. "Why is there a lock on the book?"

"That's because you're not supposed to know what it says inside," Spencer answered. "Sorry, guys. Sweet dreams."

Spencer pushed Daisy back as he drew a bottle of green solution from his janitorial belt. Holding his breath, he aimed the bottle at the whirling fan and gave half a dozen quick sprays. The classroom fan distributed the green solution much better than the bottle's spray nozzle could have.

His classmates were instantly asleep, with any memory of the book report wiped clean from their memories. Mrs. Natcher barely raised a disapproving finger before she too drifted off, an almost pleasant expression on her face as she finally got the nap she'd said she needed.

"You didn't . . ." Daisy said.

Spencer nodded. "I did." He moved around to switch off the fan. Then, holding his breath against any residual green spray, Spencer stepped past his slumbering classmates and scooped the *Manualis Custodem* out of Mrs. Natcher's lap.

"It's going to be fine," Spencer said, sliding open the window by the teacher's desk. The window had lost its screen a few months ago when Spencer had thrown his lunchbox outside to contain a chalkboard eraser explosion. "Mrs. Natcher won't remember anything about this when she wakes up."

"You're sure?" Daisy asked. "What if she remembers seeing us in the hallway?"

Spencer shrugged. "She'll just think we gave such a boring book report that everyone fell asleep."

Dez laughed as he passed them. "You guys are going to get an F."

The classroom door rattled against the lock. Spencer turned to see the Grime Sweeper compressing himself under the door. Now that the innocent observers were fast asleep, he didn't hesitate to show his powers. The Sweeper's head and shoulders had appeared in the classroom, and the rest of his body was quickly squeezing through.

Spencer cinched the straps on his backpack as Dez grabbed him and Daisy, leaping through the window, his big wings clipping painfully on the edge. Spencer and Daisy touched down running while Dez soared right above them, drawing Big Bertha's key chain from his back pocket.

In a moment, they were in the cab once more, the diesel engine firing up. "Where are we going?" Dez asked, driving the garbage truck across the parking lot.

"My house," Daisy said.

"What about your parents?" Spencer asked. Mr. and Mrs. Gates secretly knew about Toxites and the BEM, but keeping them uninvolved was the only way to ensure their safety.

"It's Wednesday afternoon," Daisy explained. "My mom's at the library, and my dad usually drives to Idaho Falls to get car parts."

"You know your parents' schedule?" Dez said. "That's creepy."

"Don't you know yours?" she asked, like such a thing should be common knowledge.

"Actually, I do," said Dez. "Ten bucks says that my dad is at the apartment right now, drunk as a skunk."

"Do skunks really get drunk?" Daisy asked. "I think you're making that up."

Dez grunted. "It's just an expression."

They arrived at the Gates home without any signs of pursuit. Either the Sweepers had given up, or they hadn't seen the kids climb into the garbage truck. Spencer was guessing the latter. He was also guessing that the Sweepers would pick up their trail soon.

"Okay," Spencer said, holding the *Manualis Custodem* in both hands. They were still sitting in Big Bertha, engine idling, as they stared out the window at the Gates property. "We've got to think of somewhere safe we can keep this. Somewhere far away."

"How about Jamaica?" Daisy suggested.

"Why Jamaica?"

She shrugged. "It's far away."

Spencer looked at the book. "We can't just dump it somewhere and hope that Mr. Clean doesn't find it," he said. "We need to leave it with someone we can trust."

"How about Bookworm?" Daisy said.

"Who the heck is Bookworm?" Dez asked.

"He's my pet Thingamajunk," answered Daisy.

"Oh, that helps." Dez's voice was dripping with sarcasm. "What the heck is a Thingamajunk?"

"But he's sick, remember?" Spencer said, completely ignoring Dez.

"Bernard told me how to make him better," answered Daisy. She seemed to be getting quite excited. "He said Bookworm was starving. Said he needed a massive trashfusion."

"What's a trashfusion?" Dez asked.

"It's like a transfusion, but with trash," Spencer said. "It's what they do to patients in the hospital sometimes. If somebody's lost a lot of blood, they can pump new blood in."

"Stop talking about blood," Daisy said. "I'm getting queasy." She shivered. "But wait a minute. Thingamajunks don't have blood."

"That's right," Spencer said. "They have garbage. Bookworm needs new garbage."

"Great!" Daisy said. "So, where do we get the garbage?"

"Hellooo?" Dez said, knocking his knuckles softly on the side of Daisy's head and making a hollow sound with his mouth. "We're sitting in a garbage truck."

Spencer pushed Dez's hand away from her head. "How do we know there's still a load back there? What if we used it up with the trashcannons?"

"Trust me," Dez said. "There's plenty back there." He rolled down the window. "It's half rotted. Can't you smell the stink?"

"Yeah, I can," said Spencer. "But I thought it was you."

"Ha ha," Dez faked a pity laugh. "You're a real comedian."

Daisy looked at Spencer in surprise. "You are?"

CHAPTER 30

"WHERE'D SHE GET IT?"

The plan to revive Bookworm was under way. Bernard had shown Daisy which controls would dump the garbage load, but first they had to get the big truck into position. Dez began the rather slow process of turning the garbage truck around in the narrow street.

"You'll have to back right up to the shed," Spencer said.

"Maybe I should get out and plunge the truck over the fence," Daisy said.

"No need," muttered Dez. He put Big Bertha in reverse and gassed it up over the curb. The rear bumper smashed through the Gateses' fence, and the heavy tires gouged into the soft grass.

Daisy's black dog ran the length of her chain and drew up, barking savagely as the garbage truck backed across the yard.

"I'm telling my dad it was you," Daisy said. "You'll be spending the whole summer putting up a new fence."

"He won't catch me," Dez said. "I'll just fly away."

Spencer was watching in the side mirror as Big Bertha drew close to the rickety wooden shed. "That'll do it," Spencer said. "Stop." Dez gave it another few inches, until the bumper touched the shed and caused the wood to creak. "I said stop!" shouted Spencer.

Dez chuckled and put Big Bertha into park. Daisy operated the controls that Bernard had shown her. The back hatch raised, and the garbage instantly began spilling through the open door of the shed.

In no time, the deed was done. Big Bertha had emptied her load of smelly trash. It filled the shed and poured out onto the lawn.

Dez rolled the truck forward and left it parked with the front tires on the sidewalk. Daisy scrambled to get out, anxious to see what effect the trash might be having on the sick Thingamajunk.

In a moment, the three kids were standing on the littered grass, staring into the clogged entrance of the shed.

"Do you think it worked?" Daisy finally asked.

"How long does it take for a trashfusion to happen?" said Dez.

There was a slight rustling in the trash pile. Spencer couldn't tell if it came from within or if the wind had disturbed the debris. He was leaning in for a closer look when the mound of garbage exploded.

Spencer was knocked backward onto the grass. Dez let

203

out an embarrassing scream and took to the sky. But Daisy stood firm, a huge smile on her face as strong garbage arms scooped her up.

Bookworm swung her around the yard like an overexuberant dance partner. The moldy covers of his textbook mouth were flapping as he grunted and mumbled in his strange way. His lunchbox head kept nuzzling against Daisy's face in what Spencer was sure was supposed to be an affectionate way, though it actually looked rather painful. Daisy didn't seem to mind a bit. She was laughing and shouting playfully.

Spencer picked himself up and glanced about, grateful that the Gateses' property was large and the neighbors were not close by. If a giant garbage figure leapt around in Spencer's Hillside Estates neighborhood, he could guarantee that it would be the talk of the town. But here, life was rolling along at the Gateses' pace, and the neighbors seemed neither to notice nor to care.

Dez lit on the ground beside Spencer. "What is that thing?"

"That is Daisy's Thingamajunk," Spencer said.

"Where'd she get it?" Dez asked, a hint of reluctance in his voice.

"PetSmart," answered Spencer.

Bookworm suddenly took notice of the Sweeper boy standing beside Spencer. His gangly trash arms rolled Daisy gently onto the grass, and he crossed the yard like a charging gorilla.

When it was clear that the Thingamajunk didn't intend to stop, Dez took flight. But Bookworm leapt a tremendous height, snatching the boy by the ankles and dragging him back to the ground.

Dez shouted for help, thrown to his back and pinned with one heavy refuse hand. Bookworm leaned over him and roared. The textbook opened, revealing nubs of pencil teeth held together with a pink dental retainer.

"Easy, Bookworm!" Daisy shouted. Spencer was a little regretful that Daisy had intervened. He was really curious to see what Bookworm was about to do to the bully.

"Bookworm," Daisy said, "meet Dez. Dez, Bookworm."

"Get him off me!" Dez said as bits of trash sloughed off the Thingamajunk's shoulder and peppered his face.

"Bookworm," Daisy said, "I know it's hard to believe, but Dez is a good guy right now. Please don't hurt him."

Bookworm gave a final snort in Dez's face and then stepped away from the boy. He draped a long arm protectively around Daisy's shoulder and mumbled something unintelligible.

"What did he say?" Dez asked, voice trembling as he dusted himself off.

Daisy shrugged. "I don't speak Thingamajunk."

"I'm guessing he wants to tear your wings off," Spencer said. "Right, Bookworm?"

The Thingamajunk nodded vigorously, to which Dez responded by tucking back his precious wings.

"How about this," Daisy said to her pet. "If Dez ever goes back to helping the BEM, you have my permission to do it."

Bookworm held out a fist, and Daisy bumped hers against it.

"You taught him to fist-bump?" Spencer said.

"No," said Daisy. "He learned that from watching TV in the shed."

"You got him a TV?"

"He was getting bored out there," Daisy said. "I used to read him stories, but that got too expensive."

"What do you mean?" Dez said. "I thought reading was free."

"Reading is," Daisy said. "But the books aren't. Every time I finished reading a story, he would eat the book. I didn't know he was starving at the time."

Spencer crossed over to the tall Thingamajunk. "How are you feeling now, buddy?"

Bookworm responded by giving what could only be interpreted as a thumbs-up. Spencer wondered what his thumb was made of. It sort of resembled a soggy waffle stick.

"I guess we should give him the *Manualis Custodem*," Spencer said.

"I wouldn't trust him with it," Dez cut in. "Didn't you just say that he eats books?"

Spencer hesitated. It wasn't just that Dez had a good point, but giving the *Manualis* to Bookworm only seemed like half of a good plan. He was a Thingamajunk from the landfill. V had described them as dim-witted on the best of days. Did they really want to leave all their hopes in the hands of a walking pile of trash?

Spencer looked at Daisy. "What's Bookworm going to do if we give him the book?"

She shrugged. "Protect it. I once told him to watch my

206

backpack, and he sat on it for three and a half days. By the time I got it back, all my homework was overdue."

"But that's the thing," Spencer said. "We can't just leave Bookworm sitting on the *Manualis Custodem*. It's too important."

"Maybe he could deliver it to somebody we trust," Daisy suggested.

"But who?" Spencer said. "All the best Rebels are trapped in the BEM laboratory."

"What about Meredith?" Daisy said. She was a Rebel lunch lady at Welcher Elementary who had helped them with little tasks in the past.

Spencer shook his head. "I'm sure Meredith would keep it for a while. But that's not good enough. We are going straight back into the heart of the BEM. Straight back to where Mr. Clean said not to go. There's a good chance none of us will be coming out of there again. Whoever takes the *Manualis* has to be someone who will use it to finish what we started."

"No one can use it," Daisy pointed out. "It's locked."

"We have Holga and one of the bronze nails in the truck," Spencer said. "We can open the *Manualis Custodem*."

"But even if we did," said Daisy, "it's written in Gloppish. Nobody knows how to read Gloppish."

"Professor DeFleur managed to translate it," Spencer said. "There's got to be someone we trust out there with enough brains to translate it again."

Spencer's train of thought had led him to answer his own question. He held up the *Manualis Custodem*. "Min!" he said. "Min Lee!"

"Wasn't he that pain-in-the-butt, know-it-all kid from New Forest Academy?" Dez asked.

"I thought that was you," Spencer said. "Min is the smartest person I know. If we can give him the *Manualis*, I'm sure he could translate it. Plus, he's so well connected with the Monitors that he knows where to find Rebel janitors all over the country."

It was the first time in a while that Spencer had felt solid about something. He would feel much more confident heading back to the BEM lab if he knew the *Manualis* was in Min's hands. In the long run, it didn't matter if Spencer and Daisy succeeded in rescuing the Rebels from Mr. Clean. At least Min could find the source of Glop and bring back the Founding Witches.

Dez sighed in annoyance. "Where does this brainiac live?"

"Sacramento," Spencer said.

"As in, California?" Dez asked. "I don't think your garbage pet can make it that far."

"Are you feeling strong enough for a journey?" Daisy asked. Bookworm nodded in excitement. He would clearly do anything for her, no matter how he felt.

"We need you to carry something important to California," Daisy explained. "Do you know where that is?"

In response, Bookworm did something strange. He wriggled his stomach, made a gurgling sound, and then barfed a piece of trash onto the grass. Stranger still, he seemed to be pleased by the fact that he had just regurgitated some of his own trash. Bookworm picked up the piece of garbage and pointed at it.

It was an empty juice pouch with a little yellow straw sticking out the top. The colorful label showed a man surfing on a whitecapped wave. Bookworm pointed to the picture and nodded his head.

"Surfing?" Daisy said.

"Yeah," said Spencer. "There's a lot of surfing in California."

"I told you, he watches a lot of TV," she said.

"Doesn't mean he knows where California is," Dez mumbled.

Bookworm's expression changed. He lowered the pouch and snarled at Dez. Then he flipped the piece of garbage around and gestured to the back. Spencer leaned forward and read.

Made in California.

"So you know how to get there because a little piece of you was made in California?" Daisy asked.

Bookworm nodded in excitement.

"That's pretty cool," Spencer said. "How fast can you get there?"

Bookworm took a deep breath and worked up another scrap of trash. This time, he spat it into his hand and held it out for the kids to see. It was a Kleenex box, or part of one. The scrap he was holding had some writing on it.

20% softer than other brands!

Daisy scratched her head. "You're softer than other Thingamajunks?"

Bookworm made an exasperated face and pointed his waffle-stick thumb at the big number 20.

"Twenty what?" Spencer said. "Twenty days? Twenty hours?"

Bookworm shook his head, chunks of garbage flinging left and right.

"Twenty minutes?" Spencer said.

Bookworm dropped the scrap of box and nodded excitedly, making strained grunting sounds.

"If he thinks he can get there in twenty minutes," Dez said, "then he definitely doesn't know where California is."

Spencer ran to Big Bertha and brought out the crinkly road map they'd used to get home. Bookworm tried to eat it, but Daisy asked him not to. Spencer spread the map on the grass.

"We're here," he said, putting his finger down on Welcher. "Sacramento is here." He touched the map again. "And you think you can get there in twenty minutes?"

Bookworm nodded slowly, as though he were sick of everyone doubting him.

Dez folded his arms. "How?"

In response, Bookworm suddenly disintegrated, his body collapsing into a lifeless heap of garbage on the grass.

CHAPTER 31

"HIS HEAD'S EMPTY."

The kids looked around the yard, but the Thingamajunk was nowhere to be seen. A second later, he burst from the garbage pile in the shed, textbook mouth curved up in a smile as he ran toward them.

Beside the map, the old, lifeless garbage still remained, but Bookworm had constructed a new body for himself. Spencer remembered how the Thingamajunks could travel at the landfill. They seemed to move fluidly through the garbage mounds.

"So," Spencer said, "you can hop from trash pile to trash pile and use the garbage to make a new body?"

Bookworm nodded, seeming grateful that someone was finally understanding him.

"How far can you go?" Spencer asked.

Bookworm thought about it for a second, then belched

out an old, plastic grocery bag. In his new body, his thumb was a glass bottle, which he used to point at a label on the bottom of the bag.

> WARNING: To avoid suffocation, keep bag away
> from babies and children.

"You have children?" Daisy said. "I didn't know you were a dad!"

If Bookworm had had eyes, Spencer thought, he would have rolled them.

"I don't think that's it, Daisy," Spencer said.

Bookworm pointed to the word *suffocation*.

"I get it," said Spencer. "If you go too far between piles of garbage, you'll run out of air. You'll suffocate."

Bookworm clapped his huge hands and nodded.

"Great," Spencer said. "So you can trash-hop over to California in twenty minutes. But if your body has to change every time, how will you carry the book we need you to take?"

Bookworm pointed at his head. Spencer noticed that, despite the body change, it was the same dented lunchbox atop that moldy, pencil-studded textbook.

"Your head always stays the same?" Spencer said.

Bookworm nodded.

"I still don't see how you can carry anything."

Bookworm reached up a hand and grabbed his lunchbox skull. Flipping aside the clasps, he opened the box, showing an open container that smelled faintly of tuna fish.

"I can't look!" Daisy said, shielding her eyes. "He's showing us his brains!"

"It's okay, Daisy," said Spencer. "His head's empty."

"That's not a very nice thing to say," Daisy said.

Spencer leaned over and looked into the open cavity. It would definitely be big enough to hold the *Manualis*. He returned once more to the garbage truck, this time to grab the old book. It would be safer to transport it sealed, but if something bad happened to the Rebels, Min would be stuck with a closed book. They needed to open it for transportation, no matter the risk.

The Dark Aurans had said that any of the bronze nails would work as a key to open the latch around the old book. "Someone else will have to open it," Spencer said. Touching the bronze would send him right into a vision.

Daisy stepped up to the task, digging Holga's nail out of the glove compartment. They knelt on the grass, the *Manualis Custodem* lying before them.

"Are you sure this is a good idea?" Daisy said. "What would Walter want us to do with the *Manualis?*"

"He would want us to keep it safe," Spencer said. "The BEM doesn't know about Min, and if something bad happens to us, he'll be able to translate the *Manualis* and finish the task. It'll be okay. Bookworm's the perfect messenger. He's impossible to track when he hops from trash to trash."

She turned to Bookworm. "Do you feel okay about it?" He gave her a clear thumbs-up and a solid nod. "What are the chances of you getting caught?" she asked.

He stepped over to the scrap of Kleenex box that he'd

used earlier. He ripped off the number 2 and held out the remainder for Daisy to see.

0%

Spencer grinned at the Thingamajunk's confidence. It seemed to settle some of Daisy's fears also. Dez looked on impassively, only aware that the *Manualis Custodem* was important because Spencer had said so.

Daisy pinched the bronze nail between her fingers and lowered it down to the small hole in the latch. "Like this?" she said.

"You're doing great," Spencer encouraged.

Daisy pressed the nail down. There was a soft click, and the latch fell open. Daisy jerked her hand away, as though fearing that something might happen. But the book just rested there in the grass, doing nothing extraordinary at all.

Spencer picked up the *Manualis Custodem*. He couldn't resist opening the leather covers and glancing over a few pages. The Gloppish writing was strange, and Spencer remembered that Professor DeFleur had described it as a combination of Latin and hieroglyphics.

"What's it say?" Dez asked.

Spencer shut the book. He couldn't read the writing. And even if he could have, he certainly wouldn't have told Dez the translation.

Spencer stepped over to Bookworm, who took a knee. Almost ceremoniously, Spencer lowered the unlatched *Manualis Custodem* into Bookworm's lunchbox head.

"One more thing," Spencer said. He reached down to his janitorial belt and unclipped a pair of Glopified walkie-talkie radios that he'd picked up in the Rebel closet. Spencer twisted the knob at the top of the device. "I'm setting these to channel 27," he said to Bookworm. "That should be a secure, private channel. Have Min radio over once you find him."

The Thingamajunk nodded to show his understanding. Spencer dropped one of the walkie-talkies into Bookworm's head and closed the lunchbox.

"California's a big place," Dez said. "How's your trash pet going to find someone he's never met before?"

"Well," Spencer reasoned, "if he can eat trash and know where it came from, then we need something that could lead him to Min."

"I have a letter in the house," Daisy said.

"From Min?" Spencer was surprised she hadn't mentioned it before. "Why did he send you a letter?"

"I don't have email," she said. "He just wanted to give me an update about the Monitors."

"But I always give you updates about the Monitors," Spencer said.

"Oooohhh," Dez butted in. "Someone's getting jealous!"

"I am *not* jealous!" Spencer said. Then he turned to Daisy before anything else could be said. "Go grab the letter."

She darted across the lawn and through the back door of her house, giving her black dog a pat on the head as she passed.

"What?" Spencer said defensively, noticing the lingering smirk on Dez's face. He turned to the Thingamajunk. "Bookworm," Spencer said, "why don't you give Dez a hug while we wait?"

"Huh?" Dez said, the grin melting off his face. "I don't want a hug!"

Bookworm lurched forward, snatched Dez in his thick garbage arms, and squeezed the kid tightly. Dez grunted and wriggled as Bookworm's hug appeared to be more of a headlock and less of a sign of affection. Now it was Spencer's turn to smirk.

When Daisy returned, both hands were occupied as she worked to clasp a piece of cheap jewelry around her neck. A white envelope was clamped tightly between her lips. She secured her necklace just as she reached Spencer and Dez.

"This is from Min," Daisy said once she'd removed the envelope from between her lips. When Bookworm heard her voice, he smiled and dropped Dez in a heap on the ground.

"That necklace?" Spencer asked.

"Huh?" Daisy looked at him, confused.

"Min gave you that necklace?" He pointed to the pendant on a chain around her neck.

Daisy giggled. "No, silly. Why would Min give me a necklace?" Daisy rubbed the shiny pendant around her neck. "It's from my grandma. I've had it forever."

"I've just never seen you wear it before," Spencer said, trying to recover before Dez pointed out his jealousy again.

"Yes you have," said Daisy. "I used to wear it all the

time, but Leslie Sharmelle broke it when we were fighting in the air vent at the school. My dad finally got around to fixing it."

"That would be cool, if I cared," Dez cut in. "Now hurry up and feed your garbage some garbage."

Daisy turned to her faithful Thingamajunk. "This is a letter from the boy you need to find," she explained. "If you eat it, will you be able to find his house?"

Bookworm nodded, and Daisy held it out for him.

"But," Spencer said, "shouldn't we read it first?" He really was curious to see what Min would say in a personal letter to Daisy.

Daisy's cheeks seemed to flush a bit and she reached out, nearly shoving the letter in Bookworm's face. He gobbled it up without hesitation.

"Know where to go?" Daisy asked.

The Thingamajunk paused for just a second as he seemed to simultaneously ponder and digest. Then he collapsed into a lifeless mound of garbage. He was on his way to Min, holding the future of education in his lunchbox head.

CHAPTER 32

"THAT'S A LAME POWER."

Spencer turned to his companions. He felt a huge weight off his shoulders, knowing he'd done all he could to get the *Manualis Custodem* safely away.

"What now?" Daisy asked.

"Now we rescue the others," Spencer said.

Daisy glanced nervously at Spencer and Dez. "I don't mean to be negative," she said. "But there are only three of us."

"Don't be such a wimp," Dez said. "We can handle it."

Spencer shook his head. "Daisy's right. We need help."

"But who?" she asked. "All our best fighters are already captured."

"Mr. Clean missed one," Spencer said, finally slipping the backpack from his shoulders. "The best fighter I know is right in here."

Daisy raised an eyebrow in surprise. "You've got a tiny person in your backpack?"

"Sort of." Spencer pulled on the zippers, and the bag fell open to reveal its contents.

The Vortex.

Spencer carefully lifted the Vortex vacuum bag from the open backpack. Almost seven months had passed since Spencer had first punctured the Vortex. The vacuum bag had unleashed a tremendous power, sucking everything inside. Several BEM workers, including a man named Garth Hadley, had disappeared. And one Rebel had been a casualty of the Vortex.

"You're going to rescue Marv?" Daisy whispered.

Marv, the Rebel janitor, had been lost to them for months now. He was alive, or had been back in November when they'd captured an audio recording of his voice. The message was simple and completely nonsensical. Marv had merely shouted, "Haha! Gutter ball!"

Spencer held the vacuum bag aloft. There was a folded note secured to the edge of the Vortex with a little paper clip. The note was from Olin, one of the Dark Aurans, who had written instructions for Spencer to rescue Marv from the bag. In the last two months, Spencer must have read the note a hundred times, studiously poring over the message with Walter.

"But Walter said we couldn't risk a rescue," Daisy quietly reminded. "He said it was too dangerous."

Spencer didn't need the reminder. Walter had decided that they should wait until the Founding Witches were back. They couldn't risk valuable time, and potentially lives, in rescuing Marv while the *Manualis Custodem* remained unsolved.

"Walter's not here now," Spencer pointed out. "We need help, and Marv is our best chance. If we get him out of the Vortex, he can help us rescue the others from Mr. Clean's lab." Spencer sounded more positive than he felt. Olin's note didn't make Marv's rescue out to be an easy task. It would be a risk. But at this point, what wasn't?

"I need a leaf blower," Spencer said.

"Why?" Daisy looked at her lawn. "There aren't even any leaves."

"It's for the Vortex," Spencer said.

Daisy looked puzzled. "I thought we tried a leaf blower on the Vortex."

"Walter did," answered Spencer. "But it wasn't right." He unclipped Olin's note from the edge of the vacuum bag.

Daisy had read it once, but she must have forgotten the message. Spencer supposed that thoughts of Marv trapped in the vacuum bag didn't weigh constantly on her mind as they did on his. It was Spencer's fault that the big janitor had spent the last seven months trapped. He had put Marv there.

"No more love notes!" Dez grabbed the paper from Spencer's hand. "Let me see that." Dez glanced over it. "Boring," he said, and dropped it to the ground.

"It's not boring," Spencer said, snatching it before the wind could blow it away. "This letter tells us exactly how to rescue Marv."

"I don't think I want to rescue him," Dez said. "He's the big hairy guy that used to work at Welcher, right? He made me clean toilets once."

"You probably deserved it," Spencer said. "Now, listen up. If we're going to survive this, we'll need to be united."

"Blah blah blah," Dez said. "Just tell me who to attack."

Spencer rolled his eyes and lifted the note. "Olin said that our earlier attempts with the leaf blower failed for two reasons," Spencer summarized. "First, Olin created the Vortex. That means it's powerful and it won't max out." He began reading Olin's carefully written words. "*Your leaf blower will need to be far stronger than anything your warlock can Glopify. Only you have the strength to create something that will match the Vortex. When charged with the Aura, your right hand has the power to Glopify. Don't hold back.*"

"Wait," Dez interrupted, pointing at Spencer. "He wrote this about *you?*"

Spencer nodded and Dez burst out in laughter. "What's so funny?" Spencer asked.

"What kind of powers does he think you have, Doofus?" asked Dez.

"Spencer's an Auran, Dez." Daisy pointed it out straight, just in case the bully had missed something along the way.

Dez shrugged. "Big deal. What does that even mean?"

"It means that I could Glopify or de-Glopify you with a single touch of my hand," Spencer said. "It means that I can live forever. It means that my inner eye can locate the exact location of the warlocks."

"Psh." Dez waved him away. "Being a Sweeper is so much cooler."

Spencer turned to Daisy. "Do you know if your dad has a leaf blower we could borrow?" He used the term *borrow* very loosely, since he probably wouldn't be giving it back.

"There's one in the garage," Daisy said.

Once again, Spencer and Dez were momentarily left alone as Daisy went to find her dad's leaf blower. A second later she emerged, holding the device above her head like a trophy. She handed it to Spencer, who set it on the ground and knelt before it.

"Now what, Mr. Auran?" asked Dez.

Spencer didn't want to admit that he'd never actually done this before. Walter had been very hesitant in letting him experiment. Spencer had de-Glopified the pump house at the landfill, but something told him that Glopifying would be different.

Olin's letter said not to hold back. Spencer only hoped he would do it right. If he messed this up, he'd have to wait a day or two for the Glop to recharge in his bloodstream before he could make a second attempt.

"You're just going to stare at it?" Dez said. "That's a lame power."

"No," Spencer said. "I'm going to spit on it."

Dez laughed. "Good one, Doofus. You actually told a funny joke!"

Spencer glared at him. "I wasn't joking."

He looked down at his hands and took a deep breath.

This was the grossest part about being an Auran. It didn't matter that the spit was his own. Spit was spit.

Spencer worked up some saliva in his mouth and spat onto his palm. The spit was stringy as he drew back his head. Spencer gagged.

"You spit like a girl," Dez said.

Daisy asked what that was supposed to mean, but Spencer was ignoring them both. He clapped his hands together and rubbed them briskly. The friction activated the trace amounts of Glop in his saliva, and he felt a tingle in his palms. Suddenly, both hands ignited into orbs of golden light.

Dez drew back in surprise, the first and only indication that he was impressed by Spencer's Auran abilities.

Spencer took a steadying breath and stretched out his right hand to touch the leaf blower lying in the grass. The moment his fingers made contact with it, he felt a connection.

It was as though a stream of Glop were flowing out of his fingers and into the leaf blower. He felt his power spread through the plastic and metal on an almost molecular level.

The blower was glowing now too. Spencer could sense its potential. He knew it could do so much more than a simple factory had designed it to do.

The magic did the work, using Spencer as little more than a conduit. The leaf blower grew stronger, the wind speed magnified and the airflow focused. The magic flowed and flowed until the blower was something altogether different.

It was no longer a simple tool in his right hand. It was an insanely powerful device, capable of blowing air at speeds previously unimaginable. Spencer knew he had succeeded, even before he let go. He knew the magic in his system had taken the leaf blower a hundred times beyond what Walter could do.

Then, all at once, it was over. The glowing Aura faded from his hands, and the leaf blower looked as ordinary as ever, lying on the grass in Daisy's backyard.

Spencer stood up, his whole body trembling. He was proud of the work he'd done and more anxious than ever to rescue Marv so he could test it out.

Daisy's eyes were wide and her mouth slightly agape. Dez had a similar shocked expression, but he snapped out of it as soon as Spencer caught him staring.

"I guess that was all right," Dez muttered. "I bet it doesn't even work."

Spencer picked up the leaf blower. He wouldn't test it here. Pointed in the wrong direction, it could blow a hole clear through Daisy's house. No, Spencer was confident enough in his work that he would only test it when the time was right.

"You know," Daisy finally said, "for some reason I thought that part would take longer. What's next?"

Suddenly, the walkie-talkie on Spencer's belt turned on. A familiar voice came through the speaker.

"Spencer? Spencer? Do you copy?"

Spencer lowered the leaf blower and unclipped the radio. "Min! Is that you?"

"Indeed," Min said. "Who else would it be?"

"So the Thingamajunk found you?" Spencer said. "You got the book?"

"If by 'Thingamajunk' you mean 'living humanoid garbage,' then yes," Min said.

"His name's Bookworm," Daisy said into the radio. "He's my pet."

"I was just finishing my homework when he came through my window," Min said. "Now I have to think up an excuse that sounds more believable than the truth."

"What happened?" Daisy asked.

"The garbage ate my homework," Min replied.

"Sorry about that. I'm just glad he found you," Spencer said. "You have the *Manualis Custodem?*"

"It's in my hands as we speak," said Min. "What would you like me to do with it?"

"We need you to start working on a translation," answered Spencer. "It's written in a made-up language called Gloppish. Like a mix of Latin and hieroglyphics. Think you can crack the code?"

"Most definitely," Min said.

"Good," Spencer answered. "But you have to keep it a secret. The BEM will be looking for it. You have to guard it with your life!"

"Please," Min said. "Calm down. It's unnecessary to shout into the walkie-talkie."

"Sorry," Spencer said, taking a deep, steadying breath. "I'm a little tired. It was a long night."

"We went to Colorado, Massachusetts, and back to Colorado last night," Daisy added.

"Hmm," said Min. "It's geographically impossible to make that journey in one night."

"We've got Glopified squeegees now," Spencer said. "As long as you have somebody in place, you can open a portal to connect two locations."

"Do I have a deadline for the translation?" Min asked, getting back to business.

"As soon as you can," answered Spencer. "Here's the thing . . . Walter and the other Rebels have been captured. It's just me, Daisy, and Dez over here."

"Dez is with you now?" Spencer could imagine Min raising an eyebrow. "Your last report clearly stated that he was . . . how did you put it? *Filthy, treacherous scum.*"

"Hey!" Dez hit Spencer in the shoulder. "I am not scum."

"My apologies, Spencer," Min said. "I didn't realize he was listening."

"All right, Min," Spencer said, getting them on topic once more. "The truth is, we might not survive this rescue mission, and we need you to carry on the Rebel work. The *Manualis Custodem* will tell you what to do."

"I understand," Min said.

"I'm going to explain the rest of the plan," Spencer said. "I'm keeping you on the radio, Min. If our rescue plan goes bad, at least you'll know what happened to us."

Daisy leaned in. "And tell my dad that it was Dez who smashed the fence."

Spencer didn't tell her that if they all died, Mr. Gates wasn't likely to care a bit about his broken fence.

"Okay," Spencer said. "I've just Glopified a leaf blower with enough power to rip a hole in the atmosphere. We'll use it to rescue Marv."

"How do we do it?" Daisy asked. "One of us has to hold the Vortex while you blast it?"

"Not it!" Dez called. "I don't want to get blown away."

"That's not how it's going to work," Spencer said. Carefully holding the talk button on the radio, he pulled out Olin's note once more. "Walter already tried blasting the bag from the outside, but it didn't work. Olin says the leaf blower must be detonated from *inside* the Vortex."

"Whoa," Daisy said. "Does that mean we have to . . . ?"

Spencer nodded. "We'll have to enter the same way Marv did."

CHAPTER 33

"THOSE ARE YOUR BICEPS."

T his sounds like a terrible plan," Dez muttered. "We're going to get sucked into the vacuum-bag-of-no-return . . . on purpose?"

"Never thought I'd say this," Daisy muttered, "but I think I'm with Dez on this one. We have no idea what it's like in there!"

"We don't," Spencer agreed. "But Olin does. He's been there before. Listen to this." Spencer held out the Dark Auran's note and began reading. *"The Vortex is a gateway to a place we call the Dustbin: an alternate dimension from which our world was created. That's where your friend is trapped. And if you want to find him, you'll have to go there. Inside the Dustbin, you can imagine and create familiar objects from ordinary dust. Only the strongest minds will succeed."*

Spencer stopped reading when Daisy cut in. "Maybe Dez shouldn't come with us," she said.

The bully fidgeted under their gaze. "What?" He ruffled his wings uncomfortably. "You think I don't have a strong mind? Just look at this!" He flexed his arms.

"Umm," Daisy said, "those are your biceps."

"Whatever," said Dez. "You should worry about yourselves in there. I'll be fine."

Spencer turned back to the letter from Olin and continued reading.

"*Creating with your mind will be hard at first, but the longer you remain in the Dustbin, the easier it gets. The Instigators have been there for hundreds of years.*"

"The alligators?" Dez said.

"The Instigators," Spencer corrected. "I don't know who they are. I'm just reading."

"What else does it say?" Daisy asked.

Spencer read on. "*The Instigators are evil. You can never hope to match the strength of their creations. Long ago, Sach, Aryl, and I were their captives. The Founding Witches rescued us and helped us escape from the Dustbin. Do not attempt to find the Instigators. Get your friend and leave as quickly as possible.*

"*Firing the leaf blower from within the Dustbin will create a Rip back to our world. It'll only work once, and you'll have only about ten minutes before it closes. You better not get stuck in there. I'm counting on you to take this blasted Pan off my neck.*

"*Best of luck—Olin*"

Spencer sighed deeply and tucked the note back into his pocket. "Well," he said to his companions. "Any questions?"

"Yeah," said Dez. "Can I have the garbage truck if I'm the only one who survives?"

"Let me make sure I got this right," Daisy said. "We get sucked into the Vortex, find Marv, create a Rip that gives us only ten minutes to get out. Then the four of us drive to Massachusetts, maneuver our way back through the traps in the construction site, enter the Port-a-Potty, break into the BEM lab, rescue the others, steal Belzora and the nail from Mr. Clean, and escape?"

Spencer nodded wordlessly. Yep. That pretty much summed it up.

Daisy smiled weakly. "Okay. Just checking."

Spencer lifted the radio to his face. "Did you get all that, Min?"

"Yes," he answered. "I managed to hear your plan *and* your quarrelsome banter."

"Is that your way of saying 'good luck'?" Spencer asked.

"Your plan is too long," Min said. "It will take much more time than you can afford. Every second wasted puts the captured Rebels in danger."

"Do you have a better idea?" Dez taunted.

"Actually, I do," said Min. "Leave a squeegee with your Thingamajunk in Welcher and take the other one with you into the Vortex. After the three of you get sucked into the vacuum bag, tell Bookworm to place the Vortex in his lunchbox head. As you spend time searching for Marv in the Dustbin, Bookworm will travel from trash to trash, arriving in Massachusetts much faster than you normally could. The Thingamajunk should easily be able to maneuver through the traps in the construction site, since he is made of nothing but Glopified garbage. He can deposit the Vortex inside the Port-a-Potty and return to Welcher. Meanwhile, you create the Rip inside the Vortex, and when you emerge with Marv, you will already be on your way into the heart of the enemy's base, taking them by complete and utter surprise, with your return to Welcher secured by the squeegee there."

Spencer was grinning by the time the boy finished his elaborate plot. "Genius, Min. Pure genius. That's why we pay you the big bucks."

"You haven't paid me anything," Min said over the radio. "Now, if you'll excuse me, I'm already late for my cello lesson."

"Jell-O lesson?" Dez scoffed.

"He said *cello*," corrected Daisy.

Dez shrugged. "What's that?"

"A musical instrument," she said.

"If it's not the tuba, it's lame."

Spencer lifted the radio one last time. "Thanks, Min. Keep that book safe. The future of education is now resting on your shoulders."

"I will not fail," he said. And then, "Min, out."

Spencer clipped the radio back onto his janitorial belt.

"We're not really going to follow his plan, right?" Dez said. "It was way confusing, with like, the Vortex in the lunchbox in the Port-a-Potty. I never know what that kid's saying."

The pile of trash in the shed erupted, and Bookworm came loping toward them, his textbook mouth curved in a grin of success. He dropped down when he reached them, and Daisy scratched the side of the lunchbox as though he were a dog.

"Okay," Spencer said. "Let's fill in Bookworm and work through the details of Min's plan. Squeegees."

"Do we have a complete set?" asked Daisy.

Spencer nodded. He unclipped one squeegee and set it on the lawn. "This is the one Earl was using. It stays here in Welcher," he said. He patted the second squeegee handle on his belt. "This is the one Agnes used to bring us over to Massachusetts. It goes with us."

"We should probably do something with Big Bertha," Daisy pointed out. "Plus it has Holga and the nail inside the glove compartment."

"Nobody can get in when it's locked," Spencer pointed out. "So the hammer should be safe. We'll leave the truck key with Bookworm. He can park it somewhere safe and out of the way."

"Garbage driving the garbage truck?" Daisy said. She looked at her pet. "Do you know how to drive?"

In answer, he hacked up an old hubcap. It rolled across the grass, and Daisy nodded.

"I'll take that as a yes."

Reluctantly, Dez pulled out the bulky key chain and tossed it to the Thingamajunk.

"Now," Spencer said, "we need to be somewhere enclosed when we puncture the Vortex."

"What about the shed?" Dez pointed.

"The suction will be too strong," Spencer answered. "It'll rip the walls right out of the ground."

"The back of Big Bertha?" Daisy suggested.

Spencer nodded. The vehicle was Glopified and reinforced. It should be able to withstand the suction. "That'll work," he said. "Once we disappear into the Vortex, Bookworm will pick us up and load the vacuum bag into his lunchbox." Spencer turned to the Thingamajunk. "You got that, buddy?"

Bookworm gave a thumbs-up. This time, his thumb was a bent spoon.

"How fast can you get to Massachusetts?" Spencer asked.

Bookworm thought about it for a second, and then hacked up a coupon that said, *$90 off!*

Daisy picked up the ripped coupon and tucked it in her pocket. "That seems like a pretty good bargain," she said.

"You don't even know what's on sale," Spencer pointed out. "Anyway, I think Bookworm was trying to say that it will take him ninety minutes to get from here to Massachusetts."

"Dumb garbage," Dez muttered. "You can't have ninety minutes. There's only sixty minutes in an hour."

Spencer rolled his eyes, resisting the urge to call Dez the dumb garbage now. "Ninety minutes is an hour and a half."

"How will he find the construction site?" Daisy asked.

Spencer was stumped for a moment. "Well, he can

locate places if he's eaten garbage from that region before. So if we had any kind of scrap from the construction site . . ."

"Will this work?" Dez asked, pulling a wad of toilet paper from his back pocket.

Spencer drew back in disgust. Toilet paper from Dez's pocket didn't seem like it could ever be a good thing.

"It's from the Port-a-Potty," Dez explained.

"Why do you have it?" Daisy asked.

"I rolled some off when we were flying over the ocean." He shrugged. "What? My nose was running."

"You don't have a nose," Daisy reminded him.

"My *beak* was running," Dez corrected. "I would have wiped it on Spencer's sleeve, but he was too far away. So I used this instead." He held out the snotty wad of toilet tissue.

"That's disgusting," Spencer said. "I'm not making Bookworm eat that."

Dez shrugged and tossed the wad on the ground. Bookworm pounced on it as though it were a piece of candy and gobbled it up in a flash.

"You know where to go now?" Daisy asked.

The Thingamajunk nodded.

"Okay," Spencer said. "So we just have to survive inside the Dustbin for an hour and a half."

"But I thought we only had ten minutes before the Rip thingy closed and we're trapped forever down there," Dez said.

"I don't have to use the leaf blower to open the Rip

right away," Spencer pointed out. "We can get inside the Dustbin and find Marv. Then, in ninety minutes, once Bookworm has dropped us in the Port-a-Potty, I can open the Rip." Spencer grinned. "This is going to work, guys. Mr. Clean won't even know what hit him."

"I don't know," Dez said. "I still see a lot of ways this could go wrong. Half the plan depends on a walking pile of garbage." He pointed at Bookworm, who snarled.

Daisy put a hand on her pet's arm. "How are you feeling about this plan, Bookworm?"

The Thingamajunk worked up an answer from deep within, spitting a chewed-up Nike sneaker on the ground.

"Nike?" Daisy said. "You're ready to run?"

But Spencer got the true meaning and smiled. "I think what Bookworm wants to say is . . ." Spencer looked at the Thingamajunk. "Just do it."

Bookworm nodded vigorously, and the plan to save Marv was finally under way.

CHAPTER 34

"DID WE DIE?"

Spencer, Daisy, and Dez stood in the back of Big Bertha. Empty now of all her trash, the Glopified Garbage Truck 2.0 still smelled awful. Spencer took it as further motivation to get the job done quickly.

He held the Vortex in one hand and a razorblade sword in the other. The highly Glopified leaf blower was strung across his back, tied in place with a piece of rope from Daisy's garage.

Big Bertha's back hatch was closed, and it was almost entirely dark inside.

"Ready when you are," Daisy said nervously.

Spencer hesitated, thinking through any last-minute aspect of his plan. There was one thing in the back of his mind. One thing he hadn't dared mention to the others.

Garth Hadley.

If Marv was in the Dustbin, then that surely meant Garth Hadley and his BEM workers would be there too. Spencer thought of the BEM representative who had tricked him so long ago. Compared to the Sweepers and Pluggers he'd faced since, Garth hardly seemed like a threat. But the man was crafty. He'd used Spencer against the Rebels from the very beginning.

If it came down to a face-to-face meeting with his old enemy, Spencer was determined not to be manipulated. He was an Auran, a Rebel, and a much more important piece of this story than Garth Hadley would ever be.

Spencer felt one of Dez's wings brush past him as the bully folded and unfolded them. "Hurry up, Doofus. It stinks back here."

Spencer's attention turned back to the vacuum bag in his hand. "Okay," he said. "Hold on." Not that holding onto anything could prevent them from getting sucked into the high-powered Vortex.

Spencer brought the razorblade up, the sharp tip hovering above the papery bag for just a moment. Then he thrust the blade into the Vortex.

There was a deafening roar, like the sound of a thousand vacuums being turned on at once. A tornado of wind and suction rose from the rend in the bag, growing until it filled the back of Big Bertha.

Daisy and Dez were instantly snatched into the whirlwind's grasp. Spencer heard Daisy scream and vaguely saw Dez's wings flapping hopelessly against the gust. The two kids circled above Spencer's head, clanging into Big Bertha's fortified walls. Then they were gone, sucked through the gateway Vortex and into the unknown of the Dustbin.

Spencer's hand slipped from the razorblade, and it was pulled out of sight. He was staring at the active hole in the bag, wondering how it was possible to fit through such a tiny tear. Would it hurt?

His left hand was clamped, sweaty, to the edge of the bag. It took more courage than Spencer expected to let go of the Vortex. The moment he did, his feet came off the floor. He spun helplessly around, two or three complete revolutions, before he was pulled headfirst into the Vortex.

He experienced a moment of sheer disorientation, completely unable to decide which way was up and which was down. He felt the wind's pressure against his skin, pushing him, pulling him. There was a tightness to it, as though his body might get ripped apart at any second. But there was no pain.

Spencer couldn't keep his eyes open, and even if he had, there was nothing to see but utter blackness. He braced himself. For what? He didn't know. This swirling, dizzying movement had to end sometime. But what if it didn't? What if this was the Dustbin? What if it was nothing more than an endless gyroscopic existence?

No sooner had Spencer considered this terrible idea than he slammed into something solid, knocking the breath from his lungs. He sat up, eyes wide and mouth agape, until he finally managed to suck in a giant gasp of air. He wondered why his coveralls hadn't protected him from the impact. He felt for the zipper, realizing that the violent wind had pulled it down a few inches.

Overhead, the twisting cyclone of the Vortex was fizzling out. Spencer's white hair tousled once in the last whip of wind. Then the suction roar faded, the air became very still, and an absolute silence settled around him.

The first thing Spencer noticed about his surroundings was the ground beneath him. At first, he thought it was soil, or maybe sand. But as he shifted his weight to stand up, he realized that the particles beneath him were much finer.

Dust.

It was soft, wrapping around his ankles and enveloping his tennis shoes like a powdery gray snow. Spencer looked up to see if he could glimpse the tear in the Vortex, but any indication of his entry point was gone.

There was no sky above him, just a colorless, shapeless cloud of dust. It hung in an unmoving haze, as though every particle of dust was suspended in time, unwilling to settle to the ground. He felt claustrophobic, his vision limited by the seemingly endless grit in the air.

Dust.

"Did we die?" Daisy's feeble voice floated up at Spencer's left. He turned to her, noticing plenty of half-buried debris littering the dust around them. It looked like they were standing in a junkyard. Daisy grabbed the edge of a broken school desk and pulled herself to her feet.

"Are we in heaven?" Daisy asked, taking a shaky step through the dust toward Spencer.

Spencer refused to think that heaven could be so bland . . . and dusty.

"Hey!" shouted another familiar voice. "I'm over here!"

Spencer saw the bully a few feet away, using his taloned hand to punch a hole through a bookshelf that was leaning against him.

"We're definitely not in heaven," Spencer said, "or Dez wouldn't be here."

Spencer expected to feel that awful, gritty taste of dust between his teeth when he opened his mouth to speak. But here, it was different. The airborne particles of dust didn't seem to bother his mouth at all, just as they didn't bother his eyes. He grasped the zipper of his jumpsuit and cinched it tight again.

Dez jumped into the air, his black wings unfurling. The flapping sent the dust particles into motion, swirling around his figure, filling in the space where he moved, and settling still once he had passed.

Dez flew high, maybe twenty or thirty yards, until Spencer and Daisy could barely see him as a dark smudge in the hazy air.

"I can't see anything!" Dez shouted. From that distance, his voice sounded muffled, like a shout in a padded room. "Where are we?"

The answer was simple. They were in the Dustbin. But what did that even mean? How would they find Marv when they could barely see what lay ahead?

Something caught Spencer's eye. It was a sheet of paper,

241

mostly buried in the soft dust. There, at the top of the page, was a handwritten name.

Spencer.

And stranger still was the fact that Spencer immediately knew who had written it. *He* had, seven months ago.

He stooped and pulled the paper from the dust. Next to his name, a small *100%* was written and circled in Mrs. Natcher's red pen.

"What's that?" Daisy asked.

"It's my spelling test," Spencer said.

"You had enough time to take a spelling test down here?" Daisy said.

"No," Spencer explained. "I took it in Mrs. Natcher's class back in September." He read off some of the words on his list. "*Pneumonia, aqueduct, colonel* . . . don't you remember this test? We took it the day after we made our mess at the ice cream social!"

"I don't get it," Daisy said. "How did your spelling test end up in the Dustbin?"

"It was in my desk when everything got sucked into the Vortex," he answered. "Look around. It's all here!"

The debris around them made sense now. Desks, bookshelves, the teacher's computer, tiles from the ceiling, strips of carpet from the floor. Even the classroom sink. Everything that had been sucked into the Vortex was here, burrowed into the thick, dusty ground.

Dez landed, sinking to his shins in the powdery dust. "I can't see a thing," he said. "It's just dust . . . everywhere."

"There has to be something out there," Spencer said. "If

the Vortex dumped its load right here, then that must mean that Marv was here too."

"That was months ago," Daisy said. "He could be any-where by now."

"Let's just forget about Marv," Dez said. He reached for the leaf blower, still strapped to Spencer's back. "Fire that thing up and blast a way out of here. This place gives me the creeps."

Spencer stepped out of Dez's reach. "We're looking for Marv," he said. "Besides, it's too soon to use the leaf blower. We have to give Bookworm at least an hour and a half to get the Vortex into the Port-a-Potty."

"So now what?" Daisy asked. "We just go wandering off into the dust?"

"Let's look for tracks," Spencer said. "Marv would have left big tracks when he went wandering off."

Spencer stepped over a splintered cabinet and started inspecting the ground. Where the Vortex tornado had de-posited them, the sedentary dust had been whipped into a dramatic swirl.

Spencer's eyes scanned across the smooth expanse ahead. It had probably been too long since Marv had walked away, assuming he'd been deposited in this spot in the first place. Any tracks the big janitor might have left behind would surely have been filled by now.

"This is a waste of time," Dez said from the other side of the debris field. "I don't see anything but dust."

The bully was right for once. It was shapeless dust as far as the eye could see. Spencer was just giving in to hopelessness when Daisy shouted behind him.

"There's something up there!"

CHAPTER 35

"IT'S BUGGING ME."

Spencer scrambled across the classroom debris to where Daisy was pointing into the hazy air.

"It's an airplane," she cried.

"Where?" Dez said, coming alongside them. "I don't see anything."

Spencer wouldn't agree out loud with Dez, but he didn't see anything either. He was wondering how he could possibly miss seeing an airplane in the formless sky when a flash of white caught his attention. Dez must have seen it at the same time. He shoved Daisy gently in the arm.

"That's not an airplane, Gullible Gates," Dez said. "That's a *paper* airplane."

"I know what it is," Daisy replied. "I never said what kind of airplane."

"But what's it doing?" Spencer asked.

The paper airplane was indeed behaving strangely. It fluttered about ten feet above their heads, dipping its wings left and right in the windless sky. The sharp center crease was angled downward, the pointy tip of the plane seeming to stare at each of their faces.

"What are you looking at?" Dez shouted up at the paper airplane.

"It's not *looking* at anything," Spencer said. "It doesn't even have eyes."

"I don't care," Dez said. "It's bugging me." He bent his knees and sprang into the air, black wings propelling him upward. One hand reached out in an obvious attempt to crumple the fragile airplane. But the paper plane's reaction was faster. It swerved out of reach just as the Sweeper kid's talons closed on empty space.

Dez grunted and dipped down for a second attempt. This time the paper airplane was ready for him. As his clumsy hands grappled with nothing, the plane zoomed forward, pecking Dez directly between the eyes with its sharp tip.

Daisy couldn't help but let out a little giggle. Spencer had to admit, it was pretty funny watching Dez get owned by a folded piece of paper. But Spencer's curiosity about the small airplane prevented him from enjoying the show.

"Leave it alone, Dez!" Spencer shouted. "Maybe it's here to help us."

But Dez wasn't going to give up now. He had a welt between his eyes and probably a bigger one to his pride. The paper airplane was buzzing circles around him while he flapped ungracefully, like a dog chasing his tail in midair.

"Get back here, you little . . ." Dez threatened.

But the paper airplane suddenly seemed to lose interest in Dez. It rose above the Sweeper's head and hovered there, fluttering like a nervous bird. Its point darted anxiously back and forth. Then it dove below Dez's feet and streaked between Spencer and Daisy before disappearing into the gritty horizon. It moved so quickly that Spencer knew it was hopeless to give chase.

Dez touched down on the soft, dusty ground.

"Way to go," Spencer said sarcastically. "You scared off the one thing in the Dustbin that wasn't dust."

"I almost had that dumb thing," Dez muttered.

"I think it was the other way around," said Daisy, rubbing the spot on her own forehead to indicate where Dez's welt was showing.

"Whatever," Dez said. "It was scared of me. Didn't you see how fast it took off?"

"I don't think it was scared of you," Spencer said.

"What else could it be afraid of?" Dez said. "We're the only ones around."

Right then, Daisy screamed as something streamed toward them through the dusty air. Spencer's hand dropped to his janitorial belt, pulling the first handle he could grasp. But before he could turn to face the incoming threat, the attack had reached him.

It was a long, unwound ribbon of toilet paper. It wrapped tightly around his arm and pulled him onto his side in the dust. Dez backed up, talons flexing. But Daisy drew a razorblade from her belt pouch and leapt forward, slashing through the thin paper and cutting Spencer free.

The toilet paper around his arm instantly disintegrated, turning to dust and hanging weightlessly in the air around him. The other end of the severed toilet paper retracted across the dusty ground. Spencer watched it retreat, following the ribbon back to its owner.

The figure was standing only yards away. It was shaped like a man and stood at least six feet high. In place of hands, the attacker sported two toilet-paper rolls on metal rods. But the toilet paper didn't stop there. It was wrapped around the figure's arms and torso, down its legs, and around its head. It wasn't a tight wrap, and the entwining strands dangled down, leaving gaps across its entire body. Through these gaps, Spencer saw no flesh or form, just emptiness, filled with the passing dust in the air.

"Mummy!" Dez shouted. And that was indeed how it appeared: a toilet-paper mummy, as if somebody's cheap Halloween costume had suddenly come to life.

Spencer had only a moment to take it in before the TP mummy was moving in on them. Spencer leveled his push-broom in defense and thrust as soon as the creature was within range. The bristles caught the mummy in the chest and sent it coiling weightlessly upward.

Its immediate reaction was to send two long streamers of toilet paper from its rolled-up hands. The paper came out like dual whips, snaring a desk from the debris field and using it as an anchor. The streamers rolled in, pulling the mummy back to the ground.

Even with its feet on the ground, the figure was still weightless and unable to successfully defend itself against Dez's attack. The Sweeper kid launched himself at the enemy, bringing his sharp talons down across the figure's chest.

The toilet paper ripped away easily, leaving an open rend in the mummy's chest. As Spencer had envisioned, the wound opened to nothingness. Instead of a tangible body, the toilet paper seemed to be wrapped around air, giving only the illusion of a human figure.

Gravity returned, and the mummy tried to step forward. Dez swiped his talons once more, severing an arm that turned instantly to dust. Off balance and torn open, the mummy lurched awkwardly, fell toward the kids, and suddenly disintegrated.

Spencer stared speechlessly at the spot where the mummy had fallen. There was absolutely no sign of it. Not even the metal rods on which the toilet-paper hands had spun. Its remains were now dust, inseparable from the countless particles hanging in the air.

"Ha! Eat that!" Dez shouted. "That wasn't even hard."

"Um, guys," Daisy said. She was pointing over the boys' shoulders, her face pale and eyes unblinking. Spencer slowly turned to face whatever it was that Daisy had spotted.

Appearing out of the dust, like wraiths from shadow, were at least a dozen toilet-paper mummies.

CHAPTER 36

"HE SAID IT."

It didn't make sense to stand and fight. They would only be defending a useless pile of classroom debris anyway. Spencer shouted the only thing that seemed logical.

"RUN!"

Dez instantly took to the sky as Spencer and Daisy sprinted away from the swirled area where the Vortex had deposited them and into the shapeless void of the Dustbin.

Spencer remembered a family vacation to the beach a few years back. He had found it hard to run fast in the loose sand. But this was worse, with every stride sinking ankle deep into the powdery dust underfoot.

Where were they running? Away. It didn't seem to matter what direction. There was nothing to be seen anywhere Spencer looked. He glanced over his shoulder to check the mummies' progress.

"Wait!" Spencer grabbed Daisy's arm, and Dez dropped out of the sky to land beside him. "Where'd they go?"

Spencer cast his eyes in all directions, but there was no sign of the toilet-paper figures.

"Maybe they run slow," Daisy said.

"Or maybe we run super fast," said Dez.

But Spencer knew it was neither. "They were right behind us," he muttered.

The stagnant particles of airborne dust began to swirl around them. The grit began knitting together and taking shape, forming into the same host of mummies that had only moments ago been behind them.

"What's happening?" Daisy cried, staggering backward. But there was no retreat. The dust behind them was also swirling, with more mummies materializing out of the haze.

"We're surrounded," Spencer muttered, readying his pushbroom while Daisy readjusted her grip on the razor-blade handle.

"Later, guys!" Dez shouted, leaping from the soft ground and spreading his wings. Spencer didn't even have time to feel enraged that Dez would desert them like this. In a flash, one of the mummies unfurled a ribbon of toilet paper, which tethered securely around Dez's ankle. His wings flapped uselessly once or twice; then he was flung back to the ground, where he landed in a heap.

The mummies formed a ring around the three kids. They stood shoulder to shoulder, their rolled hands coiling and uncoiling lengths of toilet paper, as though they were anxious for permission to lash out.

One of the mummies stepped forward. It was the same size as the others, but Spencer thought it looked a little different. Its toilet paper seemed whiter, thicker, with a quilted pattern across it.

The leader mummy tilted its head slightly to one side. The toilet paper wrapping its face parted, and a whispery voice issued an order to its comrades.

"Bring the one with white hair for questioning. Wipe out the others."

"Nobody's wiping my nose!" Dez yelled, hoisting himself to his feet. "I'm a big boy!"

"That's gross," Daisy muttered.

"Don't blame me," Dez replied. "He said it."

"I don't think that's what he meant." Something told Spencer that the order to wipe out Dez and Daisy would be far more sinister and deadly than what the bully was thinking.

"You're not taking me anywhere!" Spencer yelled. "You'll have to kill me, too!"

"Could you think of anything dumber to say?" Dez asked. Then he turned to the mummy commander. "Take me for questioning. Wipe them out!" He pointed at Spencer and Daisy.

"The Instigators do not want you," said the toilet-paper figure.

Spencer felt a chill pass through his bones. *The Instigators.* Olin's note had warned him about this. Spencer had at least hoped to find Marv before facing off with the mysterious Instigators. But the enemy had already found them—within minutes of entering the Dustbin.

The two hollow gaps in the mummy's head that served as eyes focused on Spencer. Then the mummy spoke again. "You have the needed attributes," it said. "The Instigators will use you for experiments, as they did the others."

Experiments? Olin's note hadn't mentioned what the Instigators did to the Dark Aurans. Spencer didn't want to know what kind of evil experiments had been performed on his friends before the Founding Witches had rescued Sach, Aryl, and Olin. He had to get away before the Instigators did the same to him!

Spencer stepped backward, but the mummy instantly uncoiled a length of toilet paper from its hand roll. The paper streamer shot forward like a striking snake, wrapping around Spencer's middle.

It spun him around like a dizzying carnival ride, so fast that the pushbroom fell from his hands and both arms were pinned at his sides. The leaf blower was wrapped clumsily across his back, but there was no way he could reach it, tied up as he was.

The mummy turned its face to Daisy and Dez. In that whispery voice, it gave the final order to its comrades. "Turn their flesh to dust."

No sooner had the words slipped through its wrapping than something small and white came diving through the hazy twilight sky. Even from his confinement, Spencer recognized it.

The paper airplane.

It shot straight down, faster than a diving falcon. The pointy tip drove directly through the top of the leader

mummy's head and exited through the chest, instantly reducing the toilet paper to useless dust.

The tethers that held Spencer fizzled away, and he found himself suddenly free. The deadly paper airplane came to rest at Spencer's feet, the tip sticking in the soft dust. Spencer stared down at it. There was a message scrawled across one wing, inked out in black marker by someone with really bad handwriting.

Hi, Spencer.

In the second that followed, a huge flurry of folded paper airplanes materialized out of the dusty sky. They came like a squadron of mini air-force bombers, tearing through the ranks of toilet paper mummies.

Spencer backed up, bumping into Daisy and Dez, who stood speechlessly side by side. Spencer didn't dare tell them what he'd read on the first paper plane. He didn't dare vocalize what every fiber of his soul hoped would be true.

But in the next moment, words became unnecessary. As the toilet-paper mummies broke formation to fight the attacking folded planes, the kids' rescuer came into view.

He stood not twenty yards away, a hulking, formidable silhouette in the haze. He lifted a beefy arm and flicked a paper airplane toward them. The action caused the cloud of dust to part, and Spencer saw that unmistakable, shaggy, bearded face.

Marv.

CHAPTER 37

"BUILT IT."

Spencer's feeling of victory at seeing Marv did not last long. The nearest toilet-paper mummy lunged at Daisy, knocking her sideways. Spencer scooped his fallen push-broom from the dust and slammed the bristles into the back of the mummy's head. The figure lost gravity and went skipping out of control across the soft ground.

The rest of the mummies were making a stand, using their ribbons of toilet paper to swat the folded planes out of the sky. Spencer saw several of Marv's airplanes pulverized to dust.

Another mummy sprang at the kids. Dez took to the sky as Daisy's razorblade came down in an arc, severing the creature's arm. A folded plane swooped in, its wing decapitating the mummy before the plane lost control and crashed into the dust.

"Gloves!" Spencer called to Daisy. He ducked as a toilet-paper streamer reached for his head. His hand dug into a pouch on his janitorial belt until he felt the latex glove. He didn't know if the Glopified powers would prevent the mummies from holding them, but it was certainly worth a shot.

Spencer thrust his hand into the latex glove just as a ribbon of toilet paper wrapped around his leg. He stepped away, pleased to discover that his leg slipped effortlessly through the mummy's grasp.

With this newfound advantage, Spencer and Daisy were side by side in no time, working their way through the battlefield to the spot where they had seen Marv only moments ago.

Out of his peripheral vision, Spencer saw Dez dive-bomb onto one of the mummies, the force of his impact turning the enemy to sudden dust.

Three mummies moved to bar their path, toilet-paper streamers reaching uselessly at Spencer and Daisy. The first enemy went spiraling away under Spencer's pushbroom. The second was slashed to ribbons by Daisy's razorblade. The third moved to intercept, but a big, hairy arm reached out, bare hand seizing the mummy by the neck and ripping its head clean off.

As the dust settled, Spencer and Daisy found themselves face to face with their old janitor.

Daisy flung herself at him, arms wrapping around his bearlike form in an exuberant hug. Marv patted her

awkwardly on the back and did his best to show some affection. Spencer smiled. Marv wasn't really the huggy type.

When Daisy backed away, Spencer lifted his hand into
a timid wave. He had thought that seeing the janitor alive
and well would cause his feelings of guilt to fade. Instead,
the opposite seemed to be happening. What could Spencer
say to the man he had trapped in the Dustbin for over half
a year?

"Hi, Marv." It was a lame greeting, when there were so
many other words he could have used. Then, in an attempt
to make it more meaningful, Spencer added, "I wanted to
tell you that I'm . . ."

But Marv cut him off as a mummy sprang from the side.
The big janitor lifted his hand, causing the dust to swirl and
take shape. Out of nothing, a brick wall was immediately
erected. In surprise, the mummy slammed into the wall with
such force that both brick and toilet paper were reduced to
dust.

"How did you do that?" Daisy asked, passing her hand
through the spot where the brick wall had been.

"That's what it's like down here," Marv said. "This isn't
ordinary dust." He squinted at the battlefield. Most of his
folded airplanes had been destroyed, but they had succeeded
in taking down nearly every toilet-paper mummy.

"How long have you kids been stuck down here?" Marv
asked.

Spencer checked his watch. "About fifteen minutes."

"Vortex get you too?" he asked. Spencer couldn't tell if
he was upset about it.

"We came on purpose," Daisy said. "We thought you'd be bowling."

"Bowling?" Marv said.

"Yeah," said Daisy. "We heard a recording from inside the Vortex. You said 'Gutter ball!'"

"Must have been back at the bowling alley," he said.

"There's a bowling alley down here?" Daisy asked.

"Gotta do something to stay entertained," answered Marv. "I've been down here for . . . well, who knows how long."

"About seven months," Daisy blurted, not even softening the blow.

"That's it?" he asked. "Figured it was longer. I've been down here so many years that Spencer's hair turned white."

As he always did when someone mentioned his hair, Spencer put a self-conscious hand on his head.

"He's not old," Daisy explained. "His hair turned white because Spencer's an Auran."

Marv scratched a rough hand through his thick beard. "How'd that work out?"

"It's a long story," Spencer said. This didn't seem like the right time to discuss it, even though the battle appeared to be finished.

"Looks like you're not the only one who picked up some powers," Marv said.

Dez landed beside Spencer, displacing a lot of dust as he put his feet down. "This is the guy we came looking for, right?" He pointed a hooked finger at Marv.

"I remember you," Marv said. "From detention." He narrowed his eyes suspiciously. "But you didn't have wings."

"Yeah," Dez said, unfolding and refolding his prize possessions. "These babies are new. I'm a Sweeper."

"What's that supposed to mean?" asked the janitor.

"It means I'm awesome." Dez reached for the leaf blower on Spencer's back again. "We found the dude. Let's get out of here."

Marv chuckled bitterly. "There's no way out. I've been searching since the minute I got here."

"We brought a way out," Spencer said, gesturing to the big device on his back. "But we can't use it yet. We have to give Bookworm at least another hour to get the Vortex into position."

"We won't last another hour," Marv said. "Not out here, unprotected like this. The TPs will be back. And they'll adapt to our attacks. Next time, those latex gloves won't be much use."

"Where can we go?" Daisy asked, looking around at the expanse of nothingness.

"We should get back to the fortress," Marv said.

"You found a fortress out here?" Spencer said.

"Didn't find it," said Marv. "Built it."

The burly janitor held out his hand with the palm up to the sky. He closed his eyes in concentration, and the dust above his hand began to swirl. The particles came together to form a new paper airplane, with folds crisp and even.

"How are you doing that?" Daisy asked again.

"It's the dust," Marv explained. "Down here, you can use your imagination to shape the dust into real stuff."

Olin had mentioned something like that in his letter, though Spencer hadn't known exactly what it meant until he saw Marv doing it.

"Anything?" Dez asked. Spencer didn't want to imagine what the bully was thinking about concocting.

"Has limits," said Marv. "I can only build stuff that I've seen in real life. The better I understand it, the stronger it holds up. That's why I use these." He held out the paper airplane. "Kids were always folding these at school. Tried to fly them across the hallway and land them in the trash can. 'Course, nine times out of ten, they'd miss. I spent half my work days picking up paper airplanes off the floor."

Marv stepped forward and tossed the plane. It came out of his hand like a bird taking flight. As it cut through the dusty air, it displaced the particles, leaving a clean wake behind it.

"Let's move," said Marv. "If we stay close behind the plane, the TPs won't be able to reform in front of us."

The three kids followed Marv into the clear wake of the folded airplane. Spencer glanced over his shoulder, noticing that the particles remained displaced only for a moment before settling into a thick haze once more.

"Where did those mummy guys come from?" Daisy asked.

"From somebody's imagination," answered Marv. "They form out of the dust, just like my planes."

"Who's making them?" Daisy asked.

261

"They're called the Instigators," said Marv. "Don't really have a clue who they are. When the Vortex dropped us back there, the TPs found us in minutes. Wiped out two of the BEM workers before we could blink. I got away, along with the other BEM folks."

Spencer didn't want to ask it, but he had to know. "Garth Hadley?"

"Oh, yeah," Marv said. "That scumbag's still out here somewhere."

"Do you think we'll run into him?" Spencer asked.

"Not if I can help it," said Marv. "He can turn to dust for all I care."

CHAPTER 38

"THEY'RE QUILTED, LIKE CHARMIN."

Marv's fortress wasn't at all what Spencer was expecting to see through the haze. It wasn't a castle with jagged battlements and rising turrets. There was no grand gate or formidable drawbridge. Instead, the fortress looked more like . . .

"Is that Welcher Elementary School?" Daisy asked.

"Yeah," Marv muttered. "Well, parts of it, anyway."

"You can build anything you want, and you chose to make Welcher?" Dez said. "I hate that place."

"We can only build what we know," Marv said. "Places we've actually been. Welcher was fresh on my mind when I got sucked into the Vortex, so I used the school as a basic pattern. There's bits of other places I've worked, too."

"So why are we just standing here?" Dez asked. "Why don't we go inside?"

"This is the first time I've left the fortress in months," Marv said. "Been gone at least fifteen minutes. Anything could've happened. I got to make sure it's still safe before I take you kids in there. Last thing we want is to open the door and let in a bunch of One-Plys."

"What's a One-Ply?" Spencer asked.

"It's the cheap toilet paper," answered Marv. "Just got one thin sheet with no perforations. Most of the mummies are One-Plys. They're dumb as dirt, but they put up a good fight."

Spencer remembered the mummy leader. It seemed to have been made of different tissue. "Are there other kinds?"

"Two-Plys," said Marv. "They're quilted, like Charmin. Two-Plys can talk, but they'd just as soon rip your skin off as ask about the weather."

"What is the weather like around here?" Daisy asked.

"You're seeing it." Marv gestured up to the sky. "Always the same. Never gets dark, never gets light. Dust. So much dust."

Marv's folded airplane suddenly returned. It looped around the janitor's head and perched on his broad shoulder like an obedient bird.

"What's going on over there?" he asked. "Any TPs?"

The tip of the paper airplane shook back and forth in a motion that could only be interpreted as a negative head shake.

"Good," Marv said. "Looks clear, then?"

This time the airplane nodded its tip up and down. Marv reached his big hand up and plucked the folded paper from his shoulder. "Thanks," he said. Then, soundlessly, the little paper plane dissolved to dust between his fingers.

"What happened to it?" Daisy asked.

"I didn't need it anymore," Marv said.

"But you didn't have to kill it!" she said. "Wasn't it helping you?"

"I didn't kill it," Marv said. "It was never alive. I unimagined it."

"Why?"

"Everything that I've imagined out of the dust takes effort to keep around," Marv explained. "If I'm not using it, I might as well unimagine it."

"I wish I could unimagine Spencer sometimes," said Dez.

"Come on," Marv said. He moved forward, his large feet trudging through the soft dust.

They reached the front door of the fortress in no time. It was a fairly accurate re-creation of Welcher Elementary's entrance, but something was off.

"Wait a minute," Marv said. "This isn't the right paint."

"Who cares about the paint on the door?" Dez said. "Just open it." He reached out and tugged on the handle, but it was locked.

"Paint sealed over the door," Marv said.

"Can't you just unimagine it?" Spencer asked.

"You can only do that to things that you've imagined," explained Marv. "This paint job isn't mine."

"Then who did it?" Daisy asked. "The Instigators?"

"This wasn't the Instigators," Marv muttered. "This was somebody we know."

"Garth Hadley." Spencer said the name under his breath like a curse.

Marv nodded slowly. "Locked me out of my own fortress."

"What about the walls?" Spencer asked. "You made those, right? So you can unimagine them?"

Marv was already examining the school walls. "Looks like he used the same imaginative paint over the whole structure," said the janitor. "I can't get past it to unimagine the wall underneath."

"I've got an idea," Spencer said, drawing a bottle of blue Windex from his janitorial belt. "This will turn the wall to glass so we can break through."

He leveled the spray nozzle at the wall, but Marv reached out, his thick hand holding Spencer back. "When the only thing between you and death is a little wall, you make sure nobody breaks in."

"What do you mean?" Spencer lowered the spray bottle.

"I built defenses into the walls to stop the TPs from pounding them down. If you hit that wall, it'll be the last thing you do."

"Try it anyway," Dez said. "See what happens."

Spencer wasn't about to be goaded into making a foolish mistake. He holstered the Windex as Marv explained the consequences.

"I designed the wall to backfire," said the big janitor. "Hit it, and it hits you back. Knocks the dust right out of those TPs." He scratched his beard. "These walls can't be broken down."

"So how do we get in?" Spencer asked.

"Think I'd build a fortress without a hidden door?" Marv flashed a cunning grin. "Follow me."

The janitor set off through the dust, moving quickly along the outside of the mock Welcher Elementary. Spencer thought it was strange as they passed the window that would lead to Mrs. Natcher's classroom. Garth had painted over the glass, so he couldn't see inside, but he was curious to see what else Marv had imagined up.

They quickly arrived at a section of the school that Spencer had never seen before. It definitely wasn't Welcher, and Spencer assumed that Marv had patterned this piece after another school where he used to work.

"Should be right here," Marv muttered. He waved his hand, and the movement swept aside a layer of dust to expose something that had been buried.

It was a bowling lane.

The long lane stood alone in its dusty surroundings, angled at a gentle slope toward the school. Ten pins were set up against the school's brick wall, forming their usual triangular pattern.

"Good," Marv said. "It's still here." He held out his hand, and the dust began to swirl. In a flash, it had formed into a heavy red bowling ball, Marv's thick fingers wedged into the holes.

"Ever bowled a turkey?" Marv asked, lifting the ball to eye level.

"No," Daisy said. "But we always eat one for Thanksgiving."

"You eat bowling balls for Thanksgiving?" Dez asked.

"I don't think Marv's talking about the bird," Spencer said.

"We call it a turkey when you bowl three strikes in a row," the janitor explained.

"I always thought it was three strikes and you're out," said Daisy.

"That's baseball," Spencer said. "You *want* to get strikes in bowling. It means you knock all the pins over."

"I don't see how bowling three strikes is going to get us inside your dumb fortress," Dez said to Marv.

"Besides cleaning up messes," Marv said, "I'm not too good at many things. Had to find something that I could do better than Garth." He hefted the eighteen-pound ball. "Bowling."

"So you have to bowl three strikes, and the secret door will open?" Spencer said.

Marv nodded his shaggy head. "Yep." He stepped forward, dropped his back foot, swung his arm in a smooth arc, and released the heavy red ball. It rolled gracefully down the lane, curving just the right amount to avoid the gutters and line up with the center pin.

The ball struck the first pin, which tipped, colliding with another and starting a chain reaction. Each pin clattered to the ground, turning to dust as the bowling ball tore through them. It was a perfect strike, and all ten pins were down in a heartbeat.

Marv nodded in satisfaction and reached into thin air, where he was already conjuring another bowling ball from the creative dust. At the end of the lane, ten new pins were automatically forming.

"Strikes are easy," Dez said. "Give me that ball." He reached for Marv's red ball, but the janitor swatted his hand back.

"This isn't a game, kid," Marv said. "Two more strikes and we're inside. But it only takes one pin left standing to bring down the whole fortress."

"What?" Daisy said. "If you mess up, then the whole place goes *poof*?"

Marv nodded. "Self-destructs. If I can't get back inside, then Garth shouldn't be able to use my walls for his own purposes."

"You better not mess up," Dez muttered.

"I won't," Marv said. He lifted the bowling ball to eye level again, sighting down the lane in preparation for his second strike.

But an enemy strike came first.

CHAPTER 39

"I GOT A STRIKE ONCE."

The dust swirled around them, and a group of One-Plys instantly formed. Spencer was so taken by surprise that he found himself flat on his back before he could draw a weapon.

Marv leapt away from the bowling lane, swinging his eighteen-pounder like a club. It knocked off the head of the nearest TP and ripped through the chest of the next, dissolving them both.

One of the mummies cast its toilet-paper streamers to entangle the big janitor, but Daisy's dustpan shield knocked the attack off course. Dez slammed into the back of a One-Ply, talon fingers tearing the figure apart.

Spencer saw Marv lumber back to the lane, arm cocked and ready to bowl. The heavy ball had barely left his fingers when a One-Ply pounced on him. Marv tumbled aside, and

Spencer watched with anxiety as the ball cruised down the smooth lane.

A TP moved in on Spencer, blocking his view. He found the handle of his plunger and yanked it from the U-clip on his belt. The distinct sound of clattering pins reverberated through the Dustbin, and Spencer hoped that Marv's bowl had knocked them all down.

The One-Ply came at Spencer, but the boy's plunger knocked it to dust. In the haze, Spencer saw that Marv had indeed managed to bowl a second strike.

One more to go.

TPs were appearing by the dozen. Spencer could sense their excitement at finding people outside the fortress, and they were being created at an alarming rate.

Dez was in the air, avoiding dangerous strands of toilet paper. Spencer and Daisy came back-to-back beside the bowling lane. Both held defensive dustpan shields as they slashed at the TPs with plunger and razorblade.

Marv grappled with a Two-Ply, rolling in the soft dust as each tried to gain the upper hand. The janitor had quickly created a wave of folded paper airplanes, but their effect against the mummies seemed less than what it had been previously. The mummies were adapting to the attack, just as Marv had warned.

"Bowl!" Marv shouted at Spencer and Daisy. The Two-Ply had his arms tied back, but the man was still putting up a fight. "One of you has to bowl a strike and open the door!"

Spencer and Daisy looked at each other, wordlessly debating who should take the responsibility.

271

"You any good at bowling?" Spencer finally asked.

"Only with the bumpers," said Daisy. "You?"

"I got a strike once," Spencer said. "At my ninth birthday party."

Marv finally ripped free of the Two-Ply. His arms were bleeding where the TP had bound him. He summoned a few more folded planes and moved out to intercept a pair of One-Plys.

"We can't do it, Marv," Spencer shouted. "It has to be you!"

"Can't!" answered the janitor. "Takes too much concentration just to keep these paper planes flying. Get up there and bowl a strike, kid!"

Daisy guarded him as Spencer stepped up to the lane. He had a feeling that this wasn't going to end well. He didn't even have a bowling ball!

Spencer suddenly thought of Olin's note. He'd read it so many times, he had no problem remembering what it said.

Inside the Dustbin, you can imagine and create familiar objects from ordinary dust.

Spencer took a deep breath. He guessed it was time to try out his imagination. Spencer didn't know how he was going to create a bowling ball from nothing but dust. Olin's note said it would be easier the longer he stayed in the Dustbin. But Spencer had only been here for thirty minutes, tops. He just wanted Marv to do it. Months in the Dustbin had given him plenty of practice and success.

Daisy cut back a TP hand as Spencer closed his eyes and tried to imagine a bowling ball. Round, smooth, heavy. The one in his imagination was solid blue, the three finger holes placed ideally for his grasp.

"You're doing it!" Daisy shouted, causing Spencer to open his eyes. The dust at his feet was swirling together, but his shattered concentration caused it to blast apart into useless particles once more.

Spencer slammed his eyes shut again. Round, smooth, heavy. He thought of the last time he'd been bowling, trying to draw details from his actual experiences.

"You did it!" Daisy interrupted him again. But this time it was all right. Lying in the dust at his feet was a blue, ten-pound bowling ball. He couldn't help but smile at his success. It was his. He had imagined it in perfect detail, and he knew he could unimagine it to dust in the blink of an eye.

Spencer lowered his hand to pick up the bowling ball. Just before his fingers entered the holes, he froze.

"Spencer!" Daisy shouted. "What are you waiting for?"

He said nothing, unwilling to admit it. Spencer had imagined the ball too perfectly, and now he remembered why he hadn't been bowling in over three years.

The finger holes. They were full of germs. Who knew how many kids had stuck their fingers into those same holes before him? Armpit-scratching kids, nose-picking kids . . . and how often did the bowling balls get cleaned out? Probably never.

"We're not going to last much longer out here!" Marv yelled, his deep voice rumbling Spencer back to reality. "Pick up the ball, kid!"

If Spencer had imagined the bowling ball, then the germs weren't real. Right?

Spencer took a deep breath and plunged his fingers into the holes. He lifted the ball, noticing the round depression left behind in the soft dust. Daisy was still working hard in his defense, so Spencer acted quickly now. He stepped up to the end of the lane and lifted the ball to eye level, just as he'd seen Marv do.

Staring down the long lane at the ten pins made Spencer doubt. In his entire life, he had only ever bowled one strike. And that had been pure luck. He'd thrown the ball between his legs!

Spencer exhaled slowly, trying to steady his nerves. He was actually feeling confident that he just might succeed when Dez suddenly bumped into him, wrenching the ball from his grasp.

"No, Dez!" Spencer shouted, but it was too late. Dez had thrown the bowling ball.

"You were taking too long," Dez said.

Spencer could have unimagined the ball in the blink of an eye, but it actually looked like it was on course for a strike. It slammed into the foremost pin and sent it clattering into the ones behind.

"I told you," Dez said, "strikes are easy." He turned his back on the lane as the final pin wobbled. But instead of falling, as Dez was so sure it would, the last bowling pin steadied out and remained standing at the end of the lane.

"I GOT A STRIKE ONCE."

Marv's fortress vanished in a puff of colorless dust. Months of mental construction were shattered in a single moment as walls, floor, and ceiling disintegrated without a sound.

CHAPTER 40

"OPEN UP!"

Dez turned around slowly, his face showing more surprise than Spencer could ever remember seeing.

"What happened?" Marv yelled, tearing apart a toilet-paper mummy and scrambling through the dust where his fortress had once been. Nothing was left but a crumbling shell of Garth Hadley's imagined paint, too flimsy and weak to provide them any protection from the enemy.

"I . . . I . . ." For once, Dez was speechless.

"You missed!" Spencer yelled. He didn't admit the fact that he probably wouldn't have done better. He didn't admit that he was no good at bowling. Dez had acted out of line and his arrogance had cost them big.

Daisy tumbled under the attack of a One-Ply. The mummy's streamers tied around her ankles and dragged her through the dust. Spencer didn't have time to draw a

Glopified weapon from his belt. He squinted his eyes and imagined a wall. It was his bedroom wall from Aunt Avril's house. Simple, but effective.

The dust instantly formed into a Sheetrock barrier, severing the toilet-paper ribbons and temporarily protecting Daisy from harm. An angry Two-Ply threw itself against Spencer's wall, striking angrily until it crumbled away.

Spencer pulled Daisy back to where Marv and Dez were making a stand. The janitor's arms were welted and swollen, but he didn't slow down. Folded paper airplanes flew a tight circle around them, casting aside the particles to make a clean wake in which the TPs could not materialize.

"Way to go!" Spencer said to the Sweeper boy.

"Like you could do better!" yelled Dez. "That last one should've tipped over!"

"Now we've got nowhere to hide!" said Spencer.

Daisy reached out and touched the leaf blower strapped to Spencer's back. "We'll have to use it now. We'll never survive!"

She was right. Already the TPs were finding ways to swat down the folded airplanes.

"It's too soon!" Spencer said. "Bookworm won't be ready. We'll come out inside his lunchbox head!"

"Who cares," said Dez. "Just do it!"

"Who is Bookworm?" Marv finally asked. "And what are we waiting for him to do?"

"He's my pet," Daisy said. "He's made of garbage."

Marv shook his head, as if frustrated that there wasn't time to ask for clarification. "How long does he need?"

Spencer checked his watch. "Another hour, if we want to be safe."

"There's one more place we could go," Marv said. Spencer knew exactly what the janitor meant, and he didn't like it at all.

"Garth Hadley's fortress isn't far from here," said Marv.

Spencer shook his head. "He'll never let us in. He was the one who painted you out of your own school!"

"Oh, he'll let us in," Marv said. "All we have to do is tell him we have a way out of here."

"We're not taking him with us," Spencer said firmly.

"I never said we would," Marv replied. "We just need him to let us in."

Spencer didn't like it, but they were short on options. Using the leaf blower now and coming out of the Vortex before it was in position could ruin any chance to rescue Alan, Walter, Penny, and Bernard. Spencer knew they had to stick to the original plan, even if that meant seeing Garth Hadley again.

"This way!" Marv gestured ahead, and the paper airplanes zoomed off in that direction, clearing a pathway through the dust. Without the flying defenses, the TPs closed in fast. But the Rebels were already running as quickly as their feet could churn through the soft ground.

Garth's fortress came into view much sooner than Spencer expected. It looked very different from Marv's, though every bit as ordinary. Garth's building was made of experiences and details drawn from his life as a man of the Bureau.

The fortress seemed to be patterned after an office building, like the kind Spencer had seen in Washington, D.C., as he spied on Mr. Clean through bronze visions.

It was built on a small foundation but towered at least ten stories high. Most of the exterior looked to be made of glass. Spencer didn't think a fortress with a hundred windows would be very secure, but then he remembered that here, the glass was formed of pure imagination. He had a feeling it wouldn't shatter easily.

Marv didn't even slow down as he came to the front door of the building. Any break in their pace would give the TPs an opportunity to catch up with them.

"Hadley!" bellowed the big janitor. "Open up!" He waved his hand, and the paper airplanes that had been guiding them soared upward, knocking their points against the windows.

"Well, well." Garth Hadley's charismatic voice drifted down to them. "If it isn't my long lost friends . . ."

Spencer felt his chest tighten with a surge of old memories. He scanned the tall building but couldn't see the BEM rep anywhere.

"This is going to play out better than I could ever have planned," Garth Hadley continued from his unseen place. "When you left your fortress, Marv, I knew you'd come crawling back."

"You locked me out, Hadley!" Marv thundered.

"Yes, well, what goes around, comes around," said Garth. "Isn't that what they say?"

The Rebels had reached the front door of the building, a

sea of TPs closing fast. "Open up!" Marv yelled again. "We have a way out. Let us in and we'll take you with us!"

It was silent for a whole two seconds that seemed like eternity as the TPs drew closer.

"You're lying!" shouted Garth.

Spencer took a deep breath and pulled the leaf blower from his shoulder. "He's telling the truth! All I have to do is fire this up and it will blast a way out of the Vortex!"

Whether or not it was Spencer's words that convinced Garth Hadley, the front doors to the office building suddenly opened. Dez was the first one inside, his wings brushing the metal door frame. Marv ushered Spencer and Daisy in before stepping through and pulling the doors shut behind him.

No sooner had the lock clicked than the first of the TPs slammed into the door. There was a loud crack as the building seemed to kick back, pulverizing the first wave of mummies. One of the Two-Plys shouted a command, and the others came to a begrudging halt, their wrapped faces peering hungrily through the glass doors.

Spencer clutched the leaf blower in his right hand as he turned to examine his surroundings. The Rebels were standing in a lobby with a dark tiled floor and high hanging lights. The air inside the fortress was different. It was clean and dustless, much more like air should be.

"Spencer Zumbro," Garth Hadley's voice echoed across the spacious lobby.

Spencer whirled around to find Garth descending a staircase. He was wearing a blue button-down shirt, but it was tattered and bloodstained. His usual manicured appearance was slightly disheveled, though the dapper look on his square face was intact.

The BEM rep reached the bottom of the stairs and strode toward the Rebels. "If someone had told me that Spencer Zumbro and his friends would come knocking on my fortress door, I'd never have believed it," Garth continued. "Don't get me wrong. I'm glad about this recent development. You deserve to wither away in the desolate prison of the Vortex."

"What?" Dez objected. "Spencer might deserve it, but not me. I don't even know who you are!"

"But I know you, Dezmond Rylie," Garth said. "Though I see you've changed."

Spencer was a little surprised that Garth recognized the boy as a Sweeper. Garth Hadley and Leslie Sharmelle had used Dez to plant some pink soap in the boys' bathroom for Spencer to use. That little trick had exposed Spencer's eyes to Toxites and started this whole mess.

Dez flexed his talons and fanned his large wings. "Don't hate me because I'm awesome," he said.

Garth Hadley smirked. "I don't," he said. "I hate you because you're with Spencer."

Hadley turned and took a step closer to Spencer. "Seven months, four days, and eighteen hours," said the BEM rep. "Assuming my watch still works."

Spencer knew where this conversation was going. Garth was stating exactly how long he'd been trapped in the Dustbin, a misfortune for which he no doubt blamed Spencer.

"I had no choice," Spencer said, his memory freshly recalling the details that had led up to his decision to pierce the Vortex. "I had to protect the School Board."

"Protect it?" Garth scoffed. "The School Board is property of the Bureau of Educational Maintenance. You and your Rebel warlock stole it!"

"We're not the ones ruining education!" Daisy shouted.

Garth's gaze flicked over to her. "You should never have been involved," he snapped. "Shut your mouth."

Spencer pulled the leaf blower up to his shoulder, aiming it at the man like a bazooka. Just months ago, he'd seen a leaf blower far less powerful than this one blast the jaw off an Extension Filth. Spencer wondered what kind of damage his would do if unleashed on Garth Hadley.

"Don't talk to her like that," Spencer said. "If you've got a problem, settle it with me."

Garth's cool nature never cracked. He slowly raised his broad hands in defeat. "Please," he said. "You are guests in my fortress. I find it rather impolite to threaten your host."

Marv put a hand on the leaf blower, and Spencer reluctantly lowered the powerful weapon. "Cut the fake manners, Hadley," Marv said. "We all know you'd rather have watched us get wiped out by the TPs."

Garth Hadley smiled tightly. "And I know that you'd rather have left me behind if you truly had a way to get back home. So my question is this—why did you come here?"

"Shelter," Marv said. "Spencer says we can't use the leaf

blower for another hour. Needed shelter from the TPs while we wait."

"Very well," Garth said. "I will offer you shelter. But it comes on my terms." Spencer didn't like playing by Garth's rules. But they were in his fortress, at the mercy of his limited hospitality.

"Nobody carries a weapon," said Garth. To prove that he was obeying his own rule, Garth patted his sides to show that he was defenseless. He pointed to the center of the floor in the lobby. "Put everything down slowly. You can pick it up again when we leave."

Spencer noticed how Garth said "we," including himself in their departure plans. The very thing Spencer was trying to avoid.

"Not fair," Dez said. Spencer didn't know why he was griping. Dez wasn't even packing a Glopified weapon, and his Sweeper enhancements made him dangerous enough.

"My rules," Garth repeated, pointing at the floor.

"But it's not fair," Dez said again. "You're probably just waiting until we're defenseless. Then you'll imagine something out of the dust and attack us."

Garth Hadley shook his head. "This is a noncreative zone. There's no dust in the air inside my building. No one can create anything here."

Spencer looked to Marv for affirmation. The janitor nodded. "My fortress was the same way," Marv said. "We had to create a ventilation system that pumps the dust out and keeps the air clean inside. Otherwise those TPs would just re-form right inside our walls."

"So you see I'm only being honest and fair," said Garth. Spencer scowled. The man was anything but that.

Garth waited silently until Spencer and Daisy had finished depositing their janitorial belts on the floor. Spencer tried to hold onto the leaf blower, but Garth pointed firmly. Spencer hated leaving their only ticket home lying unprotected on the lobby floor. But it was still within sight, and Garth seemed to have no inclination to steal it.

Spencer backed away from the weapons pile, his eyes on the BEM rep who stood motionless across from the Rebels.

"There," Garth said. "Now we can speak peaceably. Can I get you something to drink?"

"I'm not thirsty," Spencer said, surprised to realize that it was true.

"Of course you're not," Garth said. "In this world of dust, we have no need for food, drink, or sleep. The particles in the atmosphere rejuvenate our cells. I believe I could live forever down here."

Spencer didn't mention that he'd already beaten Garth to the whole *immortal* thing. His Auran powers kept him suspended in a state of perpetual youth.

"In fact," Garth said, stepping over to Marv, "it seems that my abilities to form the dust have improved. I suppose I should thank you. As it turns out, I'm stronger on my own than I ever was with you."

Spencer turned to Marv, a look of betrayal on his face. "You two worked together?"

CHAPTER 41

"WHERE ARE YOUR COMPANIONS?"

Spencer couldn't imagine that Marv would work with Garth Hadley, but the janitor slowly nodded his shaggy head.

"Had to stay alive," said Marv.

"How could you?" Spencer went on. "He's a bad guy! He works for the BEM!"

"There is no BEM down here, kid," said Marv. "Just a whole bunch of toilet-paper mummies that want to wipe the skin off your bones. Didn't really matter who was Rebel and who was BEM. Had to stay alive."

Spencer glanced around the lobby. He remembered more BEM workers getting sucked into the Vortex that night in September. At least half a dozen people. "Where are the others?" he asked, suddenly expecting an ambush.

"Tell him, Hadley," Marv said. "Where are your companions?"

The smug look faded from Garth's face for a moment. "Dead." He spat out the word. "The TPs were onto us within minutes of our arrival. Porter and Barlow were dead before we realized what was happening. The rest of us ran blindly through the dust, but there was no refuge. Every way we turned, the devils were forming out of thin air."

Hadley clasped his hands behind him. "In our desperation, we discovered the power of the dust. It took nothing more than a perfect imagination—the things we needed would form before our eyes. But it wasn't easy. It required immense amounts of mental focus. Our weapons were weak and our structures flawed," Garth said. "So we banded together and built a shelter against the mummies. There were five of us. We worked together to perfect our shelter. We honed our minds, and the longer we remained in this dust world, the more complex our imaginings began to be. Soon we had created an impenetrable fortress."

"And the others would still be alive if we'd stopped there!" Marv cut in. His glare toward Garth Hadley was full of disgust. "We were living peacefully."

"We were prisoners in our own fortress!" Garth shouted back. "And while you might have been content with your silly bowling alley, the rest of us were seeking real freedom."

"That's a lie, and you know it," Marv said. "Your BEM coworkers didn't care about finding the Instigators. They were just following your orders."

"You tried to find the Instigators?" Spencer said. That was precisely what Olin's note had said not to do.

"There's someone else down here," Garth said. "Another fortress out in the dust."

"You've seen it?" Daisy asked.

He nodded. "Whoever is over there has tremendous power with the dust. They've created countless TPs in a nonstop effort to destroy us. Marv wasn't interested in finding the Instigators. He thought that if we sat long enough in our fortress, the Rebels would send help. But as the weeks ticked by, I wasn't convinced."

Garth Hadley took a deep breath, as if steadying himself for the next part of the story. "I decided to find the Instigators and destroy them. It was the only way to achieve peace down here. I sent Deakin to investigate. He found the enemy fortress and sent a message, but the TPs wiped him out before he could return."

"And you waited three whole days before you sent the next poor fellow to his death," Marv said.

"Bryson knew the odds," Garth said. "He was loyal to the Bureau. And that can't be said of all my workers."

"She was afraid of you," Marv said. "You were a mad man. Obsessed! You'd just sent the others to their deaths, and she knew she was next."

"It wasn't like that," Garth said. "I went out there with her to see the Instigators' fortress for myself."

"But that's as far as you went," continued Marv. "And as soon as you ordered the girl to go inside, she turned against you."

"And I dealt with her the same way I'd deal with any traitor to the Bureau," Garth said.

"I'm guessing you didn't give her a high five," Daisy said.

"I gave her to the TPs." Garth said it without a trace of regret in his voice.

"And after all that," Marv said, "you expected me to welcome you back into our fortress?"

Garth faced Spencer. "See what kind of man your Rebel janitor is? Uncaring and unforgiving. By the time I fought my way back to our shelter, Marv had redesigned it. My walls were broken down and patched over with shoddy fragments of old school buildings. I was begging for mercy at his doorstep with an army of TPs behind me. Marv turned his back and left me to die out there. But I am resilient. From the shapeless particles around me, I formed this." He gestured grandly at his tall office building, as though it were some finely wrought piece of architecture.

"What about the Instigators?" Spencer asked. "Have you seen them?"

Marv shook his head. "They never come out of their fortress. It's just wave after wave of TPs, determined to kill. Guess they're not keen on having neighbors."

Spencer couldn't spend any more time thinking about the Instigators. Olin had said to find Marv and get out as soon as possible. So that was exactly what he intended to do.

Spencer glanced at his watch. Less than an hour remained until Bookworm had the Vortex in position. That didn't leave them much time to ditch Garth Hadley. Especially now that they were in his building.

"How much time left?" Marv asked when he saw Spencer checking. "I'm ready to get home. See the old boss."

"It might not be that simple," Spencer said. "Walter's been captured by Mr. Clean."

"By *who?*" Marv asked.

"Not the bald guy with the earring that you see on cleaning supplies," Daisy said. "This guy is way scarier. He's just using Mr. Clean as a fake name. Confusing. I know."

"We have a plan to rescue Walter and the others." Spencer glanced distrustingly at Garth Hadley, then back at Marv. "A lot has happened since you've been gone. We should go somewhere we can talk about it."

"You'll talk about it here," Garth said. "Or I open the doors and let the TPs join our conversation."

Daisy looked the way Spencer felt—nervous about revealing their plan and bringing Garth Hadley up to speed. Marv just shrugged, as if they didn't have another alternative. Dez didn't appear to be paying attention to the conversation at all anymore.

"Start with the School Board," Garth Hadley said. "Did Leslie Sharmelle manage to take it from the Rebels?"

Spencer resisted the urge to blurt out that Leslie Sharmelle was dead, shattered into tiny fragments at the Auran landfill. That part of the story would come later. For now, he needed to pick up where Marv had left off— the moment before Spencer had pounded the nail into the School Board and turned himself into an Auran.

There was indeed a lot to say.

289

CHAPTER 42

"JUST FLIP THE SWITCH!"

By the time the story was finished, Marv, Spencer, and Daisy were seated on the lobby floor. Dez was doing aerial tricks around the spacious room, and Garth stood beside the weapons pile. Spencer didn't like the way the BEM rep eyed the leaf blower, now that Hadley was convinced of its potential to get them out of the Dustbin.

"How much time left?" Marv asked.

Spencer checked his watch for the hundredth time. "Almost there," he said. "Bookworm should have the Vortex in position within the next fifteen minutes."

Marv looked over his shoulder. "What about you, Hadley? You coming with us?"

Spencer couldn't believe the janitor was asking that question. All the while he'd been talking, Spencer had been trying to think of a way to ditch the BEM rep.

"Your plan will never succeed," Garth Hadley said. "Your enemy has a reputation for cruelty. I know Reginald McClean. You can be sure that your Rebel friends are already dead."

"Clean promised not to hurt them if I stayed away," Spencer said.

Garth chuckled. "And he knew you wouldn't stay away. He's playing you, Spencer."

The BEM rep closed his eyes and seemed to think about something else for a moment. It was unnerving, and Spencer tried to shake it by saying, "It doesn't matter," even though he could think of nothing that mattered more. "We're coming out of the Vortex inside the Port-a-Potty, and we're going down to the laboratory. If it's too late for my dad and the others, then we'll still have a shot at stealing Belzora and the nail."

Of course, Spencer hadn't told Marv and Garth about the *Manualis Custodem*. He had simply explained the Rebels' need to collect all three warlock hammers. Mr. Clean's tool was the last one. After that, Spencer really didn't know what to do. If Walter didn't make it, hopefully Min would finish his translation and give them some guidance.

Dez suddenly veered downward and landed beside Spencer. "Umm, are the ceiling vents supposed to hang open like that?" He pointed upward with one hooked finger.

Spencer and the others turned their gaze toward the ceiling, and what they saw was absolutely terrible.

The vents were dangling open, and toilet-paper

mummies were climbing silently through. Already TPs covered the lobby ceiling, clinging upside down like white spiders. At every breached point, dust billowed into Garth's fortress.

As soon as the TPs realized they had been spotted, they began dropping from the ceiling, rappelling on long strands of toilet paper from their hands.

"How did they get in?" Daisy screamed.

"The ventilation system failed," Marv answered, grabbing a pair of One-Plys and knocking them together. "Dust is pouring back into the building."

In the chaos, Spencer lost sight of the weapons pile. A One-Ply struck him, sending him skidding across the hard tile. His Glopified coveralls protected him from the fall, and Daisy helped Spencer to his feet. Marv and Dez stood just feet away. Spencer scanned the sea of toilet-paper figures, but one person was nowhere to be found.

"Garth!" Spencer shouted. "Where's Garth Hadley?"

Dez leapt into the air, his bloodshot eyes darting around the lobby. "Can't see him!" shouted Dez. "He's gone!"

Spencer felt his stomach sink with despair. If Garth Hadley had gone missing, Spencer had a bad feeling that he'd taken the leaf blower with him. He had to reach the weapons pile in the middle of the lobby!

Spencer charged forward, slamming past a One-Ply and dodging the hungry streamers of a shouting Two-Ply. He dropped to his knees, sliding across the smooth tile between a TP's legs. The weapons pile came into view and Spencer's heart calmed. The leaf blower was just where he'd left it.

Spencer snatched up his janitorial belt and flung it across his middle, cinching the buckle tightly. His push-broom shimmered into view and he sent a trio of One-Plys drifting weightlessly up to the lobby ceiling.

"Daisy!" Spencer shouted, sliding the girl's belt across the tile. She strapped it on and drew a dustpan shield.

Spencer checked his watch again. They were still a few minutes ahead of schedule, but using the leaf blower to blast a pathway out of the Dustbin might be their only chance of survival. Besides, Garth had run off, and they could make a quick escape without him.

Spencer hefted the leaf blower in both hands, calling for his friends to give him some cover while he fired up the device. Marv was wielding a borrowed pushbroom, and Daisy used a mop. Even Dez rallied around Spencer, using his talons to shred the TPs.

Spencer stared at the leaf blower in his hands, realizing for the first time that he had no idea how to turn the thing on.

"It's cordless electric!" Marv shouted. "Just flip the switch!"

Spencer suddenly noticed the orange on/off switch by his thumb, feeling a little embarrassed that he hadn't seen it sooner.

"All right," Spencer shouted. He swung the leaf blower, angling the nose upward so it would blast a stream into the sky. "Here it goes!"

Spencer slid the switch into the *on* position and waited for the stream of air to roar out, ripping them a way out of the Dustbin. Instead, the leaf blower began to shudder and buck. It was malfunctioning. That much was obvious.

Spencer was struggling to hold on to the leaf blower when, all at once, it disintegrated in his grasp. It happened so suddenly that Spencer didn't even have time to call out in surprise. One moment, he was holding the blower, and the next moment it was gone.

Their only way home had just vanished into a cloud of useless particles.

CHAPTER 43

"HE DESERVES TO DIE."

Spencer swiped his hand through the little cloud of grit that had once been the Glopified leaf blower.

"What did you do?" Dez yelled.

"It just . . ." Spencer didn't know what to say. "The leaf blower just turned to dust!"

Marv grunted. "That wasn't the leaf blower."

"What do you mean?" Daisy asked. They were retreating across the lobby, fighting waves of materializing TPs.

"Stuff from the real world doesn't turn to dust like that," Marv explained. "Hadley must have made a duplicate leaf blower and switched them out when the TPs attacked."

Spencer felt awful. Once again, Garth Hadley had tricked him. Spencer should have predicted something like this. It was the same tactic Garth had used back in September when he was trying to steal the School Board.

He'd swapped Spencer's desk for a fake one, leading the Rebels to protect a useless piece of wood.

"So Garth has the real leaf blower?" Daisy said.

"Yep." Marv seemed sure of it. "And you can bet he's going to use it without us."

"We've got to stop him!" Spencer said.

Marv was staring up at the ceiling. "I don't think the ventilation system failed by accident," he said.

"Are you saying that Garth *let* the mummies inside?" Daisy asked.

"A distraction," Marv said, "so he could steal the leaf blower. Probably making his way to the upper floors where the vents are still working."

Spencer looked across the lobby to the stairs where Garth had greeted them, but the staircase was gone. Somehow, during the TP attack, Garth had unimagined the stairs, replacing the way up with a sheer wall.

"Brooms!" Spencer said, handing his spare to Marv. Daisy threw a Palm Blast of vacuum dust, pinning the closest One-Ply, and the Rebels pushed across the lobby.

Dez was already flying up to the second floor, Spencer, Daisy, and Marv close behind. Below, the TPs scrambled over one another, trying to scale the vertical wall. Two-Plys were shouting commands in an effort to organize the half-witted One-Plys. The wall bought the Rebels some time to find Garth, but the TPs would be onto the second floor in no time.

The second story of Garth's fortress was very different

from the lobby. Here, an unattractive blue carpet covered the floor, and office cubicles filled the area.

Spencer led the way down one of the aisles, noticing that the small cubicles were empty. There must have been a hundred of them, creating the ideal place for Garth Hadley to hide while operating the leaf blower.

Spencer turned a corner, looked down a long aisle, and spotted the BEM rep standing in one of the farthest cubicles. Garth Hadley saw the approaching Rebels at the same moment. He responded by angling the leaf blower upward and flipping the switch.

The sound that rumbled from the depths of the Glopified leaf blower was astounding. It shot a visible streamer of wind with so much force that the cubicle walls around Garth Hadley exploded. The leaf blower kicked out of Garth's hands, punching through carpet and embedding itself upright in the floor.

The air stream blasted a hole clean through the ceiling and continued upward, demolishing each floor it passed through until it smashed out the roof of Garth's fortress.

The BEM rep rose to his feet. In the splintering destruction, Spencer hadn't even noticed that Garth had been knocked aside. His shirt was whipping wildly as he stared up at the slipstream air current.

Spencer set off at a run, but he knew he wouldn't be fast enough. A dark blur passed over his head. Sweeper Dez slammed into Garth Hadley, knocking him away from the escape stream.

In the next moment, Spencer was there, pinning Garth

with a Funnel Throw of vac dust. On top of that, Daisy's mop strings licked out, entangling the BEM rep and leaving him helpless on the floor.

Marv stood at the edge of the slipstream, his long hair caught in an updraft. Spencer understood the look on the big man's face: a mixture of gratitude and disbelief that a way home had finally opened.

"What now?" Daisy yelled over the windy torrent.

Olin hadn't explained it in his note, but the ride home seemed fairly obvious. "I think we jump into the wind and ride it up to the Rip," Spencer said.

Marv and the three kids stood in a circle around the slipstream. It was much wider than the narrow nozzle of the leaf blower. Wide enough that even Marv would fit easily in the vertical wind tunnel.

Spencer was about to step forward when a choked cry came from behind.

"Wait!" It was Garth Hadley, struggling against the Glopified mop strings around his arms. "You can't leave me here!"

Spencer couldn't believe that Garth was begging. After all the tricks and deception, after attempting to use the leaf blower without them . . . now he was pleading for the Rebels to take him home.

"I'll be your prisoner," he begged. "I'll do anything you ask."

Daisy's dad had once described people like Garth Hadley. Hadley was a chameleon, always changing his story and adding lies, like a lizard changed colors. Garth would say anything to anyone as long as he got his way.

Garth's head suddenly turned, and Spencer followed his gaze across the floor. The TPs had reached the second floor. They were moving toward the group, ripping apart cubicle walls with their toilet-paper hands.

"You don't know what they'll do to me!" Garth continued. "Please! Show me some mercy!"

Marv stepped over to him, fist clenched. "How much mercy did you show your own workers? Didn't she beg before you turned her over to the TPs?" Marv spat on the floor. "What goes around, comes around. Isn't that what they say?"

But Marv's words suddenly wrought the opposite effect in Daisy. She stepped over to Spencer, her large eyes full of sincerity. "We have to take him," she said.

"What?" Spencer said. "He deserves to die."

"If we leave him here, then we're no better than he is," Daisy continued. "If we're really the good guys, shouldn't we be good?"

Spencer had been in enough situations with Daisy to know when she was right. As much as he hated it, this was one of those moments. And he had to act fast with the TPs closing in.

Spencer took a knee in front of Garth Hadley. "All right," he said. "We'll take you home."

Dez moaned. "You've got to be kidding me. . . ."

"But you go as our prisoner." Spencer reached into his janitorial belt and withdrew a roll of Glopified duct tape to bind Garth Hadley's hands and cover his mouth. Daisy uncoiled the mop strings, and Marv hoisted Hadley to his feet, holding the BEM rep in an iron grip.

Spencer ripped off the first length of duct tape. As he reached out to bind the man's wrists, he noticed that something was wrong.

Garth Hadley was smiling.

"I think you're missing something from your belt pouch, Spencer," Garth said, freely offering his wrists. Spencer looked down.

Garth Hadley was wearing Spencer's latex glove! He must have taken it when he had swapped the fake leaf blower.

Spencer shouted a warning, but Garth was already on the move. He slipped out of Marv's grasp without any difficulty and leapt past Daisy and Dez. A victorious laugh escaped his lips as he jumped into the leaf blower's airstream.

Spencer and the others watched in stunned horror as he rose, arms outstretched in the current and a smug grin on his face. But as he neared the ceiling of the second floor, his hand reached out a bit too far, dangling momentarily outside the slipstream.

In that moment, a Two-Ply leapt from the top of a cubicle wall, flinging dual ribbons of toilet paper. The attack caught Garth Hadley's exposed hand, finding solid grip now that the TPs had adapted to overcome the Glopified latex glove.

Garth was jerked from the slipstream, crying out in surprise as the Two-Ply reeled him in. The TP hit the floor, wrapping toilet paper around Garth Hadley's body like a spider would wrap a fly. He managed to scream once, and then the toilet paper covered his face and head.

All was silent for a moment as the Two-Ply hunched over its bundled prey. Then the mummy reared back, tearing away the bindings and dropping Garth Hadley to the floor.

Daisy screamed at the sight of the BEM rep, and Spencer shut his eyes. Even Dez looked horrified by the sudden turn of events.

Garth Hadley was not the man he'd been a moment ago. All that remained of him was a lifeless skeleton.

A pile of dusty bones.

CHAPTER 44

"WHERE ARE THE REBELS?"

Spencer was too shocked to move. He stood rooted in place, unaware that the oncoming TPs were about to do to him what they'd just done to Garth Hadley. All around them, the office building began to deteriorate, unable to hold its form after the death of its creator.

Rough hands caught Spencer by the shoulders, shaking him back to reality. "Keep your arms and legs tucked close," Marv said. Then the janitor tossed him directly into the leaf-blower slipstream.

Spencer felt a strong upward pull that tempted him to throw out his arms to stabilize himself. But he remembered Marv's warning, and the memory of Garth's demise was fresh.

Spencer kept his arms at his sides and shot upward like Superman. He passed through the crumbling ceiling of the second floor, gathering speed as he rose. Garth's building was coming down, the upper floors already dissolved back into the dust from which they were made.

Carefully, Spencer craned his neck downward to find Daisy and Dez rising beneath him. Marv had also entered the slipstream, struggling to keep his broad shoulders inside the air current.

In seconds, they were clear of the crumbling building. The slipstream paved a clean pathway upward, throwing aside dust particles and giving the Rebels safe passage. Spencer saw a number of TPs materialize in the hazy air, only to plummet to the ground when they failed to reach into the air current.

Higher and higher they rose, until the dust of the air and the dust of the ground became indistinguishable. In every direction, it was nothing but a wash of gray.

As Spencer looked across the never-ending expanse of the Dustbin, he saw something in the distance. At first it seemed like nothing more than a smudge of black in the haze. But as the slipstream lifted him higher, his aerial view brought some clarity.

It was a building, or rather a series of buildings, black with age and soot. Spencer knew at once what it must be.

The fortress of the Instigators.

Spencer squinted through the wind and grit. There was a peculiar light rising from the center of the evil fortress, like a beacon of multicolored energy. The column twisted upward as high as Spencer could see.

The beam of magic seemed to exude a wicked aura, and

Spencer shivered to think that he would have been taken to that fortress if the TPs had succeeded in capturing him. Sach, Olin, and Aryl hadn't been so lucky when they had fallen into the Dustbin so many years ago. The Founding Witches had rescued the Dark Auran boys, but not before the Instigators had performed experiments upon them. Spencer shook his head, trying to rid himself of the dark thoughts.

At last, the Rip came into view, only yards ahead. It was a dark hole at the end of the slipstream. The jagged border of their exit glowed a deep and magical purple.

Spencer took a deep breath as the rushing wind seemed to grow louder.

He tensed his muscles, bracing himself to pass through. If Bookworm had succeeded, then they were all about to find themselves back inside the Port-a-Potty.

Everything went dark for a second, accompanied by absolute silence. Then Spencer found himself lying facedown on a hard floor. He scrambled to his knees, blinking hard for his eyes to adjust to the darkness.

He was not in the Port-a-Potty; that much was sure. Spencer fought a wave of despair at finding himself in an unknown environment. He rose to his feet, running his hands along the wall until he found a light switch. As a fluorescent bulb flickered to life, Spencer realized that he was in some sort of janitorial supply closet. The small room was packed with Glopified weaponry hanging from hooks and shoved onto cluttered shelves.

Spencer was looking for the Vortex when Daisy

suddenly appeared out of a shelf by his knee. He scrambled backward as his friend dropped to the floor.

"This isn't the Port-a-Potty," she said, squinting against the artificial light. "Where are we?"

"I don't know," Spencer whispered. He bent down and found the Vortex on the shelf where Daisy had appeared. The vacuum bag looked normal, except for one small hole in the center of the paper material. Spencer held his hand above the hole, feeling a strong wind leaking out.

Suddenly, Dez's head emerged out of the hole in the Vortex. Spencer jerked his hand away, watching the boy squeeze through a tear no bigger than the diameter of a pencil.

Dez flopped awkwardly onto the floor. His big wings stretched out, scattering the contents of a nearby shelf to the floor.

"Quiet!" Spencer hissed. Stealth was more important than ever since none of them had a clue where they were.

Of course, Dez's clumsy arrival instantly drew unwanted attention. Spencer froze as the three kids heard the unmistakable sound of a key being inserted into a lock.

Spencer's gaze turned to the closet door. The knob turned and the hinges squeaked. Spencer reached back to the shelf and grabbed the Vortex just as a Filth Sweeper entered the janitorial closet.

The look of surprise on the Sweeper's face lasted only for a split second before it changed to aggression.

"Who are you?" the Sweeper asked. "How'd you get in here?" His breath was making Spencer dizzy with sudden

305

fatigue. Daisy saw the effect and reached for the air freshener on her belt.

"Nobody moves!" the Sweeper demanded. His rodent eyes studied Spencer. "Give me that vac bag."

Spencer was so tired, he gave in without an argument. He tossed the Vortex forward, and the Sweeper caught it carefully in his clawed hands. At the same moment, Marv's shaggy head appeared through the hole in the bag. The Sweeper let out a cry of dismay and tried to drop the Vortex. But Marv's strong arms had already come through, and he grabbed the Sweeper in a viselike choke hold.

The Vortex fell to the floor as Marv's entire body finally worked free of his prison. The Sweeper, even with his Filth enhancements, was still no match for Marv's strength.

Daisy released a blast of vanilla air freshener to counteract the Filth breath for Spencer's sake. Then she stepped around the wrestling pair and quietly closed the closet door.

The Sweeper was gasping for breath, his entire body shuddering. In a final move of desperation, he launched the quills from his back. The kids took cover as the arrowlike projectiles pinged off the walls of the closet. Marv grunted but held on, forcing the Sweeper to his knees.

"Tell me where we are," Marv demanded. He let up on the Sweeper's neck just enough for the man to gasp out an answer.

"BEM . . ." he tried. "BEM laboratory . . ."

"We're already inside!" Spencer said. For once, part of the plan had gone *better* than expected.

"How'd we get here?" Daisy asked, glancing around the supply closet.

"Found . . . the vac bag . . ." the Sweeper said. "In the Port-a-Pot . . . thought it was BEM . . . brought it here."

Marv looked at the kids as though putting a Sweeper in a choke hold was just another day at work. "Anything else you want to ask this guy?"

Spencer stepped over to their prisoner. "Where are the Rebels?"

The Sweeper forced a painful smile. Then, instead of answering, he spat on the floor in defiance.

Spencer quickly drew a bottle of green spray from his belt and misted the Sweeper in the face. The little bit of consciousness he still had faded instantly, and Marv dropped him to the ground.

The Rebel janitor grunted again as he stepped away from the still body. His hand went to his side, and he drew in a pained breath.

"You're hurt!" Daisy said.

Two of the Sweeper's quills had pierced Marv in the side, staining his shirt crimson. "I'll be fine," Marv said through gritted teeth.

Daisy drew her orange healing spray and stepped over to him. "This might sting a little." She pulled the quills out of the janitor's side and quickly sprayed over the wounded area.

"Now, that's a handy spray," Marv said, as the injury began to heal.

"One of Walter's best," Daisy said.

"Where is the old boss?" Marv asked.

"He's here somewhere," Spencer said. "And I think I know how to find him."

Marv and Dez worked on tying up the unconscious Sweeper while Spencer and Daisy searched the closet for any piece of bronze. Spencer was about to give up when Daisy found a box full of old hardware. Spencer rooted around until he found a small cupboard handle. He knew it was bronze as soon as he touched it.

The janitor's closet faded to white, and Spencer focused on thoughts of Walter Jamison. When the vision cleared, Spencer was looking through the old warlock's eyes, with an immediate fix on his location.

Walter was in a bare room, one floor down, third door from the end of the hallway. Penny and Bernard were there too. They looked worn and afraid, with not a word exchanged between them.

Spencer was instantly relieved that they were alive. But at the same time, the scene brought an overload of worry.

Where was his dad?

Spencer watched through Walter's eyes long enough to be sure that his dad was not in the room. He tried not to let panic take over. He refused to assume the worst. The BEM lab had six floors. Just because Alan wasn't being held with the other Rebels didn't mean he was . . .

Spencer decided to switch perspectives. With Director Garcia dead, there was only one other warlock to spy on. And it was just as important to know Mr. Clean's location as it was to know Walter's.

His vision cleared, and Spencer was surprised to recognize the room. The Sweeper warlock was on the bottommost floor, in the room with the round sea window and the bronze nail.

A Rubbish Sweeper woman stood before Mr. Clean, fidgeting, as everyone seemed to do in his presence.

"That is no concern of yours," Mr. Clean said. Spencer hated coming into the middle of these conversations and trying to piece together the meaning. "I will kill him when the time is right. For now, I want Zumbro alive. Have you separated him from the others?"

"Yes, sir," the woman said. "Just as you asked."

"Excellent." The warlock's deep voice rumbled out. "Keep him under guard. Now that he's out of the way, it's time to pay a visit to Jamison."

CHAPTER 45

"I'M NOT WEARING THIS."

Spencer released the bronze hardware and found himself back inside the janitor supply closet. It took him a moment to realize that Daisy, Dez, and Marv were staring at him, awaiting a report. He slipped the bronze handle into his pocket.

"Good news," Spencer said. "My dad is alive. Bad news—I don't know where he is." He shrugged. "Good news—I *do* know where Walter and the others are. Bad news—Mr. Clean's on his way to see them right now."

Spencer thought back on the conversation. Why was it so important to separate his dad? It was only after this was done that Mr. Clean was willing to see the other Rebels. Something didn't make sense. Spencer felt like he was missing part of the story.

"So what are we going to do?" Daisy asked.

"We're going to get there before Clean does," Spencer said. He reached onto one of the shelves and withdrew two extra spray bottles with green solution. Handing them to Dez and Marv, he said, "We have to move quickly and silently. All we have is the element of surprise. Once we're discovered, we'll be too outnumbered."

They took a minute to gear up, scavenging through the supply closet. Spencer and Daisy replenished their belts, while Dez pocketed some razorblades. Spencer yawned, surprised that he felt tired at such a moment as this. Then he remembered the Sweeper in the closet. Even though the man was unconscious, he was still breathing, and the effects were clouding Spencer's focus.

He let out a spritz of air freshener and shook his head. It was going to be tough with so many Sweepers in the BEM lab. Rattling his air freshener, he realized that his aerosol can was nearly empty. Mr. Clean wouldn't stock a product that was meant only to benefit the kids. But the BEM warlock did have something else that might be useful.

Spencer dug in his belt until he found the white dust mask. He hadn't thought much about it since the last time he was at the lab. He'd taken it from the elevator when Mr. Clean had paralyzed the others with the chalkboard eraser bomb.

Spencer quickly sorted through the shelves until he found a few more masks. He handed one to Daisy and another to Dez.

"We should probably put these on," he said. "This place is crawling with Sweepers, and we can't afford to get distracted. Mr. Clean said these masks will provide pure oxygen. Last time I wore one, it blocked the Toxite breath."

Spencer stretched the small elastic and pulled the mask over his head. When Daisy did the same, Dez burst out laughing.

"You guys look like dorks," Dez said. "I'm not wearing this." He handed the dust mask back to Spencer. "Besides, I'm not affected by Toxite breath. The Rubbish used to get me sometimes, but now I am one."

Spencer rolled his eyes. Dez's invincibility complex was going to get him in trouble. He slipped the extra mask into his belt and turned to Marv, who had just found a janitorial belt of his own. The buckle wouldn't quite reach around the big man's stomach, so Marv tore off a small strip of duct tape and bridged the gap, giving a satisfied grunt when all was in place.

As an afterthought, Marv stooped down and picked up the Vortex. Spencer wondered if it still had power after the Rip. The hairy janitor held the vacuum bag in silence. Spencer didn't know what Marv was thinking, but the big man seemed deep in thought.

Spencer saw Marv shrug away his thoughts, and the janitor tossed the Vortex into the corner of the closet. "Leave it for the BEM," he said. "I never want to see that thing again."

They slipped into the hallway, scanning both directions but seeing no one. Spencer had to lead, since he was the only one who knew where the Rebels were being held. The bronze vision hadn't shown him which route to take, but Spencer knew they were headed in the right direction.

As they rounded a corner, Spencer found himself face-to-face with a surprised Grime Sweeper. Before the enemy could move, an emerald mist sprayed into his face and he collapsed with a gap in his memory.

Marv peeked into a nearby room and, finding it empty, dragged the unconscious Sweeper inside. There wasn't time to tie him up, which meant their entire rescue operation needed to be done in about fifteen minutes.

They found the elevator rather quickly, but Spencer didn't want to use it. They'd been trapped in there before, and he didn't want to repeat the mistake now. Besides, Mr. Clean would probably be using the elevator to get from the sixth floor up to the second. Stairs were a better option.

Daisy spotted the stairwell at the end of the hallway. They moved as quickly as they could manage without making a sound. Just as they reached the stairwell door, voices drifted up to them.

They recoiled from the doorway, Marv pressing the three kids against the wall and trying to flatten himself beside them. The door swung open, and three Sweepers stepped into the hallway. They moved straight away, never bothering to check over their shoulders. If they had done so, they would have seen four Rebels quietly slipping through the open door and down the stairs.

They emerged onto the second floor, entering the hallway behind an unsuspecting Filth Sweeper. Dez gestured that he would handle it. Silently opening his wings, the boy jumped forward, gliding the distance to the Sweeper without a footfall. The guard collapsed in a cloud of green spray, and Marv dragged him back, depositing the body in the stairwell.

Spencer pointed straight ahead down the hallway. "Third door from the end," he said.

A short distance to the right, the elevator chimed in an unwanted announcement that Mr. Clean had arrived. The Rebels dropped into a dead sprint, caring less about stealth and more about reaching the room before Mr. Clean spotted them.

There were two Sweeper guards outside the door, and the Rebels engaged them before they could call for backup. Daisy conquered one with a shot of vac dust and a mist of green spray. Marv took down the other, thrusting a plunger against the Sweeper's chest with bone-breaking force. His Glopified half vanished, leaving him unconscious, blind, and plainly human.

One of the Sweepers wore a key on a lanyard around his neck. Spencer ripped it off, inserted the key into the lock, and pushed open the door. Marv and Dez flung the unconscious Sweepers into the room. The three kids ducked inside, followed closely by the big janitor, who swiftly shut the door behind him.

Stunned silence greeted the rescue party as Walter, Penny, and Bernard rose to their feet. They stared at Marv, and Spencer could see the absolute disbelief on their faces.

"Marv Bills," Walter finally muttered, a genuine smile spreading across his weary face. "I don't believe my eyes."

Marv gave a curt nod and grunted, suddenly uncomfortable with all the attention. "Better make a plan," he said, getting back to the comfort of business. "Mr. Clean's right outside the door."

"I have a way out," Spencer said. He pulled the dust mask off his face, and Daisy did the same. "I've got a squeegee," Spencer said, patting the handle on his belt. "Bookworm's got the other one in Welcher."

"So the Thingamajunk is feeling better?" Bernard asked.

Daisy nodded. "We gave him a trashfusion of new garbage, just like you said."

"But we've got to find my dad," Spencer said. "How long ago did they take him away?"

"Probably an hour or two," Penny said. "But we don't know where they took him."

Walter held out a hand for silence as Mr. Clean's voice sounded in the hallway outside.

"Head down to staffing and find out who is scheduled for guard duty here," the warlock said. "I'll have them punished for this negligence."

Walter whispered to the other Rebels, "We have to stop him from opening that door."

The knob rattled as Mr. Clean used his master key. It was unnecessary, since the door was unlocked, but it gave the Rebels just enough time to come up with a plan.

Spencer peeled off a long strip of Glopified duct tape and pasted it along the edge of the door, securing it closed. No sooner had he stuck it down than Mr. Clean twisted the knob and attempted to push the door open.

Daisy ripped off another strip of tape, fortifying the other side of the door as Mr. Clean threw his weight against it. Marv triple-secured the entrance, running a third piece along the bottom threshold.

"The Rebels have blocked the door!" Mr. Clean shouted, a thread of anger in his voice. "Fetch me a bottle of Windex." He pounded against the door twice more, but the tape was impenetrable.

"I'm beginning to question your rescue operation," Bernard said. "It would appear that we are now all trapped in the same room."

"Not all of us," Spencer said, his thoughts turning to his dad.

Mr. Clean was speaking again, but his voice was too low to understand the words. Even when Spencer pressed his ear to the door, he could hear only the rumble of the man's voice.

Mr. Clean didn't deserve to have a private conversation, not with Spencer standing nearby. He reached into his pocket and felt the bronze hardware that he'd taken from the supply closet. Channeling his energy, Spencer found himself looking through Mr. Clean's eyes, hearing every word the warlock said.

The same woman Sweeper Spencer had seen earlier was standing before Mr. Clean, her Rubbish wings folded back. The warlock stared down at her, his voice soft.

"The time has come sooner than expected," Mr. Clean said. "Where did you lock Zumbro?"

"He's down on the fourth floor, sir," said the woman. "No chance of escape."

"I want you down there," Mr. Clean said. "The moment I radio the order, kill him."

"You don't want to speak with him first?" she asked.

"That's the last thing I want," he muttered. "Go."

The Rubbish Sweeper moved down the hallway, and Spencer brought the vision to a quick close.

"Good news," Spencer said. "I know where they're keeping my dad. He's somewhere down on the fourth floor."

"What's the bad news?" Daisy asked.

"They're going to kill him."

Penny stepped forward. "You guys should get down there and get Alan out."

Bernard shot her a surprised sideways glance. "And what are you going to do?"

"We've got to remember what we came here for," Penny said, her voice soft. "Mr. Clean is right outside that door, and he doesn't have a lot of backup. If we strike before he's ready, we have a good chance of taking Belzora."

"And a good chance of dying," Bernard added. Then he shrugged. "Fine. I guess I'll stay here and take on the war-lock with you."

"I'm staying too," Spencer announced. "After we steal Belzora, I can use bronze to find Walter so we can meet up with the rest of you and get back to Welcher together."

"Alan's being held on the fourth floor?" Walter veri-fied, dropping to a knee in the center of the room. He asked Marv for a bottle of Windex and misted a spot on the floor.

317

In a moment, the Rebels were looking through the transparent floorboards and into an empty room on the third floor below them.

Marv clamped a broad hand on Walter's shoulder, a grin parting his beard. "Here we go, boss. Like old times."

Walter nodded, though he looked far less enthusiastic about the plan. "Daisy, Dezmond," he said. "Stay close. We won't get out of this without a fight."

Dez cracked his knuckles. "I love fighting."

Then Marv smashed his big foot down, sending shards of glass falling into the room below.

CHAPTER 46

"WE NEED MORE WEAPONS!"

Spencer, Penny, and Bernard waited until the others had moved out of sight down below. Then the garbologist straightened his duct-tape tie.

"All right," Bernard said. "Three of us, sharing one janitorial belt, against the most powerful warlock in BEM history. I hope someone has a plan."

"We need to attack from an angle he won't suspect," Penny said.

Bernard glanced down the hole in the floor. "What if we strike from below?"

"What do you mean?" Penny asked.

"We spray the floor under Mr. Clean's feet," Bernard explained. "He falls through, separated from his backup Sweepers, giving us time to swipe the hammer."

Penny shook her head. "We could never be that

precise," she said. "There's no way we can tell exactly where he's standing up there."

"Actually," Spencer said, "there is."

They didn't have long to act on the plan. As soon as re-inforcements came with Windex, Mr. Clean would discover that the Rebels had escaped through the floor.

Using the brooms from Spencer's belt, the three Rebels dropped through the opening. On this lower floor, the door to the hallway was already ajar from Walter and the others. They peered into the hall and, finding all quiet, moved out.

Each had a very specific job in order for the plan to succeed. Bernard held a broom and a bottle of Windex. Penny had a mop and a pinch of vac dust. They nodded to Spencer, and he thrust his hand into his pocket, gripping the bronze hardware.

Mr. Clean was pacing the floor above them. Three Sweepers lurked against the wall, trying to remain unnoticed while the warlock was in his obvious rage. Back and forth he stepped, glancing from time to time at the door where he believed the Rebels were still locked away.

Spencer felt his heart rate quicken. This wasn't going to work unless Mr. Clean stood still. Little did the warlock know that his angry pacing was currently his best protection.

Through Clean's ears, Spencer heard footsteps. At last, the warlock stopped, turning to face the reinforcements— four Sweepers laden with Glopified supplies.

"You've kept me waiting," Mr. Clean said. "Use the Windex to . . ."

There was no time to listen to another word. Spencer severed his link with the bronze, pulling his hand from his pocket and pointing directly to the spot on the ceiling where Mr. Clean stood above them.

Bernard tapped the broom bristles and drifted upward. He aimed the spray bottle and looked to Spencer for affirmation.

"A little farther to the right," Spencer whispered, hoping that the warlock hadn't moved in the brief second since the vision had ended.

Bernard adjusted his aim and misted the floor. As the blue glow shimmered away, a pair of feet became visible, standing perfectly centered over the glass spot.

Penny flicked her mop at full force. The strings stretched upward, cracking into the glass and smashing it to bits. Mr. Clean fell, a surprised gasp leaving his lips. But the warlock Sweeper's instincts were too quick.

His Grime-like hands stretched out, and he caught himself on the edge of the shattered floor. With swiftness and ease, he began to hoist himself back up, but Penny's Funnel Throw of vacuum dust caught his legs, drawing him in a downward suction.

Mr. Clean's sticky fingers slipped, and he dropped heavily into the hallway as Bernard touched down on his broom. Penny leapt onto the warlock, easily forcing back his arms as the vacuum suction still strained against him.

Spencer bent down and pulled open Clean's white lab coat. He felt the weight in one of the pockets and instantly knew that Belzora was within reach.

Another Grime Sweeper dropped through the hole above. Bernard recovered Penny's mop and lassoed him mid-fall, slamming him against the wall.

Spencer reached into Mr. Clean's pocket and felt the smooth, cold bronze of the hammer in his grasp. Immediately, a rush of white pinpricks clawed into his eyesight, forcing him into a vision. He jerked his hand backward, and there was a loud *clang* as Belzora slipped from his grasp and clattered across the hard floor.

Spencer's eyesight returned in time to see Mr. Clean forcing Penny back as he struggled into an upright position. Bernard retreated, waving his mop at an incoming Rubbish Sweeper.

Spencer crawled across the floor to the spot where he'd dropped the hammer. He needed a way to pick it up without his skin touching the bronze. He slipped on a latex glove that he'd taken from the supply closet. It would stop the visions and would also help him escape.

Spencer scooped up the hammer and dropped it into his largest belt pouch. Bernard was racing toward him, but Penny was still struggling in Mr. Clean's grasp. Spencer unclipped a pushbroom and took aim. Hurling it like a spear, he saw the bristles smash into Mr. Clean and send him spinning down the hall.

The three Rebels made their escape, sprinting toward the stairwell ahead. The sound of pursuit was thick behind them, but they had a good head start. Spencer hoped it would be enough.

Down the stairs they went, leaping three at a time.

"Where's Walter?" Penny asked, throwing her last pinch of vacuum dust over her shoulder at a Rubbish Sweeper who had flown too close.

Spencer knew he couldn't maintain a vision while at a full sprint. He took the briefest of seconds to lean against the wall, maneuvering his non-gloved hand into his pocket.

The first thing Spencer saw through Walter's eyes was his dad. Instant relief flooded through him. The Rebels had rescued him! Alan Zumbro had slipped away from death's doorstep once more.

A Filth Sweeper leapt into view. Then, in Walter's peripheral vision, Spencer saw Marv throw the enemy back and topple a filing cabinet onto a pile of debris.

Strong, slimy fingers clamped onto Spencer's arm, abruptly ending his vision. He twisted away, the latex glove allowing him an easy escape. Bernard knocked the Grime Sweeper aside with the mop, and they were running again.

"This way!" Spencer said, shoving open the door to the fourth floor and exiting the stairwell. It was suddenly obvious where the other Rebels were. There was chaos ahead, with the unmistakable sounds of battle.

Spencer, Penny, and Bernard plowed into the attacking Sweepers from behind, forcing their way into a large laboratory room. In a moment, the two Rebel groups had reunited.

Walter and the others had created a barricade in one corner of the lab. Filing cabinets, desks, and overturned tables and chairs formed a decently defensible location.

Alan rustled Spencer's white hair as he ducked behind the barricade. "Glad you could join us," he said. The situation looked grim. The Sweepers were swarming, and it wouldn't be long before the barricade crumbled under their onslaught.

Spencer cast his eyes along the barricade, making sure all the Rebels were safe. Dez was hunched at the far end, Daisy standing beside him. Spencer quickly made his way over to them.

"You guys all right?" he asked.

Daisy's hands were on her hips, and she stared down at Dez with a disapproving expression. She seemed relieved to see Spencer. "Good," Daisy said. "Maybe you can talk him into helping. He wouldn't lift a finger to build the barricade."

Dez was on his knees, using both hands to try to pry open a mini fridge that formed part of the blockade. "I don't like working on an empty stomach," he said.

"Where did you get that?" Spencer pointed to the small refrigerator.

Dez shrugged casually. "I dunno. I think Walter pulled it over when they were putting the barricade together. But he didn't even check it for snacks."

At last, the door to the mini fridge popped open. Dez rocked back on his heels, a pleased expression spreading across his Sweeper face. "Oh, yeah!" he shouted. "It's loaded!"

Spencer stepped forward and slammed the fridge door.

"Hey!" Dez protested. "There was a Mountain Dew in there!"

Daisy chimed in. "You shouldn't drink that. My dad says Mountain Dew makes kids hyper."

"Whatever," Dez grumbled, pulling open the mini fridge door again. "It doesn't do anything to me." He reached inside and withdrew a bottle of Mountain Dew.

"If you think you can drink it while you fight, then be my guest," Spencer said. "But have you noticed the color of that stuff?" He shrugged. "It's my personal rule never to drink anything that happens to be the exact same color as—"

"We need more weapons!" Penny shouted. Spencer whirled around to find Marv taking on a pair of Sweepers as they tried to breach the barricade. The rescued Rebels still didn't have weapons, and Spencer didn't know where the nearest janitorial closet would be. Even if he knew, they probably wouldn't be able to reach it without gear.

Then he had another idea. Spencer fumbled with a handle on his janitorial belt. If he could use the squeegee, they could step back into Welcher and arm themselves with gear from Walter's own closet. Then, with the proper supplies, they could make the final push to steal Belzora's nail.

Spencer crawled toward the back wall, his Windex already misting the cinderblock. When the transformation to glass was complete, he dragged the squeegee down the smooth surface, hoping that Bookworm had been diligent in keeping his end of the portal open.

"What are you doing?" Bernard asked. "We've still got to find the nail!"

"But we need weapons first," Spencer said. "This is just

temporary. We can open the portal again after we steal the nail."

The linkage was successful. As the portal's frame glowed an eerie green, the view into Welcher Elementary School was clear and open. Bookworm's dented lunchbox head ducked into view. When he saw Daisy hunkered behind the barricade, his textbook mouth curved in his classic grin, showing the pink retainer.

"Hi, Bookworm!" Daisy said. "You did a good job!"

He waggled his head as though happily embarrassed by her praise. Then he muttered something unintelligible and waved for the Rebels to step through the portal and join him in Welcher.

"We'll hold 'em!" Marv yelled, slamming a pushbroom into a Filth Sweeper. "Head in there and get geared up!"

Penny rolled through the portal, clearly anxious to strap on a belt and get back into the action. Walter, Alan, and Bernard moved swiftly after her.

Spencer grinned, holding the squeegee at his side. With all the Rebels armed, it would certainly even the fight.

Something shot over the barricade, slimy and wet. It was the tongue of a Grime Sweeper, and it coiled around the squeegee handle before Spencer knew what was happening. The squeegee ripped from his grasp, flinging back to the mouth of a Sweeper woman who was crouched atop the barricade. She caught the tool in her teeth.

Spencer drew his mop and aimed the strings directly at her, but the damage was already done. The squeegee fell from the Sweeper's mouth, the handle broken in half and the rubber scraper smoldering with Grime venom.

The mop attack went wide as the Sweeper woman bounded out of view. Spencer raced to the broken squeegee, but he couldn't pick it up because it was soaked in acid. He watched in disbelief as the rubber melted away, ruined forever.

He heard Walter's voice issuing an order from behind him. "All right," the old warlock said. "Let's smash this portal and find that nail!"

"Wait!" Spencer yelled, whirling around just in time to stop Penny from putting a razorblade through the portal's glass border. "That's our only way back," he explained. "They destroyed the squeegee."

It was silent for a moment, and everyone seemed to ponder and dismiss a number of alternatives.

"What about another squeegee?" Penny asked. "Leave one with Bookworm and we'll take the other in search of the nail."

Walter shook his head. "The squeegee formula was complicated," he said. "I didn't make very many."

"What are you saying?" Bernard asked.

"I'm saying that there aren't any more squeegees," Walter said. "Not until I can mix another batch of Glop formula."

"Maybe we can find a janitorial closet," Penny said. "Spencer might be able to use his Glopifying powers on a regular squeegee."

But Spencer shook his head. "I'm all out of power," he

said. It had been only a few hours since he had Glopified that leaf blower. It would be at least another day before his abilities recharged.

"That's it, then," Alan said. "We have to leave now." He pointed back at the magical doorway to Welcher. "Everyone through the portal before it closes!"

"What about the nail?" Spencer said. He was feeling responsible. He had chosen to open the portal now, and he had lost the squeegee to that Grime Sweeper.

Alan and Walter glanced at one another. They were the only two who knew exactly what was in the *Manualis Custodem*. The looks on their faces told Spencer that nothing was more important than getting Belzora and the nail.

"I know right where it is," Spencer said. "How long will the portal stay open?"

"About fifteen minutes," Walter said.

"That's enough time," said Spencer. "We can get there and back before it closes."

"Unless one of those Sweepers breaks the glass," Penny said. "Then we're all stuck here."

Spencer shut his eyes, trying to think through it all. "I'll go," he said. "The rest of you stay here and guard the portal until I get back."

"Absolutely not," Walter said. "If anything—"

But Alan cut him off. He put a hand on his son's shoulder. "We're wasting precious time," Alan said. "Spencer and I will get the nail; the rest of you protect the portal."

No one argued with Spencer's dad, though Walter's expression was far from approving. Spencer checked to make sure that Belzora was resting safely in his belt pouch. Then he followed his dad to the edge of the barricade and peered over a downed table.

The room was full of Sweepers. There were far too many to outmaneuver, even with the latex gloves that Alan and Spencer were wearing.

"We need some cover to get to the stairs," Alan muttered.

It was Dez who answered. "Wait a minute." He had a pinched look on his face, and one taloned hand gripped his large middle. His other hand held the bottle of Mountain Dew. Spencer was surprised to see that it was already empty. Dez must have really chugged the stuff. "I think I'm working something up."

"What are you talking about?" Spencer said. Then he heard Dez's stomach gurgle loudly. "Uh-oh."

Dez Rylie belched. The fizzy drink sent it rumbling up from his stomach, but this wasn't a normal burp. When the Sweeper kid opened his mouth, a puff of black dust came spewing out, like fire from a dragon.

"Whoa!" Dez said, clamping both hands over his mouth and sealing the blast.

"Could you get any more disgusting?" Spencer shouted.

"What was that?" Daisy asked.

Dez was grinning now. "Just another Sweeper superpower!"

"I told you not to drink that soda," Daisy said.

"Whatever!" He spread his wings, laughing. "I can burp dust!" Then he sprang into the air, landing just atop the barricade. His stomach rumbled and he let out the longest belch Spencer had ever heard.

Billowing black dust streamed out of his mouth, falling across the crowd of attacking BEM Sweepers. The enemy fell back, choking and blinded, while Dez laughed from his perch.

The attack, no matter how unconventional, was just what Spencer and his dad needed. In the chaos, they leapt over the barricade and sprinted toward the stairwell.

"You can thank me later!" Dez shouted. Then he seemed to gag, and he spat off the top of the barricade. "Ugh," Spencer heard the bully say. "Bad aftertaste."

CHAPTER 47

"YOU . . ."

Spencer and his dad actually reached the sixth floor much faster than anticipated. They came across only two Sweepers in the stairwell, one of which left a painful gash on Alan's arm. Spencer had paused long enough to mist the wound with orange spray. Then they were kicking open the door and sprinting down an empty hallway.

The bottommost floor of the BEM laboratory had been bustling with Sweepers yesterday, when Spencer had been caged and carried to his interview with Mr. Clean. Now the level was nearly vacant. It seemed that most of the fight had been drawn to the Rebels on the fourth floor.

They took down only two more Sweepers before Spencer and his dad came to the double doors at the end of the hall. Only a day had passed since Spencer had seen the bronze nail in the wall above the round window. Spencer hoped with all his might that it hadn't been moved since then.

Spencer shoved against the doors and was surprised to find them unlocked. The two Zumbros stepped into the room, and Spencer noted that everything was just as he remembered it. A simple desk in the center of the room, empty except for the intercom that Mr. Clean had used to communicate with them in the elevator.

On the far wall was that large sea window, taller than Spencer and perfectly round. He thought he saw a fish swim by, illuminated by an exterior deep-sea light.

And above the window, a twinkle of bronze glittered in the room's soft lamplight.

Alan quietly shut the doors as Spencer crossed toward the nail. "Hope this doesn't take long," Alan said. "That portal's only going to stay open for another ten minutes or so."

Back in September, Spencer had used Ninfa to pull out a bronze nail in Welcher. It had been a quick and rather effortless process. And Daisy hadn't had any trouble using Holga to draw the nail in New Forest Academy. Spencer hoped this would be the same.

Reaching into his belt pouch, Spencer used his gloved hand to withdraw Belzora. The hammer felt comfortable in his grip, but he could feel that it was much more powerful than its plain appearance would indicate.

As he stepped around Mr. Clean's desk, Spencer realized that he wouldn't quite be able to reach the nail above the sea window. He grabbed the desk chair as he passed, pulling it over to the wall and stepping up onto the seat.

Rising onto his tiptoes, Spencer stretched Belzora as high as he could until the blunt end of the hammer touched the small nail in the wall. A golden glow began to form between hammer and nail. Spencer felt the power surge down his arm as the magic began to extract the ancient nail.

The small piece of metal slipped from the wall and fell to the floor with a tinkle. In his excitement, Spencer leapt off the chair, scooped up the nail, and tucked it into his belt pouch.

"Got it!" Spencer said, turning to his dad. But Alan Zumbro was not wearing the same victorious expression as his son. He was standing in the center of the room, staring at the double doors, which had just flung open.

There must have been at least twenty Sweepers crowding in the hallway outside the door. Spencer couldn't count them, but he knew it was an impossible number to withstand. They were cornered. It was over.

Alan began to take a step back toward his son, but froze as the crowd of Sweepers parted. A familiar figure slipped into view, white lab coat draped across his broad frame.

It was Mr. Clean.

Spencer tensed himself against the enemy warlock, but Alan went rigid. Spencer could tell his dad was trying to say something, but his mouth just kept opening and closing in total dismay.

"You . . ." Alan finally mustered, as Mr. Clean came toward him. "You . . ."

"Surprised to see me, old friend?" Mr. Clean asked. "The years have not been kind to you."

"Dad?" Spencer interrupted. "What's going on? You . . . know him?"

"Know him?" Alan said. "This man was my partner." He swallowed hard. "This is Rod Grush."

CHAPTER 48

"I DON'T BELIEVE YOU WILL."

Spencer stood in stunned silence as Mr. Clean stepped closer to his dad. It made sense now. The reason Mr. Clean had sent Leslie Sharmelle to eliminate Alan instead of coming himself. The reason Mr. Clean had been so quick to use green spray when Alan seemed to recognize him on the night they met Professor DeFleur. The reason Clean had separated Alan from the rest of the Rebels. He didn't want his true identity to be known.

He was Rod Grush—the man who supposedly had sacrificed everything to solve the thirteen Auran clues with Alan.

"I don't understand," Alan said. "I thought you were dead."

"You thought what I wanted you to think," Mr. Clean

335

said. "From the moment we met till the moment our partnership ended."

Alan shook his head. "You didn't want me to find the thirteenth clue? You were behind the attack at the school? I thought they killed you!"

"I was behind everything," Mr. Clean said.

"But the warlocks hired us to solve the clues. . . ."

"*I* was the commanding warlock," said Mr. Clean. "I opened the Warlocks Box and used your expertise to help me solve the Auran clues."

"No," Alan said. "You wouldn't do that. You were my friend."

Mr. Clean's mouth curved in a belittling smile. "You were my puppet," he said. "There is no such thing as a friend in this corrupted world." Mr. Clean stepped swiftly forward and seized Alan by the wrist.

"Dad!" Spencer shouted. Why didn't he pull away from the Sweeper warlock? Alan was still wearing his latex glove.

"It's all right, Spence," his dad said. His voice was surprisingly calm, considering the hopeless circumstances. "He won't hurt me. This is Rod Grush." He said it as if he were still trying to convince himself. "He was my friend."

Mr. Clean reached into his white lab coat and withdrew a dirty rag. He held the corner and gently twirled it, letting gravity wind the rag into a deadly weapon. Spencer had seen the warlock use it before. He was going to kill Alan, just as he'd killed Director Garcia. He was going to kill him the Clean Way, and not a trace would be left of Alan Zumbro.

"Your faith in me is warming," Mr. Clean said, "though

poorly placed. I will do this and feel no regret. I will kill you, *friend*."

Alan squared his shoulders and looked the big man in the eyes. "I don't believe you will."

Standing across the room, Spencer did not share an ounce of his dad's hopeful belief in Mr. Clean's mercy. The man holding his dad was Mr. Clean. As far as Spencer was concerned, Rod Grush no longer existed.

The Sweeper warlock raised his deadly rag, and Spencer reacted without hesitation. He wielded Belzora like a war hammer, smashing the bronze tool into the circular deep-sea window as hard as he could. It struck the thick glass with a solid *smack*, instantly sending spiderweb cracks across the smooth surface.

Mr. Clean froze as the insurmountable pressure of the Atlantic depths pressed against the weakened window. Spencer stepped aside just as the water pressure became too great. The glass shattered, and a horizontal column of ocean water shot into the BEM lab with unbelievable force.

Spencer barely had time to draw a breath before the entire room was full of icy water. Swept off his feet, Spencer slammed into the wall, barely managing to hang onto the bronze hammer. The impact surely would have broken his bones if it weren't for the protection of his Glopified coveralls. The lamps in the office exploded, plunging the room into darkness, with shadowy figures thrashing in the deep.

It took Spencer a moment to orient himself. There was light coming from the hallway, though it too was completely underwater. He assumed that the entire sixth floor was already flooded. And it wouldn't take long for the water to rise.

Mr. Clean and the Sweepers were gone, knocked away by the violent rush of water. A few Sweepers bobbed unconscious, the Glop knocked out of them. But there was nothing Spencer could do about that. He had to find his dad and swim up to the fourth floor before the squeegee portal closed.

The rushing water whipped Spencer forward, tossing him into an eddy beside the doorway. He found his dad there, fighting to tread water and not get sucked into the current. Spencer assumed that the panicked look on his dad's face was mirrored in his own. Smashing the window had been a thoughtless reaction to save his dad from Mr. Clean's rag. The Sweeper warlock was nowhere in sight, swept away by the torrent.

But Spencer and his dad were hardly safe! Now they were treading water deep under the ocean's surface with nowhere to draw a breath. Spencer was a fairly good swimmer, but he knew there was no way he could make it to the portal when his lungs already felt like bursting!

They needed oxygen. They had to get a breath of air before their lungs burst! Spencer's hand plunged into his janitorial belt and closed around the dust mask. His chance of survival now rested on an item that Mr. Clean had given him when the chalkboard eraser had exploded in the elevator. But the Sweeper warlock had said that the mask would provide pure air under any circumstance.

Spencer pulled the thin elastic band over his head and

fit the mask snugly over his mouth and nose. Immediately, the water drained out of the mask and his lips felt dry. He parted them just slightly. Finding that no water filled his mouth, he took a gasping breath.

It worked! Spencer found it ironic that Mr. Clean had given him the very thing he needed to survive the destruction of the BEM laboratory.

Spencer dug in his belt for a second mask, the one Dez had handed him when he refused to wear it in the janitorial closet. In a flash, Alan had it on.

"We've got to hurry!" his dad said. Spencer could understand every word, though Alan's voice sounded distant and muffled through the mask and water. Bracing himself for the long swim, Spencer and his dad allowed themselves to get pulled through the doorway and out into the hall, whipped along by the rushing flood.

It was strange to see the building underwater. Spencer was surprised to find that some of the lights still worked. It seemed as though the secret lab had been built with the knowledge that a total flood was possible. And if that was the case, then Spencer assumed the Sweepers would have some way to safely escape.

The breakneck current pulled them helplessly down the hallway, the force making it impossible to swim against the rush.

"We'll never make it back!" Spencer yelled. They didn't have much time before the portal closed, and Spencer knew he wasn't a fast enough swimmer to make it against the current.

"Plunger!" his dad yelled. Spencer scrambled for the handles on his janitorial belt. His dad's tool was already out, and Alan slammed his toilet plunger against the wall, the rubber cup anchoring him in place.

Spencer's plunger snapped out of the U-clip, and he gripped the handle tightly. He tried twice to clamp onto the wall, but the fast water prevented a good suction. At last, the rubber end clamped tight to a wooden door.

Spencer's body trailed out behind him as he fought the current, struggling to keep a grip on the plunger handle. He could see his dad anchored a dozen yards ahead of him in the hallway. Before Spencer could wonder how to catch up, the wooden door cracked under the pressure of the water.

Spencer let out of cry of alarm as the door ripped open on its hinges, loosening the plunger's suction and sending the boy tumbling through the water once more, the contents of the room flooding out after him.

Spencer pushed against a broom that bumped into his side. A dustpan clanked painfully against the side of his head, and he realized that he must have opened a janitorial supply closet. It wasn't unlikely, since every other room at the BEM lab seemed to be full of Glopified gear.

In the flood of waterlogged cleaning supplies, Spencer suddenly found his fingers wrapping around a familiar object. It was a toilet brush, with a plastic handle and bristly white scrubbers on one end.

He had seen such an item only once before. The Aurans used toilet brushes to power their recycle-bin boats across the Glop lagoon. If this was anything like those, then a simple twist of the handle should set the brush twirling.

Spencer felt the brush activate in his hand. The bristles spun like the propeller of a motorboat, instantly pushing him back up the hallway.

Spencer grinned behind his dust mask. Tucking the toilet brush close to his body, he stretched out, streaming against the current with the ease of a fish.

He reached his dad in no time. Alan popped his plunger off the wall and accepted Spencer's outstretched hand. They idled in the hallway for a moment, Spencer twisting down on the throttle just enough to hold them against the current.

"We can swim up the elevator shaft," his dad said, gesturing across the hallway with his plunger. It would probably be a much faster and more direct route than winding up the stairwell, which was surely already full of water.

Spencer towed his dad across the hallway, and Alan clamped his plunger to the elevator door. It slid open about two feet, a few trapped air bubbles gurgling upward as the passageway opened. Spencer was about to squeeze into the elevator shaft when his dad shouted.

Spencer whirled around to find something swimming toward them at an alarming rate. It was a Grime Sweeper, moving through the water as though it had been born there. Spencer knew Grimes were amphibious, living comfortably on land or water. He'd hoped that characteristic hadn't been passed to the Sweepers, but the one coming toward them looked to be in no need of air.

"Is it Clean?" Alan asked.

Spencer squinted through the water. "Nope. Just a random Sweeper. Let's get out of here!" He opened the throttle on the toilet brush and squeezed through the opening. But his dad, whose shoulders were much broader than Spencer's, caught in the narrow doorway.

Before Spencer could tow him through, the Sweeper hit Alan, peeling him away from the elevator door and hurling him through the water.

Spencer angled himself back through the door, twisting the toilet-brush handle and speeding through the water as fast as he could. Alan had managed to clamp onto the wall again, anchored helplessly against the attacking Grime.

As Spencer torpedoed toward the enemy, his razorblade clicked out in his left hand. The blade's sharp edge sliced through the water, nicking into the Sweeper's shoulder.

A pale, yellow goo oozed from the wound. It hung suspended in the seawater around the Sweeper as he let out a bubbly cry of pain. He turned toward Spencer, bulging eyes full of malice.

Spencer leaned back, twisting the toilet brush into a full retreat. The Grime Sweeper leapt off the wall to dive for him but suddenly recoiled like a dog hitting the end of its leash.

"Into the elevator!" Alan shouted through his mask. He released his plunger's suction, and Spencer was there to pull his dad safely away from the Grime Sweeper.

"What about him?" Spencer asked. The Sweeper was

thrashing and swimming frantically but didn't appear to be going anywhere.

"Duct tape," Alan explained. Spencer looked back just long enough to see that his dad had pasted a strip of tape across the Sweeper's tail, pinning him to the wall. The enemy wouldn't be following them now. Not unless he cut off his own tail.

Spencer towed his dad, pressing through the narrow gap between the elevator doors and streaming straight up into the darkness of the flooded shaft. It was nearly pitch-black when Alan clamped his toilet plunger and hefted open the elevator door.

They swam through the fourth floor of the BEM lab, finding no sign of the enemy in the flood. Spencer maneuvered them through the flotsam, dodging debris as the toilet brush pulled them along faster than any human could swim.

The barricade came into view. Some of the material that had formed the Rebel shelter had drifted off, and Spencer was counting the seconds, unsure if they'd been fast enough. But as Spencer and his dad propelled around the overturned tables, they saw the portal, still intact. Its glowing border seemed to flicker, as though it might extinguish at any second.

There was a new current here, sucking water toward the opening into Welcher. Spencer let the toilet brush wind down, releasing his dad's hand and allowing himself to get dragged in by the current. Ducking his head and putting his arms straight forward, Spencer passed through the portal.

Once on the other side, he twisted the toilet brush and powered upward until his head rose above the waterline.

His dad was right behind him, and not a moment too soon. Suddenly, the squeegee portal folded in on itself. For a second, the wall was made of glass. Then the Windex wore off and the wall became solid red brick.

Spencer and his dad found themselves treading water in the Rebels' janitorial closet. Boxes and bags bobbed all around them, and little waves lapped at the stairs where Walter and the others waited, watching the basement fill up.

The flood was over now. The BEM laboratory was destroyed. And Spencer hoped they would never have to explain why the janitor's closet at Welcher Elementary School was full of water from the Atlantic Ocean.

CHAPTER 49

"TONIGHT WE TURN THE TABLES."

The Rebels were sitting in Mrs. Natcher's room. It wasn't the most secure location, but, seeing as how the janitorial closet was full of ocean water, it would have to suffice. Daisy had asked Bookworm to guard the door, and Spencer could see his garbage-pile silhouette in the doorway.

It was nearing midnight in Welcher, but there was still so much to be done before they could sleep.

"I can't believe you used to be friends with that weirdo," Dez said when Alan had finished explaining what had happened.

"Rod Grush was nothing like Mr. Clean," Alan said.

"I thought you said Rod Grush *was* Mr. Clean," said Daisy.

"He is," Alan admitted. "But I never thought my old partner could be capable of such crimes."

"Why do you suppose he tried so hard to keep his identity a secret from you?" Walter asked.

Marv grunted. "Coward, is my guess."

But Alan shook his head. "Rod Grush was anything but a coward. I knew him better than anyone. We went through a lot together. I know how he acts and how he thinks. That's probably why Mr. Clean didn't want me to know who he really was."

"So how can we use this to our advantage?" Penny said. "If Rod Grush just had his hideout destroyed and his hammer stolen, what would he do next?"

The look on Alan's face became very somber. "He'd come here."

"Then I guess we'd better skedaddle," Bernard said.

"It doesn't matter where we go," Alan said. "He'll find us and take revenge for what we've done."

"The time for running is past," Walter said. "The Rebel Underground has survived under a rock, avoiding the BEM and trying to stay hidden. No more. Tonight we turn the tables."

Bernard raised his hand. "I hate to be the pessimist in the group," he said. "But there are only nine of us here, if you count the Thingamajunk. What kind of tables can we turn against the entire Bureau of Educational Maintenance?"

In reply, Walter laid a blue binder on the desk he was occupying. Spencer recognized it as Professor DeFleur's translation of the *Manualis Custodem*. Spencer had wondered if the binder had survived the flood, but he hadn't dared ask about it in front of the others. Apparently, Walter had untaped the binder and moved it to safety before the water came through.

"You've all been very patient," Walter said. "And I thank you for trusting my orders. Our reason for stealing all three bronze hammers is much greater than a desire to take away the BEM's warlocks."

He opened the binder. "This is a translation of the *Manualis Custodem*—an original first-edition *Janitor Handbook* penned in Gloppish by the Founding Witches themselves."

"How long have you had this?" Penny asked, looking a touch hurt that she hadn't heard about it until now.

"Since the landfill," Walter answered. "Though the translation was only completed a few days ago."

"So what does it say?" asked Bernard, sitting forward on the edge of a desk.

"It says that the Founding Witches are not dead," Walter said. "They are trapped in the source of all Glop, counting on us to free them back into the world."

It was silent for a moment. Penny, Bernard, and Marv looked wide-eyed at the news. Even Dez stopped grooming his wing long enough to stare at the binder on Walter's desk.

"So that's how we're turning the tables?" Bernard asked. "We're bringing back the Founding Witches?"

Alan nodded. "Exactly. And we need to do it tonight. Before Mr. Clean can recover from the blow of losing his laboratory."

"Where's the source?" Marv asked.

"Tonight," Walter said, "the source of all Glop is going to be right here in Welcher Elementary School."

CHAPTER 50

"WHAT IF SOMEONE GETS THIRSTY?"

How is that possible?" Spencer asked. Hadn't the janitors covered every inch of Welcher Elementary? If the Glop source had been at the school, surely they would have found it before now.

"According to the *Manualis Custodem*," Walter explained, "the source of all Glop does not currently exist."

"I'm confused," said Daisy. "How are we going to find it here if it doesn't even exist?"

"We are going to create it," Walter said.

Alan stepped in for a little explanation. "A long time ago, there was a natural source where all Glop came from. When the Founding Witches left, they took the source with them, sealing it off so that no one could find them before the time was right."

"The *Manualis Custodem* clearly states that the source

349

must be reopened for the Witches to return," Walter said. "And that is what we are going to do tonight."

Spencer was deep in thought. All this time they'd been searching for a source that didn't even exist. All the Glop in the world was being recycled by the Aurans at the landfill, but the real natural source had been closed off since the Witches' departure.

"How do we open the source?" Penny asked.

"The return of the Witches is based on a Glop formula," Walter said. "Every time a warlock Glopifies something, he must experiment with a formula. It usually starts with a cup of raw Glop, mixed together with a myriad of strange ingredients until we reach the desired result."

"Like a good old-fashioned witch's brew," Bernard said.

Walter nodded. "Then the Glop formula is applied to the specific cleaning supply, and the magic takes effect."

"What do we have to Glopify for the source to open?" Spencer asked.

"This time it's a little different," Walter said. "Instead of depending on the warlocks to experiment with a formula, the Founding Witches left the exact recipe in the *Manualis Custodem*."

He thumbed through the pages of the translated binder until he found the recipe.

To Reopen the Source of All Glop

Fountain of pure water
Cup of raw Glop
Tail of Grime

Quill of Filth
Wing of Rubbish
Ash of the School Board
Keys of a warlock
Spit of an Auran

"As you can see," Walter said, "we have all the ingredients we need right here at Welcher Elementary."

Spencer took a deep breath as he saw his part in this. For someone who hated spitting, he sure had to do it a lot to save the world.

"Fountain of pure water?" Marv asked.

"Anciently, the Witches probably would have used a well or a spring," Walter said. "But this is the twenty-first century. We're going to use a drinking fountain."

"We're going to turn a drinking fountain into the source of all Glop?" Daisy asked.

Walter nodded. "There's one in the hallway just outside this classroom. It ought to work nicely."

"But we can't ruin a drinking fountain," Daisy protested. "What if someone gets thirsty?"

"Which would you rather have," Bernard said, "a few mildly dehydrated students, or the end of the world?"

"I guess they can use water bottles," Daisy said.

"What happens after we reopen the source?" Penny asked.

"That's why we needed the hammers," Alan said. "The *Manualis* says that the Witches used the hammers to lock their souls away. Whoever was holding the hammer

351

received some of the powers and abilities of the Witches. That's why warlocks can handle the Glop and come up with successful formulas. But the Founding Witches can't return while their souls are tied to the hammers. To release the Witches, we have to drop the hammers into the Glop source."

"What about the nails?" Spencer asked. "If the Witches' souls are tied only to the hammers, then why did we need the bronze nails?"

"Holding a bronze hammer gave me abilities and inspiration," Walter said, "but I needed a nail to have the real power. This was also true of the Witches. They were indeed gifted women, but their true power rested in their wands."

"So the three bronze nails are just representations of the Witches' magic wands?" Penny asked.

"Precisely," said Walter. "Toss the hammers into the source, and the Witches return. Toss the nails into the source, and the Witches receive their wands of power once more."

"Wands of power," Bernard said. "I like the sound of that! The BEM won't stand a chance."

CHAPTER 51

"LEAVE?"

Nearly an hour had passed by the time everyone gathered around the drinking fountain in the hallway outside Mrs. Natcher's room.

There were many ingredients needed for the Glop formula that would bring back the Witches, and everyone arrived with his or her specific assignment fulfilled.

Walter had taken Ninfa and extracted the bronze nail from its hiding place in Welcher. As a result, his domain momentarily collapsed, preventing him from using raw Glop. Since he would need that ability to reopen the source, Walter pounded the nail in a new spot: right beside the drinking fountain, next to a large hallway mirror.

With his domain quickly reestablished, Walter next needed some raw Glop. The Aurans were tasked with keeping all the warlocks stocked with the magical substance, and

353

Walter had received an anonymous delivery from one of the girls just last week.

Daisy and Dez had gone back to the Gateses' home, where Big Bertha was still parked. Spencer would have been worried about the two of them, but of course Bookworm went with them, encouraging Dez to be his best self so the Thingamajunk didn't rip his wings off. They had retrieved Holga and the nail from the glove compartment and returned to the school without any trouble.

Spencer and his dad went out to the school parking lot. Walter had given them the keys to his janitorial van with instructions on how to peel up the floor mat and find the School Board he'd been hiding.

Marv, Penny, and Bernard were the last to return to the drinking fountain. They had prowled the school, hunting a Rubbish, a Filth, and a Grime. It was tricky, since they needed to bring them back alive in order to use the proper parts of the Toxites. Marv carried the three trapped creatures in an Agitation Bucket. It was probably the most secure method of keeping Toxites trapped, but the side effect of the bucket caused the captive monsters to feel relocated and grow angry.

Penny released a shot of vanilla air freshener to counteract the Toxite breath for Spencer and Daisy. Then it grew quiet, and Walter exchanged a heavy look with Alan. Spencer's dad nodded and turned to the others.

"All right," Alan said. "Thank you all for your contributions. Unfortunately, before the source can be reopened, we have to leave."

"Leave?" Daisy said. "Then who's going to mix all the ingredients into the drinking fountain?"

"The instructions in the *Manualis Custodem* are very clear about this," Alan said. "Only two people can be present when the source reopens: a warlock," then his gaze shifted to Spencer, "and an Auran."

"What?" Dez moaned. "No fair! Why does Spencer get to stay?"

"The formula needs his spit," Alan explained.

"I can spit too, you know," said Dez. To prove his point, he spat on the floor.

Dez wasn't the only one who didn't seem keen on leaving. Penny was silently pouting, and Bernard was scratching his head, a look of disappointment on his face.

"Don't like this, boss," Marv said. "What if the BEM finds you before you can get the formula together?"

"You don't have to go far," Walter said to the Rebels. "You can stand guard around the school. Marv's right: Mr. Clean and his Sweepers could be on to us soon."

"Nobody'll get past us," Marv said.

"Yeah," Dez agreed. "If anybody shows up, I'll just burp dust at them."

Marv set the Agitation Bucket at his boss's feet and gave a quick nod of his shaggy head. "I'll cover the south doors and around the outside by the cafeteria."

Alan passed the School Board to Spencer. It was the first time he'd touched the ancient piece of wood since he had used Ninfa to pound the nail that had transformed him into an Auran.

Spencer turned the Board over in his hands to find the clumsy etching that Marv had made in an attempt to disguise the wood as part of Spencer's desk.

Mrs. N Smells like cabbige

Spencer smiled. Marv wasn't great at spelling.

Daisy handed Holga and the nail to Walter. She patted Spencer on the arm as she passed by, Bookworm close behind. "Good luck," she said.

"Don't mess up the formula, Doofus," Dez said to Spencer.

Spencer didn't say anything. He watched his dad and friends disappear down the darkened hallway until only he and Walter Jamison remained. The old warlock put a steady hand on the boy's shoulder.

"Ready to make history?" Walter asked.

CHAPTER 52

"THIS IS FINAL, SPENCER."

Walter laid the translated binder on the floor beside the drinking fountain. It was open to the page with the Glop recipe, and Spencer quickly read over the ingredients to make sure they had everything.

Fountain of pure water

Walter pressed the button on the drinking fountain, and a crystal stream of water flowed out of the spigot. It was a far cry from the natural spring that the Witches would be expecting, but Walter seemed to think it would work just fine.

On instruction from Walter, Spencer tore off a little piece of duct tape and pasted it over the button so the drinking fountain continued to shoot a stream of water even though neither of them was holding it. Spencer turned back to the list in the binder.

Cup of raw Glop

Walter had to handle this one, since only warlocks were authorized to touch Glop without consequences. The old warlock had a dented coffee can half full of gurgling, sludge-like Glop. Not long ago, Spencer had sailed across an entire lagoon of the magical stuff. Now it was hard to be impressed by a half-empty can.

Walter took a plastic cup and dipped into the substance. Spencer crinkled his nose at the sulfuric smell. The warlock lifted the dripping cup to the fountain and dribbled the contents into the streaming water.

It hissed and threw a plume of vapor as Glop met water. Then the grayish sludge oozed down until it plugged the drain, causing the fresh water to swirl back in little eddies.

"This is where it gets ugly," Walter said, pointing back to the ingredient list.

Tail of Grime

"Have you ever tried to hold one of these slippery monsters?" Walter asked, peering into the Agitation Bucket.

Spencer had, on several occasions through his Toxite-fighting adventures. It wasn't easy. Grimes were designed to slip through tight situations.

"Would you rather hold it," Walter asked, "or cut off its tail?"

The second option sounded repulsive. "I'll hold it," Spencer said. He pulled on a latex glove to protect his hand against the acidic fingertips of the Grime. He looked into the bucket and waited until the Grime was holding still, clinging to the plastic side.

Spencer thrust his hand inside, gripping the little creature around the middle and jerking it from the Agitation Bucket. It wriggled wildly in his grasp. Spencer felt himself losing control as Walter stepped forward, razorblade extended.

The Grime's wide mouth clamped down on Spencer's thumb, jagged teeth biting through the thin glove. He grunted in pain, letting up just enough that the Grime slithered free. But as it leapt to the floor, Spencer's left hand came around, snatching the monster from its flight and pinning it against the wall. He felt the burn of venom on his gloveless hand, but he held tight.

Walter seized the tip of its slippery tail and made a deft slice with his razorblade. In Spencer's hand, the Grime exploded in a spattering of yellow slime. But Walter quickly tossed the twitching tail into the drinking fountain.

Spencer held out his dripping hand, trying not to think about the Grime germs that had just exploded between his fingers. He wiped the residue on the leg of his jeans.

"This next one shouldn't be so bad," Walter said, "though you'll probably want an extra shot of air freshener."

Quill of Filth

Spencer pulled out his aerosol can of vanilla air freshener and sprayed a stream into the air above the Agitation Bucket. He couldn't afford any sleepiness with a task like this.

The Agitated Filth was nearly impossible to pick up. Every time Spencer reached into the bucket, the little beast would flare its sharp quills like a scared porcupine. After a few failed attempts, Spencer changed his strategy.

He drew a plunger from his belt and, turning it over, pressed the wooden handle into the bucket. Spencer prodded the Filth, increasing its anger until finally it snapped its buckteeth into the handle. As soon as the dusty Toxite had a firm bite, Spencer pulled the plunger handle from the bucket, lifting the Filth with it.

Walter reached out, pinching a long gray quill between two fingers. He plucked the sharp spike from the Filth's back just as the creature released its bite on the plunger handle. It dropped to its clawed feet and scurried off down the hallway.

Walter lifted the Filth's quill triumphantly, nodding his approval to Spencer before dropping the spike into the drinking fountain.

"One more Toxite part," Spencer said, checking the list of ingredients in the binder.

Wing of Rubbish

Spencer had learned his lesson with the Grime. If he reached into the bucket for the Rubbish, he was likely to end up with another bloody finger. Instead, Spencer drew a pinch of vacuum dust from his belt and kicked over the Agitation Bucket.

The angry Rubbish took flight, winging around and diving toward Walter's exposed head. The warlock stepped back as Spencer threw a Palm Blast, dropping the little Toxite to the floor with vacuum suction.

Walter bent over the downed Rubbish. Spencer saw the razorblade slice, and when the warlock stepped back, he was holding a leathery, black Rubbish wing.

Walter stepped over to the drinking fountain and dropped it into the mixture. The concoction seemed to be at a full boil by this point. The individual ingredients had melted away in the Glop, leaving the liquid a disgusting muddy color.

The next ingredient seemed puzzling to Spencer.

Ash of the School Board

"There's no turning back now," Walter said, sliding the School Board into the middle of the hallway. He withdrew a lighter from his back pocket.

"We have to burn the School Board?" Spencer asked. It seemed obvious, but he thought he must be missing something.

"It's the only way to make ash," Walter said. "I disabled the hallway smoke detectors. The last thing we need is the local fire department checking in on us."

Walter sparked the lighter, and a little flame appeared.

He lowered it toward the School Board but paused just before it touched the wood. Walter glanced up, and Spencer thought he saw a need for validation in the old man's eyes.

"This is final, Spencer," Walter said. "If we burn the School Board, there can be no new warlocks."

Spencer took a deep breath and nodded his understanding. "If we succeed, there won't be hammers or nails, either. We won't need warlocks," Spencer reassured. "We'll have the Witches."

Without another word, Walter Jamison touched the little flame to the School Board.

Spencer had seen various ways of starting campfires. His dad used to try to ignite a fire with a single match and one piece of newspaper. Daisy's dad liked to douse the wood in lighter fluid. But the School Board lit like nothing Spencer had ever seen before.

It caught fire immediately, large flames lapping across the wooden surface. The colors were unusual, too. The flames flickered between deep purple and hues of brilliant green.

"Why does it burn like that?" Spencer finally asked.

"The *Manualis Custodem* says that the School Board was cut from an ancient piece of wood growing at the heart of a Glop lagoon," Walter said.

Spencer looked at him in surprise. "The Broomstaff?"

The old warlock nodded. "The Board was cut from the Broomstaff and brought into civilization as a way to regulate the transfer of power from one warlock to another."

Spencer knew the process. When one of the bronze

hammers was passed on to another person, the new warlock had to reset the power by driving the nail into the School Board and pulling it out again.

"I always thought I understood the purpose of the School Board," Walter continued. "I thought it was for *us*, the warlocks. But now I realize that *this*," he pointed to the blazing wood, "is what it was made for." The warlock nodded. "The School Board *wants* to burn. The Witches knew we would need its ash to bring them back."

Spencer and Walter stood in silence, transfixed by the multicolored flames as the School Board burned. Then it began to smolder. The wood turned to ashen embers that blazed a fierce golden when Walter knelt down and breathed on them.

Walter prodded the charred School Board with his razorblade until it cracked in half, weakened to charcoal from the magical flames that had consumed it. Nudging the ruined wood with his foot, Walter slid the smoldering remains aside, leaving a little pile of white ash in the middle of the hallway.

The old warlock drew a dustpan from his belt. Instead of opening it into a magical shield, he used it for its original purpose. Once Walter finished scooping the ashes into the dustpan, he stepped over to the drinking fountain and upended it into the brew.

The School Board ashes swirled into the viscous liquid, and the whole mixture began to glow a deep red. Thick bubbles rose and splattered like magma, with bits of the glowing substance dripping down the side of the fountain.

Two more ingredients to go.

Keys of a warlock

Walter reached down to the ring of keys that was always hooked through his pants belt loop. Spencer didn't know why he carried so many keys, but there were certainly a lot of doors in Welcher Elementary School, and he figured the janitor had a key for every lock.

Walter stretched out his arm until the keys were dangling above the lavalike Glop formula. He took a deep breath and dropped them. The keys landed with a *clink* in the drinking fountain, though there was so much vapor and smoke that Spencer couldn't see where they fell. The mixture accepted the keys with an aerial shower of sparks, like Fourth of July fireworks in the hallway.

Walter stepped away from the drinking fountain. "It's up to you for the last ingredient," he said.

Spit of an Auran

Spencer swished a bit of saliva in his mouth. At least he didn't have to spit on his hand this time. He secretly wondered if his spit would work in the formula. It hadn't been very long since he'd Glopified the leaf blower. And the Glop in his system took time to recharge. Besides, the Founding Witches would surely be expecting one of the original Aurans to spit into the mixture. Would this suffice?

Spencer stepped up to the drinking fountain, feeling the heat of the gurgling Glop formula on his face. He'd seen lots of kids spit into the water fountains at school. That was one of the main reasons why Spencer vowed never to drink from one.

He told himself that this was different. If he and Walter succeeded in turning this water fountain into the source of all Glop, then Spencer was pretty sure no one would be drinking from it again.

Spencer leaned forward. If he waited any longer, his mouth would dry up from the heat of the Glop and the anticipation of what was about to happen.

Spencer opened his mouth and spat into the drinking fountain.

The final ingredient in the Witches' recipe hit the mixture with a loud *pop!* Spencer staggered backward as black smoke began billowing out. The red glow brightened until Spencer was forced to squint. Then all went dark and silent, and the smoke cleared.

Gurgling out the top of the ruined drinking fountain was the source of all Glop.

CHAPTER 53

"THAT IS INCORRECT."

Spencer and Walter stood side by side in the hallway, watching the Glop bubbling upward. The lower half of the drinking fountain looked the same, but the top had melted away, spigot, drain, metal, and all. In its place was a deep opening, Glop spewing upward from the unknown depths.

"I suppose it's time," Walter said, drawing Ninfa from his pocket. He took a moment of silent reprieve with the bronze hammer. Spencer understood. As soon as Walter extracted the nail, his domain would collapse. But even more than that, the moment he threw the hammer into the mixture, Walter would give up his warlock powers forever.

Walter stepped over to the large mirror beside the fountain. His reflection looked worn and weary—a man burdened by the huge responsibility of saving the future of education.

Walter sighed as he placed Ninfa against the nail. The magic bond formed and the nail slipped easily from the wall beside the mirror.

Spencer withdrew Belzora and the nail from his belt pouch. The latex glove he still wore prevented him from going into a vision. Walter took the items, gripping the nails in one hand while holding all three hammers in the other. Ninfa, Holga, and Belzora.

It was strange to see the complete set of bronze hammers in one place. They weren't large, and each was slightly different. But they seemed to radiate an unseen power.

Walter looked at Spencer, their faces alight in the magical luminescence of the Glop source. Then, suddenly, the silence was broken by a bit of static radio noise. The static cut out and a voice came through.

"Spencer? Spencer, do you copy?"

It was Min. And at a time like this!

Spencer had almost forgotten about the walkie-talkie on his belt. Since they'd succeeded in rescuing Walter, he hadn't given any thought to Min and his efforts to translate the *Manualis Custodem*.

Spencer unclipped the radio and pressed it to his lips. "I'm here, Min. Reading you loud and clear."

"I have nearly completed the translation you asked for," the boy said. "All but the final chapter."

Spencer smiled. "Why are you even awake? It's the middle of the night."

"I have worked nonstop," Min said. "You told me it was urgent."

"Not too urgent anymore," Spencer said. "We did it, Min. Walter and I just reopened the source of all Glop."

"Just you and Walter?" Min said. "Where is Daisy? Where are the others?"

"They're waiting outside," Spencer answered. "Walter and I had to do this alone, just like the *Manualis* said."

"The *Manualis Custodem* said nothing about that," Min said.

Spencer paused, confused. He looked to Walter, who stooped over the translated binder and turned back a page.

"Says it right here," Spencer said into the radio. "On the page before the Glop formula recipe." Walter pointed to the line and Spencer read it: "*Only a warlock and an Auran are permitted to be present at the time of the source's opening.*"

"That is incorrect." Min said it so matter-of-factly that Spencer instantly believed him. "That sentence is not written on that page of the *Manualis Custodem*."

Walter leaned in to say something, and Spencer pressed the button for him. "Perhaps you made a mistake."

Spencer could imagine Min shaking his head. "It's much more likely that your first translator made a mistake."

"Professor DeFleur?" Spencer said. "That's a pretty big mistake to write in there."

"Unless, of course, it wasn't a mistake," Min said. "Perhaps this professor wanted to isolate you and Walter Jamison from the rest of the Rebels."

"But why would he do that?" Spencer said. "He died trying to help us escape with the translation."

"You saw him die?" Min asked.

"Yeah," said Spencer. "Mr. Clean swallowed him whole."

There was a sound behind Spencer and Walter, a shuffling footfall punctuated by the click of a cane. Spencer turned to find himself staring at a figure he had never expected to see again.

Professor Dustin DeFleur hobbled forward, his thin cane tapping across the hard floor. He paused beside the smoldering remnants of the School Board and turned his wizened face toward them.

There was a little grin on his face as he spoke. "Did you know that a small person can survive for several minutes inside the belly of a Grime?" Professor DeFleur said. "Quite an unpleasant experience, I must say."

"How did you get in here?" Walter asked. Spencer was wondering the same thing. It seemed unlikely that the old professor could have been stealthy enough to slip past the Rebels standing guard outside.

"I've been here all day," said Professor DeFleur, "waiting in the gym for you Rebels to show up. I work here now. Principal Poach just hired me to be the new P.E. teacher."

Spencer scoffed. "You?" he said, pointing at the hunched man's cane. "The P.E. teacher? You're like a hundred years old!"

"I'm faster than I look," said Professor DeFleur. He swung his cane, hidden metal prongs extending from the tip to form a rake. He slammed his concealed rake at Spencer's feet, the impact knocking the walkie-talkie from the boy's grasp. The metal bars folded around Spencer in a heartbeat, and the momentum from the attack sent his cage sliding across the hallway and clattering into the wall.

Walter was still free, his entire body tense as he guarded the drinking fountain, standing firmly between Professor DeFleur and Spencer's cage.

The old professor drew a razorblade from the pocket of his linen shirt. The blade extended, and he thrust the tip into the fallen walkie-talkie, crushing the Glopified device in a spray of sparks.

"We trusted you," Walter muttered, but the professor ignored him.

Professor DeFleur turned his gaze upon the drinking fountain. "Is that it?" He pointed a crooked finger at the gurgling mess. "Is that the source of all Glop?"

Spencer couldn't believe that the old professor was alive! And even more unbelievable—he had turned against the Rebels. Spencer gripped the bars of his cage, staring speechlessly at the old man standing alone in the hallway. He was terrified by his arrival and disgusted by the fact that DeFleur's death had been a lie.

Professor DeFleur took a step closer to the drinking fountain. "Stay back!" Walter threatened, reaching for his janitorial belt. "We have help waiting outside. You're alone and outnumbered."

The professor's bushy white eyebrows raised. "How *alone* am I?" he asked.

His wrinkly hand flashed to his side, drawing a short-handled rubber squeegee that had been tucked in his belt. Leaning forward, DeFleur dragged the squeegee across the large hallway mirror beside the drinking fountain.

Walter stepped backward, bumping into Spencer's cage as a magical portal opened. In a moment, the two Rebels were outnumbered as a dozen Sweepers poured into the hallway.

The last to arrive was Mr. Clean, his white lab coat still damp from the flooded laboratory.

The Sweeper warlock greeted Professor DeFleur with a nod before turning to Walter and Spencer. "Your Rebel uprising ends tonight," he said.

Professor DeFleur chuckled and looked at Walter. "Now it seems *you* are alone and outnumbered."

"But you've made a mistake," Walter said. "We're not alone either."

Then Walter turned and flung the bronze hammers into the bubbling Glop source.

CHAPTER 54

"THERE'S WORK TO BE DONE."

The first Witch emerged rather suddenly, rising up out of the Glop. The sludge spat her onto the ground, where she rose to her knees, dripping.

She was old, with bony fingers that she used to brush the snarly gray hair from her wrinkled face. Her thin frame was draped in a thick cloak of black, with a hood bunched around her neck.

Spencer had barely looked her over when the next Witch bubbled up out of the Glop source. She landed beside her sister, wiping sticky Glop from her eyes and tugging at the ill-fitting black dress she wore.

In no time at all, the final Witch gurgled into view. She landed more gracefully than the previous two and stomped her feet to shake the Glop from her tall leather boots. She lifted her arms, as if to embrace her freedom, and Spencer saw more than a dozen shiny bangle bracelets adorning her right wrist.

"This is ridiculous!" exclaimed the middle Witch. "Whoever thought of this exit plan, anyway? My dress is utterly ruined!"

"Oh, shut up, Holga," said the first Witch. She was patting the pockets of her cloak. "I simply must find my wand. There's work to be done."

Holga began to laugh, a true witch's cackle. "Please, Ninfa," she said to the first Witch. "You haven't done a day of work in your life! I wouldn't be surprised if your wand grew legs and walked away, it felt so neglected."

"Liar!" Ninfa shouted. "My wand was always prettier than yours. You finally grew jealous enough to steal it! Now give it back!"

Belzora finally stepped between them, her voice sharp and commanding. "Silence your bickering!" Ninfa and Holga suddenly seemed to grow aware that other people stood nearby.

Belzora lowered her voice. "One of these mortals holds our wands."

"I have them." Walter stepped forward, opening his palm and showing the three bronze nails. An excited look passed over Belzora's face.

"Are you a warlock?" she asked.

Walter nodded his bald head. "Yes."

"Have you done what was asked in the Warlocks Box?" Belzora pressed.

Spencer felt a pang of worry pass through him. Walter

knew nothing of the Warlocks Box. Mr. Clean had opened it before Walter had stolen Ninfa and the nail.

"Yes," Spencer said from the confines of his rake cage. "We have solved the thirteen clues from the Warlocks Box."

Belzora turned her long, wrinkly face toward him. "And who are you, young lad?"

"My name is Spencer Zumbro."

Holga took a shuffling step closer, sniffing the air. "White hair," she muttered. "White hair and the ageless smell of Auran about him."

"I am an Auran," he said. "I'm new. But I'm friends with Olin, Sach, and Aryl."

"Aww," Ninfa said. "How are the children?"

"Good, I guess," Spencer said.

"Are they getting along?"

It seemed weird to be talking about it while Mr. Clean and his BEM Sweepers stood watching in silence. "Well," Spencer said, "the girls panned the boys about two hundred years ago, and they've been archenemies ever since."

"Oh," Ninfa said with a sweet smile. "That's nice."

"Enough chat," Belzora said. "Has everything else been prepared for our arrival?"

Spencer and Walter exchanged a puzzled glance.

"What do you mean?" Walter asked.

"The other instructions in the Warlocks Box," Belzora asked. "Did you fulfill them all?"

Spencer's head turned slowly to Mr. Clean, whose lips were curling in a gradual smirk. The big Sweeper stepped forward. The Witches turned to him as he dropped respectfully onto one knee in the hallway.

"New Forest Academy is ready," Mr. Clean said. "Just as you commanded."

Spencer felt his heart stop. A flush of fear and shock crawled across his skin as the Founding Witches nodded their approval at Mr. Clean's words.

"One more thing," Professor DeFleur muttered to Spencer and Walter. "I never gave you the translation of the final chapter—the part where it explains that the Founding Witches are on *our* side."

CHAPTER 55

"GIVE ME
THE NAILS!"

Spencer felt the panic, causing him to rattle and shake at the bars of his rake cage. They needed to run. But he was trapped, and Walter seemed frozen. The Rebel warlock closed his hand tightly around the three bronze nails. "What is going on?" he finally muttered.

"We are ready to visit the Academy," Belzora said. She turned to Walter. "Give us our wands."

Walter took an unsteady step backward. "You know about New Forest Academy?"

"Obviously," Belzora said. "We left specific instructions for the Academy to be started in the Hopeless Day."

"Is that today?" Holga asked.

"Of course it's today," Ninfa said. "Otherwise they wouldn't have opened the Warlocks Box, and we wouldn't be here."

Walter looked so confused. Mr. Clean had told Spencer a little bit about the Warlocks Box, though apparently not everything. He had said that the Witches had prophesied of a Hopeless Day, when there would be nothing but sin and corruption in the world. That was why Mr. Clean and Garcia had opened the Warlocks Box. But it wasn't right!

"There's been a mistake," Spencer said. "It's not the Hopeless Day. There's still a lot of good in the world out there!"

Mr. Clean stood up, whirling to face the boy. "Your lies are evidence of the Hopeless Day!" he bellowed, causing Spencer to shrink to the back of his cage.

Then, lowering his voice, Clean turned back to the Witches. "There is no good left in the world. But we have done everything you asked. The Bureau of Educational Maintenance has followed every instruction found in the Warlocks Box. We allowed Toxites to take over schools. We raised a private Academy in the mountains, protecting only the most cunning students. We followed the thirteen clues to find the Auran landfill and the *Manualis Custodem*. We have brought you back into this corrupt world so you can rule it and set things right again."

Belzora nodded. "A sensible follower. What is your name?"

"They call me Mr. Clean," he answered, which brought a cackle from Holga. Spencer had never seen anyone laugh at the Sweeper warlock and live to tell about it. But Mr. Clean was no longer in charge. "Reginald McClean," he amended, head slightly bowed.

Walter was shaking his head, face ashen white. "This was planned?" he mumbled.

"Don't you see?" Mr. Clean said to Walter and Spencer. "You've been set up."

"It was a trap." Walter's voice was barely audible, the shock and disappointment ripe in his expression.

"Much more than a trap," answered Mr. Clean. "This was a way to get you to do the hard work. Professor DeFleur's translation told you just what you wanted to hear. We *let* you steal Holga and Belzora. You already had the School Board," he said. "And we didn't know how else to get the spit of an Auran." He grinned. "We used you to reopen the source and bring back the Witches."

Belzora turned to Walter. "You did not welcome our arrival, warlock?"

Walter shook his head. "Not like this. It wasn't supposed to be like this."

"Your majesties," Mr. Clean said to the Witches. "This man is a traitor to your cause. He has raised an organization of Rebels who ignore my orders and continue to fight Toxites."

"Rebel!" Ninfa shouted, pointing a finger at Walter.

"Heretic!" Holga shrieked.

Belzora remained calm. "Is this true, warlock?"

"Yes," Walter said. "The Rebel Underground works to uphold education. We thought it was the desire of the Founding Witches."

"Now you see you are mistaken," Belzora said. "We mean to cleanse the world. To start civilization anew with our chosen students at the Academy." She reached out her thin hand. "Give me the bronze nails."

Walter drew his clenched fist over his heart. "You will not have them."

"Do you really think you can resist us?" asked Belzora. "Give me the nails!"

Walter stepped behind Spencer's cage. With his free hand, he reached through the bars and twisted the rake handle. The metal prongs snapped away and the rake fell to the hallway floor.

Finally free, Spencer instantly reached for the weapons on his janitorial belt. But Walter, standing close behind, rested a reassuring hand on the boy's shoulder. He lowered his head and spoke quietly in Spencer's ear. "You're a good boy, Spencer Zumbro. I'm proud of you." He patted Spencer softly on the back.

"Give me the nails!" Belzora was screaming, ratty black hair shaking in her fury.

Walter Jamison stepped away from Spencer, hand clenched impossibly tight. "I will not give in to your demands." Spencer saw the Rebel warlock swallow, his Adam's apple sliding nervously along his throat. "There is so much good in this world," he said. "And I will never stop fighting for that."

"So be it," Belzora said. "You have made new enemies today."

Her hand shot out with alarming speed, catching Walter by the wrist. Spencer heard his elbow crack, and Walter cried out in pain. Belzora pulled him, twisting his arm until his clenched fist was just above the gurgling Glop source.

Through the pain and intensity, Walter's eyes found Spencer. The old warlock opened his mouth and whispered one word.

"Run."

Then Belzora forced Walter's hand open. The Witch's mouth twisted in a cry of dismay at what she found.

The bronze nails were not there! Walter's hand was empty!

The Founding Witches screamed in unison, their shriek an awful harpy sound.

"Kill!" Belzora yelled. "Kill him!"

Mr. Clean stepped forward, his deadly rag already twisted into a tight rope. Spencer opened his mouth to scream, but his lungs seemed unable to draw air.

Clean's rag snapped through the air, rippling with magic as it struck Walter in the chest with a terrible *crack!* Then he was gone without a trace. That goodly old man, Spencer's friend and mentor, reduced instantly to a wisp of nothingness.

Walter Jamison was dead.

CHAPTER 56

"RETREAT!"

Spencer's mind was numb. It was as though all his senses had turned off. He stared blindly at the spot where Walter had stood.

This couldn't be real. Not Walter.

Then Belzora turned her wrinkled face toward him, and Walter's final word echoed in Spencer's mind.

"Run."

Spencer leapt forward, extending his razorblade and slashing through the nearest Sweeper. The Filth man fell, his Glopified half melting away and leaving him unconscious. Several others tried to lay their hands on him, but the latex glove worked its magic, helping him slide easily through their grasp.

Spencer's feet thundered through the hallway. His senses seemed heightened now, and he was painfully aware of the pursuing Sweepers right behind. He'd never be able to outrun them. They would capture him, and Walter's death would be for nothing.

Tears streamed down Spencer's cheeks, and his heart raced as he fought the urge to throw up. He stumbled and went down, striking his knee on the hard floor.

He lay there, waiting for death. Waiting for the evil Witches to overtake him.

A Rubbish Sweeper dove from above. But before her talon hands could rend him, Marv leapt around the corner, delivering a powerful blow with a pushbroom.

The big janitor seized Spencer with one hand and pulled him around the corner. Penny, Dez, and Bookworm rushed past them, meeting the incoming Sweepers head-on. Dez opened his mouth, using a stored-up belch to fill the hallway with black dust.

"What happened?" Daisy asked.

Spencer was shaking. He couldn't speak.

"Where's the boss?" Marv asked. "Where's Walter?"

"He's . . ." Spencer squinted his eyes shut. "Dead." The last word was barely audible. Daisy gasped, her big eyes instantly filling with tears. Spencer took a sobbing gasp of air and tried to explain the horror of their situation. "The Witches . . . they killed him."

Spencer sensed the fear unravel in his companions. Spencer opened his eyes again. Closing them only made him relive Walter's final moment. Belzora had opened the warlock's hand, but the bronze nails weren't there.

Then Spencer remembered something—a soft pat on the back as Walter had whispered in his ear.

Spencer reached around, putting his hand into the spill-proof pouch on the back of his janitorial belt. Even with his latex glove on, Spencer could clearly feel the three sharp bronze nails that Walter had slipped into his pouch.

Spencer held the nails out for the others to see. "We can't let the Witches get these," he said. "Walter died for that."

Marv was slumped against the wall, the strength seeming to have leaked out of him. His eyes were full of tears, but he blinked them away, jaw tightening in rage.

"Marv," Alan tried to say, but the janitor leapt to his feet, a terrible force to be reckoned with. Drawing a razorblade and a dustpan shield, he let out a roar of grief and jumped around the corner, fighting with the strength of ten men.

"We have to go," Spencer said, rising on shaky legs. "We have to get away from them."

Alan nodded, pulling Daisy and Spencer into a tight hug. "Bernard is on his way," said Alan. "He went to get the truck."

Just then, Big Bertha's headlights glinted through the glass doors at the end of the hallway.

"Retreat!" Alan yelled, pulling the kids toward the exit. Spencer went without hesitation, the bronze nails now clenched firmly in his own fist.

Still unaware of Walter's death, Dez, Penny, and the

Thingamajunk fell into a quick retreat. But Marv refused to fall back, determined to avenge his old boss.

"Bookworm," Daisy said, when she saw what was happening. "Go get Marv!"

The Thingamajunk bounded back into the fray, seizing the hefty janitor with one trash arm and dragging him down the hallway.

Bernard flung open the school doors, and the Rebels began piling into the cab of the garbage truck. The trash-cannons were armed and ready, and as soon as the Rebels were clear, Bernard slammed his fist on the red button, firing a high-speed slug of garbage at the Sweepers in the hallway.

Big Bertha peeled away from Welcher Elementary School, leaving behind the source of all Glop and the Founding Witches who were supposed to be their allies.

Everything had gone wrong. Walter was dead. The Witches were bad.

Spencer took a deep breath and forced the tears to stop. He stared at the three little bronze nails in his gloved palm.

An old memory came back to Spencer. At the very beginning of all this, Walter Jamison had told Spencer that he feared a war was brewing. It seemed the warlock was right. The war was upon them now. And Spencer was determined to win.

He closed his fist around the nails. He would win it for Walter.

ACKNOWLEDGMENTS

Thank you, reader, for sticking with this series. I wouldn't be anywhere without you. It's been a pleasure meeting you at schools and book signings. I hope you enjoyed *Strike of the Sweepers*.

I was a Sweeper once. No, seriously! Many of my ideas for this series came while I worked as a part-time custodian at a local middle school. Since I worked only a few hours each evening, I never earned the official title of janitor. The nightly crew was called something else: We were Sweepers.

The team at Shadow Mountain continue to amaze me with their support and attention. Thanks to Chris Schoebinger and Heidi Taylor for their direction and guidance, to Emily Watts for her editorial work, to Richard Erickson for his art direction, and to Karen Zelnick and Mary Beth Allen for organizing many of my events and tours.

Thanks to Brandon Dorman, whom I finally met face to face! There isn't a nicer guy out there. Thanks for providing another eye-catching cover. Dez would be very pleased with his rippling muscles and black talons.

Thanks to Rubin Pfeffer for representing my work in the Janitors series. His advice and guidance have meant so much to me over the years.

ACKNOWLEDGMENTS

I want to thank fellow author Chad Morris (Cragbridge Hall series) and the Jammin' Janitors—Sam, Doug, and Mike—for spending lots of time and effort to help launch past books.

To my neighborhood friends growing up—Aubrey, Lance, Nate, Andrew, and Nick. Our countless hours of imaginative games helped shape me into the writer that I am today. Thanks for always coming along on another adventure.

Thanks to my parents and to my brother and sisters and their families. Thanks for always being interested in my many projects.

And the greatest thanks goes to Connie, for always being there. I could never do this without you!

Keep reading! Keep imagining! I can promise a lot of excitement in the final book!

1. Glopified squeegees open portals to let people travel great distances quickly. If you could use a squeegee to instantly travel anywhere, where would you go?

2. If you were holding a Sweeper potion, would you choose to take it and transform? Or would you choose to stay human? Why?

3. Which kind of Sweeper do you think is most powerful: Rubbish, Filth, or Grime? Why? If you had to become a Sweeper, what kind would you want to be? Why do you think Dez made the choice he did?

4. Spencer learns that Mr. Clean is known by several names. If you had a fake name, what would it be? Who would you tell it to?

5. The BEM's secret laboratory is hidden deep in the Atlantic Ocean. If you built a secret laboratory, where would you hide it? What would it be like?

6. When Spencer needs someone to take care of the *Manualis Custodem*, he chooses Min. Who would you trust to take care of something that is valuable to you?

7. The Dustbin allows you to use your imagination to create familiar objects out of dust. What would you create?

8. The Rebels show mercy and try to save Garth Hadley

from the TPs. Have you ever helped someone who was un-kind to you? How did it make you feel?

9. What's your favorite magical janitorial weapon used by the Rebels? If you had access to magical glop, what jani-torial tool or item would you make magical, and what could it do?

10. The arrival of the Founding Witches turned out not to have the effect the Rebels were hoping for. Have you ever been disappointed by something or someone? What did you do to deal with it?

WHITE   **ROB**
Whitesides, Tyler,
Strike of the sweepers /

ROBINSON
09/14